Wish I May

Justine Picardie writes for *Vogue* and the *Daily Telegraph*. Her best-selling memoir *If the Spirit Moves You*, was published by Picador in 2002. She lives with her husband and two sons in London.

'A child's eye view steeped in an English Edwardian literary air reminiscent of Rosamond Lehmann and P. L. Travers, tightly written and promisingly observed' Ali Smith, *Guardian*

'Beautifully buoyant, *Wish I May* explores the gorgeous, impossible jigsaw of happiness that has us all hooked. Justine Picardie writes with a deft, elegant and warm power, wrestling with the muscular spell memory casts over everyday moments, chasing precarious and precious glimpses of hope. She invites us into a life only too real and messy, yet tickled by magic in ways everyone can, with shivers of pleasure and meaning, recognize' Andrea Ashworth, author of *Once in a House on Fire*

'Picardie is an assured and elegant stylist. She has written a thoughtful novel about the perils of growing up among the smart, and the depressed' Emma Hagestadt, *Independent*

'Arch and evocative writing' Alice Fisher, *Time Out*

'Picardie's prose has a singsong clarity' Eithne Farry, *Zembla* magazine

'An insightful exploration of family intrigues' *Sainsbury's Magazine*

'A touching and intelligent read' *Good Housekeeping*

'A magical and imaginative book . . . She writes with a beautifully clear simplicity, conjuring up a truly enchanted atmosphere' *Waterstone's Magazine*

Also by Justine Picardie

If The Spirit Moves You

Justine Picardie

Wish I May

PICADOR

First published 2004 by Picador

This paperback edition published 2004 by Picador
an imprint of Pan Macmillan Ltd
Pan Macmillan, 20 New Wharf Road, London N1 9RR
Basingstoke and Oxford
Associated companies throughout the world
www.panmacmillan.com

ISBN 0 330 41222 1

Copyright © Justine Picardie 2004

Typeset by Intype Libra Ltd
Printed and bound in Great Britain by
Mackays of Chatham plc, Chatham, Kent

All Pan Macmillan titles are available from www.panmacmillan.com
or from Book post by telephoning 01624 677 237

For Neill, Jamie and Tom

'It's a poor sort of memory that only works backwards,' the Queen remarked.

'What sort of things do you remember best?' Alice ventured to ask.

'Oh, things that happened the week after next,' the Queen replied in a careless tone.

Through the Looking Glass, Lewis Carroll

Star Light, Star Bright,
First Star I See Tonight.
Wish I May,
Wish I Might,
Wish Upon a Star Tonight.

One

The gates to the house lay on a blind curve in the road. It was easy to miss it, to go on towards the sea, where the road ended and the water met the sky. Even though she had been coming here since she was a baby, still, sometimes those gates were a surprise.

Beyond the rusted iron gates lay a long drive that seemed to lead nowhere. The dark trees obscured everything for a quarter of a mile or so, and then suddenly, there was a clearing, and you could see the house. It was grey stone and symmetrical, the kind a child might draw: a front door at the centre, with identical eight-paned windows in a row to either side and above, topped by smaller attic windows set into the slate roof. It was a house engraved inside Kate's head; a house that she walked through when she could not sleep at home in London; a place preserved as the single fixed point in what might otherwise be the blurred land-scape of memory; the last house, before the land gave way to waves. Nothing seemed to change inside the house – the polished wooden floors; the rust mark where the tap had dripped forever in the nursery enamel bath; the clocks that chimed not quite in time with each other; the willow-pattern plate hanging on the dining-room wall, with a faint crack across the middle, the lines of which Kate knew off by heart. Only the people inside the house changed, though Kate half hoped they would not.

The house belonged to Kate's uncle and aunt. Her uncle Charles had been born here – the eldest of two boys – and now he lived in the house with his family. Charles was married to Bella, who was Kate's mother's sister. Kate had fitted these things together in her head when she was about five, like an intricate jigsaw. She was part of the jigsaw – which made her feel safe, because there were holes in the rest of her life; absences and blank bits and places that fell away into nothing.

Her uncle and aunt had built a family as apparently symmetrical as their house: boy, girl, boy, girl – two years between each raven-haired child. Paul was the oldest; then came Isabel, Julian and Harriet. Julian was the same age as Kate, though he was bigger than her. But when she went to stay with her cousins, she shared the girls' bedroom with Isabel and Harriet, tucked into a truckle bed between the two of them, safe inside clean, freshly ironed linen sheets.

Truckle. That was a word Kate learnt the summer that she was seven, when she spent the holidays in the house without her parents, the time she could not forget (even though, years later, she wondered if her memory of that summer was somehow flawed, like the willow-pattern plate). Her mother had explained that they were separating. Kate remembered that – the sound of the word, how it fell apart into bits (and how was it that the plate did not separate, but held together, despite its cracks?). At first Kate thought she meant that the three of them – this already too small family – were separating from each other, severed, to live alone; but her mother said no, after the summer Kate would come home to London to live in the same flat as before, with her mother, though her father would be somewhere else. Kate didn't know what to think. She felt hollow inside, and guilty as well: a sort of sick, sinking feeling. Truckle, she said to herself, to fill the space: tucked up in a truckle bed.

Kate's mother was called Judith. She and Bella were twins. It seemed to Kate that having a twin must be a magical thing: exciting, yet also safe, more solid than your reflection in the mirror. There was safety in numbers, which was why Kate did not like hearing herself described as an only child. Kate's father, Sebastian, was also an only child – and he seemed to her to be a strange, solitary creature, not a father, exactly; not like the way her uncle was a father to his children. Sometimes Sebastian roared; sometimes he cried. Father. She spelt the word out in her head, but sometimes it turned into farther.

The night before she had come to her uncle's house, she had heard her father weeping. Kate was supposed to be sleeping, but she could hear him on the other side of the wall – too close, as if the bricks and plaster had dissolved in his tears. 'What were you doing in the water?' he cried. 'What were you thinking of?' Kate heard her mother's voice murmuring – no words, just something soft. What was her mother thinking? Kate didn't know. When she fell asleep, at last, she dreamt that her mother was porcelain white, standing at the top of the high stairs in her uncle's house, and then Kate watched her fall down the stairs – did she fall, or jump, or was she pushed? – and at the bottom, her mother was cracked; not crumpled, but broken; her face was broken into jagged pieces, all separated now, no blood, no flesh, just broken china. And when Kate tried to speak – to scream – no sound came out, her throat closed up, and she was silent, like her broken mother.

In the morning, after the dream, her uncle's brother, Luke, came to the flat and Kate said goodbye to her parents. Luke lived in London, but Kate didn't know him very well. He was younger than Charles and had no children of his own; he looked at Kate as if she might bite, or was he looking at her father? Her father wasn't looking at anyone; he was just sitting in the corner, staring at the floor, rocking himself, making a low moaning sound that frightened Kate. She got into the back seat of Luke's car, and her throat was hurting like it had done in the dream, burning, tight, but she wasn't dreaming. This was real, though the world looked different through the rear window as she waved to her mother; wrong, somehow, as if she had slipped through the crack in the willow-pattern plate, to a skewed and shifting place.

Luke drove her to the house. The house was called Elverson House. That was its address: Elverson House, Elverson, Norfolk, England, Great Britain, the World, the Universe, Infinity. Julian told her that. She wrote it in the red writing book that her mother had given her for the summer holidays. Then she wrote her name on the next line, as neatly as she could, to avoid the possibility of mistakes (not like last year, when she'd got confused, mixed some letters up the wrong way round). Kate Linden. Aged seven.

Paul, Isabel, Julian, Harriet. There were so many of

them. Kate felt shy at first, but Isabel and Harriet held her hands, Isabel on the left, Harriet on the right. 'Katie, Katie, kiss me, Kate,' said Julian. 'Don't be stupid,' said Paul, who was eleven, so he was going to big school in September. Bella had made a cake for tea. It had strawberries in the middle, dripping pink into the cream. 'I picked the strawberries this morning, didn't I,' said Harriet, 'in the garden, all by myself?' Bella smiled at Harriet. 'Sweetpea,' she said, 'what a lovely girl you are.'

'What about me?' said Julian, pulling at his mother's arms while Paul pulled a face at him.

'You're lovely, too,' said Bella. 'You all are. Five lovely children. How lucky I am.' She smiled, again, and Kate searched her face for clues about her mother. Bella and Judith were meant to be identical twins – that's what other people said – but Kate knew differently. They both had hazel eyes and light brown hair ('mouse,' said Judith; 'honey,' said Bella), just like Kate did, but her mother's hair was short and feathery, while her aunt's came below her shoulders. Judith was skinnier; Bella was softer. Bella had freckles scattered across warm tawny skin; Judith was pale-faced and always felt the cold. They were quite old now; Kate knew that. They were thirty-three years old. Kate was seven years and one month. Julian was two months older than her, and two inches taller. She tried to keep on top of these figures. They were important to her.

After the strawberry cake, Bella told the children to go into the garden, and they played hide-and-seek. Kate hid behind the oak tree that had been there since before her uncle Charles was born. Maybe it was older than his parents, who were really old, thirty-eight, maybe, but it wasn't polite to ask. They lived up the road now, nearer to the village, in another house with fewer rooms. They weren't Kate's grandparents; they belonged to Paul and Isabel and Julian and Harriet. It didn't seem fair. Kate only had two grandparents – her mother's parents, who lived in Sussex – because her father's parents were sort of dead. 'Dead to me,' said her father, 'monstrous people.' Kate did not like to think of these half-dead monsters.

When it was getting darker, after bath time, her uncle came home. Sometimes he worked at home, in his study with his books, but sometimes he went to the university, to look at the stars. That was his job – the stars. Kate's mother had taught her a rhyme about the evening star: a magic rhyme that meant you could have a wish if you said it right, in the twilight. Kate knew it off by heart, like a prayer: 'Star light, star bright, first star I see tonight, wish I may, wish I might, wish upon a star tonight.' Sometimes, when she stared hard at the first star in the sky, she wondered if it was just a tiny hole in the darkness, a pinprick that let the light behind shine through, heaven's light, perhaps; but maybe that was wrong, and the star was the only bright thing in the black night and there was nothing else out there, nothing beyond the sky, only the end of everything, for ever and ever, Amen.

Bella and Judith had learnt the starlight rhyme from their mother, too, but Charles didn't believe in it. He believed in physics, not magic, he said. Physics was a hard word to spell, and his job was even harder: physicist; only Paul could spell the job properly, without help from Bella. Her uncle's name was Dr Charles Reid. She could spell that (but you had to remember the spelling broke the rules, because usually it was *i* before *e*, except after *c*. 'It's an exception that proves a rule,' said her mother, which Kate didn't really understand, even though she had nodded, to show how good she was at listening). Charles was tall – taller than her father, taller than her mother, like the oak tree – and he leant down, as if from a great height, to kiss Kate on the tip of her nose. 'How nice to see you,' he said when he walked into the kitchen. 'Thank you for having me,' she said, like her mother had reminded her to say. Her uncle laughed.

Charles looked like his children; or did they look like him? Kate wasn't sure which was the right way round. They had dark hair – almost black, but not quite – and grey-blue eyes, like the evening sky before the stars came out in winter. He smelt of soap when she hugged him; and something else, something cold, which she told herself was starlight. 'The summer has started,' he said, and it was as if God had spoken.

In the morning Kate picked raspberries from the kitchen garden with Bella and Isabel. They put the raspberries in a blue china bowl, decorated with the same willow pattern as the plate that hung on the dining-room wall, but it wasn't broken – not like the plate, which was cracked in the middle of the picture of a little bridge across the water. You couldn't see what was on the other side of the painted river; there was just a path that disappeared between the willow trees, a hidden place that Kate longed to see. (Once, not this summer, another time, her uncle had found her looking at the plate and he'd told her that it wasn't really broken, the line across the picture was called a hairline fracture. Kate didn't know what fracture meant, but later Paul said it was

7

broken bones, and Kate wondered if the tiny person she could see in the picture had a fractured head, underneath her hair, perhaps.)

Inside the house Mrs Cox the cleaning lady was polishing the floors with beeswax. Nobody polished floors in the flat where Kate lived. Judith was busy trying to write a book ('a fairy tale about the stars,' she told Kate, 'but not for children') and Sebastian said that housework was irrelevant. Sebastian was a Marxist; Kate didn't understand what that word meant, either. He worked in a university, like her uncle, but a different one. He didn't look at the stars. 'I deal in the real world,' he used to say. Kate's mother sometimes smiled when he said that. Sebastian said she had a mocking smile. Mocking, locking, rocking, shocking. Kate made up rhymes in her head when her parents shouted at each other.

Nobody seemed to shout at Elverson House. Bella hummed; Harriet sang; Julian whistled. Charles was teaching Paul to play chess in the drawing room. The drawing room was not for drawing (even though Kate sometimes imagined that the green leafy wallpaper was a picture, like the willow pattern, and if you found the right place, you could slip away into it and hide, lost in the leaves). The drawing room was for sitting and being quiet in, said Bella. Kate was quiet – her words were silent inside her, swallowed by her hollow stomach. Outside, Julian climbed up the oak tree. He was very brave. 'Don't go too high,' said Kate. 'You might fall.'

'I won't fall,' said Julian. 'I'm very safe.'

Kate went to find Bella, who was clipping the lavender bushes that grew in a circle around the rose garden. The cat lay in the warm grass beside her, twitching its whiskers as a bee came too close. You had to be careful with cats. Sometimes they patted you, with claws safely in; sometimes you got scratched. 'When is my mum coming here?' said Kate.

'In a while,' replied Bella. 'She's got lots of things to sort out right now.'

'Next week?' said Kate.

'Maybe the week after that,' said Bella.

'OK,' said Kate, looking at her fingertips, instead of her aunt. The raspberry juice had stained them red, like blood. She walked back to the oak tree, but Julian was hidden in the branches, almost as high as the sky. She nibbled the knuckles on her hand. Knuckle, truckle, dead. Dead didn't rhyme right. She bit her hand harder. It didn't hurt, however hard she bit. Once her mother had told her a bedtime story that she had made up out of her own head, about a little girl who washed in a bowl of starlight, instead of water, and afterwards she never ever bled again, even when she cut herself with a knife.

For lunch they had egg-and-cress sandwiches. Isabel's chickens had laid the eggs, but there weren't any chicks inside, just yolks. Paul had grown the cress from seeds planted in wet cotton wool, for his science homework project. Kate tried not to think of the cotton wool or the baby chickens when she ate her sandwich, because she still felt sick, and her tongue tasted of metal. Afterwards, she helped Mrs Cox do the drying up. 'What a good girl you are,' said Mrs Cox, 'just like your auntie.'

'My mum's good, too,' said Kate, but she wasn't sure if this was true. Her mother seemed shadowy now that Kate was here, in the sunlight.

'You need plenty of fresh air,' said Mrs Cox. 'Brighten you up before you go home to London. Out you go, dear, go and play in the garden.'

The afternoon seemed to go on forever, but then it was tomorrow, and the next day, and the day after that. Kate's mum still didn't arrive, though her grandparents – Bella and Judith's parents – came to visit for a weekend. Their names were Mr and Mrs Michael Scott, but Kate called them grandma and grandpa. They were quite grand, actually: rather tall and thin, with lots of silvery white hair swept back from their faces, and sharp noses like birds. Grandma said that Kate was a dear child. She gave Kate a little silver cross on a chain to wear around her neck, and reminded her to say the Lord's Prayer at bedtime. 'Sebastian won't approve,' said Bella.

'Sebastian is neither here nor there,' said Grandma. This was true. Where had he gone to, exactly? Her father (not Our Father, who art in heaven – but what did that mean, did he paint pictures in the sky?) wasn't in the flat; he had moved out – Kate's mum said so. One night Kate dreamt that she met her father beside the stream that ran through the Elverson grounds and down to the church. It wasn't a deep stream, but he held her face beneath the water so that she couldn't breathe. In the dream she seemed to be in two places at once, floating in the air above herself, watching her father push her down, a silent wide-eyed doll child in the water. She woke up from the dream in the middle of the night, choking and sweating and even more guilty. The sheets of the truckle bed had come untucked.

The next morning – or it might have been another one, these things got mixed up – Charles drove Bella and the children, all squashed in the back of his big car, to the sandy beach. It wasn't the nearest beach, the one you could cycle to from Elverson – that beach had round pebbles on it, they made a noise like broken bones – but a bigger one along the coast road. Charles parked the car, and then they had to walk a long, long way, past the pine trees and through some muddy bits, and then there was the sand. It stretched so far, Kate could hardly see the sea at the end of the sand. The wind blew; it nearly blew her dream away. 'Come on,' said Julian, taking her hand. He pulled her up the highest sand dune. They stood at the top, and they could see the sea, silvery, not blue like in the pictures Kate painted at school. 'I'm the king of the castle and you're the dirty rascal!' shouted Julian.

'I'm not a rascal,' said Kate.

'OK,' said Julian, 'you're the queen of the castle.' He laced his warm fingers through hers, and then pulled again, and they were running down the sand dune, faster than she had ever run before, all the way down, but they couldn't stop and they ran and ran towards the sea. 'Be careful in the water!' cried Bella behind them, her voice small in the wind. The sea was cold, and Kate didn't want to go too deep, she let go of Julian's hand, and he kept running, splashing, till he was just a dark head bobbing in the water, Paul on one side, their father on the other. Kate looked for shells along the water's edge, like she always did. The best ones to find had a little hole in them, so you could thread them together into a seaside necklace. She didn't want the broken shells, or cracked ones, or razor shells, which might cut your fingers, or your neck. After a while, Isabel came to help Kate, and she found a small grey cowrie, tiny edges curved in on each other, so you couldn't see inside. 'Maybe there is a secret in the shell,' said Kate.

'Like a message in a bottle?' said Isabel, who was clever. 'A sea fairy would have had to put it there – people are too big and clumsy.'

'Or a child,' said Kate. 'A sea child.' Isabel regarded her, unblinking even though she had a few grains of sand at the end of her dark eyelashes.

Then Julian came out of the water, dripping wet, shaking off the sea from his brown body, black hair in tendrils as he pushed it away from his eyes. 'Look at my footprints,' he said to Kate. 'Put your feet on my footprints and see if they fit.' She stepped into them, carefully, balancing, but her feet were just a little bit smaller than his. 'Do you think there is anyone in the world that has exactly the same footprints as me?' said Julian.

'Probably not,' said Isabel, shrugging.

'In the whole universe, there must be two people with the same footprints.' he said. 'That's what infinity means, that's what Dad says.'

'No, he *doesn't*,' said Isabel.

'Does,' said Julian.

'You think you know everything,' said Isabel, and walked away.

'Look, Julian, mine are nearly the same as yours,' said Kate, still standing in his footprints in the sand.

'Very nearly,' said Julian. 'Maybe you are almost me . . .' Kate did not reply, just looked at her feet, sinking slightly in the sand, as the tide began to turn and the water washed the footprints away.

Two

8 River Lane, Crouch End, London N8, England, Great Britain, Europe, the World, the Universe.

Kate looked at her son's new diary. This could be seen as an invasion of his privacy, but apart from the address and the date – January 1st – he had so far written nothing apart from a short list of New Year's resolutions: (1) get a dog, (2) learn how to do magic, (3) swim across the sea. Kate had not committed her own list to paper, but she told herself that she was resolved, even so, to: (1) go swimming at the local pool twice a week, and do yoga at weekends, (2) be mindful of the beauty and joy in small things, (3) meet an accountant; fall in love and marry him.

Sam was seven, an apparently uncomplicated child; 'sunny-natured and even-tempered' said his end-of-term report from school. (Kate sometimes wondered if that meant his teacher thought he was boring, unremarkable, *ordinary;* not that ordinariness was necessarily a bad thing.) Still, Kate wanted some more clues. Did Sam hide a secret unhappiness, given that his father did not live with them? Was he a lonely only child? What was her son thinking, in the quiet corners of his mind, between the empty lines?

Upstairs Sam slept peacefully, the cat curled up beside him. He breathed so gently that Kate reached out to touch his warm cheek, to check that he was still alive. He smiled equably, eyes closed, unreachable behind translucent lids in a place she could not see. Kate stood there for a moment, adoring her sleeping child, before returning downstairs to the kitchen to read her horoscope for the coming month. She was a Gemini – a thirty-five-year-old Gemini – with one son, one cat and one ex-husband. 'Time for your unique brand of original thinking,' said the horoscope in her magazine (hers, in that she wrote for the magazine, as well as read it). 'You know you have great ideas to share with the world – so go ahead, be brave, shine!' Kate had some knowledge of the inside workings of these horoscopes – as a former assistant editor on the magazine, a glossy monthly which concerned itself more with Hollywood stars than those of the firmament, she had, nevertheless, when necessary, polished up the astrologer's eccentric prose (an avalanche of clauses, and not much in the way of full stops). These days, as a part-time feature writer, she only went in to the office once a month, or less: uncomfortable occasions, when she felt badly dressed and out of place, dull, alongside the girls with shiny hair and wide smiles and expensive names that ended in 'a', like Angelica. (It seemed improbable that she had once looked like them; but she had – or at least an approximation of a girl like that, in low-slung Calvin Klein jeans that now no longer fitted her.) Mostly she worked from home while Sam was at school, mooching from desk to fridge and back again in sagging baggy tracksuit bottoms, talking to nobody for hours at a time except her computer screen, or the occasional bright-voiced yet faceless PR person ringing with news of the latest skin cream or fashion show. Tonight, having got behind with her paltry schedule in the Christmas holidays, Kate knew she should be finishing her feature on celebrity morning beauty routines ('How the Brightest Stars Rise!'). But it was too depressing for words.

She considered ringing her cousin Julian instead, but that might also be depressing, in a more damaging way. Julian was married to Jessica and lived in an immaculate Georgian rectory in Suffolk. Jessica did not work – she didn't need to, with Julian's substantial City salary – and stayed at home instead, to care for their two children: four-year-old Rafael ('an angel,' said his father, at every opportunity, with no apparent sense of irony) and Madeleine, who was almost two. Julian was still handsome, and Jessica – a former stylist at a glossy interiors magazine – was beautiful, and their children were growing up in an unbroken family, blessed with a large garden, a swimming pool and two white ponies, that, like Jessica, never appeared ungroomed in any way. It was the sodding ponies that always got Kate in the end. When she was eight she had spent hours filling in the forms for the W.H. Smith 'Win A Pony' competition, composing careful sentences of less than ten words, as specified in the rules, concerning the various merits of different equine breeds; but nothing had ever come of it. Kate did not win competitions. Her five premium bonds – bought for her by her maternal grandparents when she was born – had failed, resolutely, to bring in any prize money at all. Her lottery tickets were equally unproductive and Sam's school raffle tickets proved to be consistent failures, as well. She was ill-starred, clearly. Shining was not an option right now.

It might have been more comforting to ring Julian's older sister, Isabel, but she was not yet back from the Maldives (Kate did not begrudge her this, as she begrudged Julian the ponies, because Isabel was never smug and lived alone, and deserved a break from her job as a psychiatrist in an underfunded north London hospital where mad people shouted at her all day). Instead, Kate knew she should speak to her parents, much as she dreaded the prospect. She started with her father.

'Hello, Dad,' she said, when he picked up the phone on the other side of England, in a cottage halfway up a windswept Herefordshire hillside. 'It's me.'

'Who?' said her father.

'Me, your daughter, Kate,' she said, trying not to sound irritable. 'Happy New Year! How are you?'

'Oh, you know, depressed,' said her father, who did not like the winter, 'and plagued with an irritable bowel, or maybe it's worms inside me. But I'm trying to sleep my way through January. And you – how are you and Sam?'

'Fine,' she said.

'Good,' he said, and sighed, so deeply that Kate held the phone away from her ear for a second, as if his breath were somehow contagious. 'I've written another poem. I'll post it to Sam tomorrow, OK?'

Her father, who had retired from his university post as a history lecturer last year, had taken to writing very gloomy poetry, much of it concerning the Holocaust. The last poem he had sent Sam – whom he adored, from a distance – was about a little boy who finds himself on a train to a nameless destination, probably a concentration camp, where death awaited him.

'That would be lovely,' said Kate, who did not want to hurt her father's feelings at this, the bleakest time of year, when he was crabbiest (claws out, yet also somehow defenceless). 'Would you like to come and stay with us next weekend?'

'I am penniless,' said her father, which was true, as he had donated most of his small pension to the Socialist Workers Party, even though he professed himself to be a nihilist. 'And I hate London. It reminds me of all that is anomic in the world. You can feel the chaos and despair in the air that you breathe.'

'It's not that bad,' said Kate. 'But never mind, we'll see you soon.' She put the phone down feeling quite relieved – firstly, that she had done her duty as a daughter, by offering hospitality; secondly, that her father had turned her down, as usual; and thirdly, that she wasn't as miserable as he was. Unlike Julian and Jessica, who were constantly receiving windfalls from deceased distant relatives, Kate told herself she had inherited nothing – neither her father's clinical depression, nor the mania that followed it, nor her mother's propensity for silent despair. In a recent card that approximated as a Christmas greeting from her father (it had Munch's *The Scream* on the front), he had suggested she might like to know the details of his current medication, given that manic depression was doubtless genetic. She did not, however, take Prozac – unlike many of her friends – and though she liked little better than to go to bed with a sleeping pill, she had just managed a fortnight without a prescription, which was an achievement, definitely. Her pots of lavender in the front garden appeared to have survived last night's heavy frost, and a few snowdrops were already flowering in the back – those that had escaped the rapacious squirrels – and while a bitter east wind was blowing litter across the filthy city pavements, at least the sun had shone today; and she and Sam had seen a robin perched outside on the kitchen window ledge. (There had been a single, baleful magpie, as well – 'one for sorrow,' her mother used to say – but Kate had negated the potential bad luck that accompanied the bird by whispering, as she always did on such sightings, 'Hello, Mr Magpie. Give my regards to your wife and family.') Tonight her house was peaceful – quiet and far more calm than it had been when her ex-husband the photographer was still living there, filling it up with all his shiny cameras, magpie-like himself – and she told herself that she was peaceful, too. Almost, maybe . . .

But as midnight drew nearer, the whisper of anxiety in her head grew louder, as it often did at this time of night. Sam seemed happy enough, but could something bad be brewing? What about money? Her ex-husband (christened Sneaky Pete by Julian – not that her cousin had any right to be rude, given his own imperfect record) had agreed that she should stay in the house, but he might change his mind and demand they sell up, if his series of affairs turned into another marriage, and another child. Quite apart from all of that, where was she going in life? There would be no place for a forty-year-old feature writer on a magazine engaged primarily with the cult of blessed youth; and even if there were, it was too shaming a prospect – though Kate had learnt the value of the apparently meaningless. ('There is safety in the shallows,' she told her father some time ago, after he had remarked that she might do more with her first-class degree in English literature.)

It was now too late to ring her mother for advice – late, in every sense, because her mother was dead, though not gone – and anyway, what would her mother have to say? 'Mum,' she said, out loud, 'what were you thinking of?' Kate tapped her nails on the table, an unintelligible Morse code to the Other Side. Her mother died before Sam was born – before he was even imagined; though Kate believes that he must have lived inside her, before he was conceived (just as her mother seems to still). Her mother drove off a road on her way back to London from Elverson House when Kate had just embarked upon her second term at university. A blind bend, it must have been; another one, as treacherous as the way that led to Elverson. (Blind, mind, unkind, wrote a childish hand inside her head, from force of habit; round the bend, round the twist, round the houses . . .) It was an icy night, like tonight; the kind of night when green leaves shrivel in the cold.

The morning after her mother died, her uncle came to Cambridge to tell Kate what had happened, and she sat and stared out of the window of her college room. There was nothing in the sky – no message, nothing but the grey. Charles had held her in his arms, briefly, but his face was empty, and then he left. Not long after, Julian arrived, out of breath from running. 'I just heard,' he said, and he took her hand. He kept her hand in his for the rest of the day, as if she might otherwise disappear; and that night she said to him, 'Don't leave me,' and he climbed into her bed, her narrow college bed. 'I love you,' he said, but she could not speak, there was nothing but tears inside her, and then they were spilling everywhere, warm tears on her face, and on his.

The next morning he drove her to Elverson House, and they were all there, together again – Charles and Bella and Paul and Isabel and Julian and Harriet and Kate. Her father came the following day, looking smaller than she remembered him, shrunken inside a black winter coat (a greybeard, rather than Bluebeard, after all). Everyone was wearing black; bloodless white faces against black clothes for the funeral; like magpies, thought Kate. Bella had picked snowdrops for the grave. ('Bad luck,' said Mrs Cox, shaking her head. 'Don't bring those collywobble white flowers in the house, or we'll see another shroud before the year is out.') They went in a procession of undertaker's cars, all polished and dark, driving so very slowly to the nearby church that she wanted to scream, or laugh; but she was silent, as silent as the rest of the mourners in the back seats, their sighs misting up the windows, though Kate felt as if she were holding her breath. Her mother was ahead of them, leading the way from inside her hearse. Kate had not seen her mother's body, but she imagined it as wax, like the unreal-looking white lilies that covered her coffin; a porcelain head on the wax-doll body, her face cracked, though not yet fallen apart. When the vicar said 'ashes to ashes, dust to dust', Kate imagined only china dust, the powder scattered on the floor after a plate is broken.

Kate walked back from the grave, along the footpath that led from the church to the house. The January mud had gone, turned to ice, and the stream was frozen over so you could not see what lay beneath. Julian walked beside her, but she did not look into his eyes. Her hands were cold, deep inside her pockets, clenched so hard her shoulders ached, and the ache spread down her legs. By then the sky had filled with clouds, rose tinted and ragged against the fading blue, drifting towards the sea. When it was dark, the last of the violet clouds sinking with the wintry sun, everyone was gathered in the house; but she followed her uncle outside again, onto the stone terrace that looked over the rose garden, with its bare black spikes cut low to the ground, the lavender flowers all gone now. 'Is there an equation that explains accidents?' asked Kate, knowing that his mind moved in mathematical ways.

'We are all made of stardust,' he said, gazing up into the unlit night. 'That is where we come from and where we return.'

'No figures?' she said.

'No words,' he replied.

Kate can't remember much more. She saw her grandfather crying, for the first and last time; and her grandmother said, no, I couldn't eat a thing, but Kate was hungry – well, not hungry, exactly, but empty, so she ate the dense fruit cake that Mrs Cox had baked, and drank sweet tea. That night she slept alone, in a spare bedroom, and dreamt that her mother was swimming away from the shore, out to sea. Charles was standing at the edge of the water and he said to Kate, 'You can't follow her.' And there were words written on the sand, but she couldn't read them, and numbers in the sky, but the wind blew them away.

Ho hum. No use dwelling on what was long gone. 1 January. A new year, a new beginning. Time marches on. ('Darling, do try to avoid clichés,' said her mother's voice in her head. 'You can talk,' said Kate. 'But I don't,' said her mother. 'Talk, that is.')

Three

Day two of the New Year: how many left to go? Kate was
bad with numbers. It was time for her tax return, and nothing added up. Now that she was no longer on the staff of
the magazine – merely an anxious contributor, her freelance
income supplemented by occasional book reviews for a
Sunday newspaper – the tax return was unavoidable, yet
insurmountable. She gazed at her dwindling bank statements, which didn't seem to make any sense – surely she
had not spent so much last month; could the bank be steal-
ing from her in a complicated computer fraud? – and then
decided to give up until next week, when Sam was back
at school. Today she was driving them both to Elverson
House, having made an excuse to avoid Christmas there.
(Quite a good excuse, really – Pete had come round on
Christmas morning with presents for Sam, which was fine,
fortified as she was by a small dose of Valium borrowed
from her friend and neighbour Maria, who needed larger
doses to cope with the seasonal deluge of in-laws, outgoings
and ill-will.)

New Year's Eve had passed off without incident as well

– a few hours across the road at another neighbour's house, with Sam and lots of other children and parents from his school. The talk was of street crime spiralling with property prices, of organic paint and linen sofas, and whether the world would be taken over by tiny sinister robots in the next decade (yes, said a journalist who lived around the corner, and had written a gloomy newspaper piece saying so; no, said a local aromatherapist, who believed that the earth would heal itself, because that was the natural order of things; bollocks to all that, said Maria's husband, we'll all be drowned in the rain, but then Maria told him it was whisky he was drowning in, and a robot would be more fun to live with). Kate had felt exhausted by ten o'clock, unlike Sam, who was high on excitement and lemonade, but she'd managed to last out until ten past midnight, and then insisted they both come home – much to Sam's disgust – to the quiet comforts of their respective beds. (Sleeping alone had much to recommend it, she told herself, in her familiar mantra against bedtime loneliness, given that Pete had snored and sweated through the night, kicking against her presence, or so it had seemed at the time.)

Kate was inclined to agree with Sam, who said that New Year's Eve came too soon after Christmas (why not have it after the summer holidays, he'd suggested, when grownups weren't so tired?). But there was no escaping the relentless New Year, not entirely, even though it felt stale already on its second day, after she'd stuffed her crumpled invoices and bank statements back in their box underneath her desk; and by 11 a.m. she had done the washing-up, reminded Maria to feed the cat, found Sam's favourite teddy, and packed them both a bag. She double-locked the front door, got into the car, got out again to check that she had, in fact, locked the back door, re-locked the front door, got back into the car, checked for the third time that Sam's safety belt was securely fastened, and set off towards the motorway. (Why couldn't these obsessive symptoms manifest themselves in more useful ways, she wondered? A loss of appetite would be better than the double-locking compulsion, or how about an urge to visit the gym instead?) Sam was dozing before long, as London faded behind them; so that left Kate in the silence, without the comforting familiarity of his chatter or the radio (she didn't want to disturb Sam and, anyway, the signal crackled and was lost once you were halfway up the motorway). At times like this, in the car, Kate was sometimes sure that she felt her mother's cold breath on the back of her neck; that if she turned round fast enough she might catch a glimpse of her face. This was partly reassuring – 'Yes, Mum, I am driving carefully,' she muttered out loud – but there was an undertow of fear, because if she did turn her head to look behind her, her eyes would not be on the road.

As she drove north beyond the city, the muddy fields that lined the road turned white with hoarfrost, and by Stansted there was a thin covering of snow on the ground, sparkling white against the pearl-grey sky. Sam loved the snow – for its rarity, and the miraculous cold. 'I love winter,' he said, often; though he loved the summer, too. Others might consider Kate unlucky in life – unfortunate, at any rate – but she felt herself to be so blessed by Sam and his good humour (not constant, for he was a child rather than an angel, but comforting nevertheless), that it was impossible to agree with those who pitied her. Whatever Pete had done wrong – wherever she had failed, as well, in her haphazard mothering – Sam appeared relatively unscathed, so far; and for that she was grateful – if not to God, then to fate. (But might she be tempting fate to say so? Or was there a rational physics of fate, which ruled these matters? She must ask her uncle.)

Two hours out of London she turned onto the road that led to the place where her mother had died. You came through the woods – except her mother would have been coming in the opposite direction and not yet in the forest when she crashed – and out onto the other side, and there you were. Here you are. 'You couldn't see the woods for the trees,' whispered a papery voice in Kate's head – as it had done often before, so she ignored it (and found herself thinking instead of something her uncle had once said: that our minds were not necessarily in our heads, we only imagined them there – but he did not explain where our minds might otherwise be, which troubled Kate, for where was her mind now, if not in her brain? Floating free from the car, perhaps, though surely that would not make for safe driving).

She switched on the radio to drown out the workings of her mind – it didn't matter if Sam woke up now – and listened to the weather forecast, hoping for some familiar certainties. Snow in eastern England overnight, though not in coastal areas. Elverson was probably too close to the sea – and there was no snow to be seen now, and they were only twenty miles or so away from the house – but still, she prayed, for Sam's sake, if not her own. 'God,' she said, feeling faintly embarrassed, as she did when she talked to solitary magpies, 'I don't ask you for much, but I am asking you now, please, out of the goodness of your heart, to allow the snow to fall out of the heavens. Thank you. Amen.'

Bella believed in God; Charles said he did not, though the little Kate knew of his physics seemed, to her at least, to have a mystical slant. He had become a Cambridge professor – grand enough to be interviewed on Sunday night television programmes about the mystery of the universe – and even though he cited lengthy mathematical equations by way of explanation, his apparent belief that the universe was a thing of beauty, order and perfect symmetry suggested that God might lie at the unspoken heart of it. Not that Kate was ever quite sure what her uncle was *actually* thinking. He, like God, was a mystery.

Five more miles to Elverson, and the sun slanted low over the fields – another winter sun, from a distant place beyond a break in the clouds. (When she was little, she had drawn a picture: three lines; the sky at the top, where God was, and the earth, where she lived, and down below the black line, where who knows what preyed.) And then she was there, here, at the blind bend, and her heart quickened, just a beat, and she had not missed it this time, she was through the gates and driving past the trees and up towards the house. Behind her, Sam opened his eyes – clear blue eyes, his own colour, not hers, beneath red-gold hair quite unlike anyone else's in the family – and she smiled at him in the rear-view mirror, and he smiled back at her.

It was bitterly cold when they climbed out of the car – Norfolk in winter always felt ten degrees below London – so she hurried Sam to the front door, out of the wind. Bella's dog, a rough-haired, sweet-faced Jack Russell called Poppy, reached them first – barking and licking and jumping up on hind legs in a frenzy of joy. (Kate had so far managed to avoid Sam's pressing requests for a puppy – Poppy's puppy, in fact, which was what he had *really* wanted for Christmas, though the skateboard she bought him seemed to just about fill the breach – by explaining that he would have to wait until Poppy got pregnant, an event that Kate dreaded most of the time.) After Poppy came Bella, in one of the well-washed navy sailor's sweaters that she seemed to have been wearing since Kate was old enough to notice other people's clothes. 'Kate, Sam, how lovely to see you,' said Bella. 'You must be longing for some lunch.'

They followed her down the hall, which smelt of beeswax and lavender, as ever, and into the kitchen, where Harriet was making a large pot of tea. Sam looked a bit shy – he hadn't seen Harriet since Guy Fawkes' Night – but went to her, nevertheless, when she beckoned him. 'I have a very special Christmas present for you,' said Harriet, who had no children of her own, and was good at avoiding boring, educational, guilt-ridden gifts. She handed him a small package, which he unwrapped before taking his coat off; inside was a new Gameboy – of such high playground status that Sam's face broke into a wide smile. 'Wow, that's wicked!' he said.

'Say thank you,' said Kate, automatically.

'He has,' said Harriet, and gave her a hug.

Harriet's job was something to do with computers that Kate didn't understand; but she did know that Harriet enjoyed it and made a great deal of money. She lived in Primrose Hill in the sort of covetable flat that Kate imagined herself in, if she was single and childless (creamy suede sofas draped with dove-coloured cashmere throws; ash-blond

Justine Picardie

floors, unmarked by scuffing feet or sticky fingers; and a
well-stocked walk-in wardrobe lined with fragrant cedar-
wood, to keep her new season Prada free of moths and
dust). Harriet, like her flat, was very fashionable, in a way
that Kate admired – never looking as if she had tried too
hard, in faded jeans that showed half an inch of her tanned,
taut stomach (the result of thrice-weekly yoga and no doubt
athletic sex with a part-time boyfriend, who was currently
residing in Seattle). Harriet, unlike Kate, had no need of
baggy jumpers to cover up her waist, let alone her thighs;
moreover, Harriet had beautifully cut glossy dark hair and
clean unbroken nails and not a trace of a shadow beneath
her almond eyes; yet for all that, Kate loved her.

'Cool,' said Sam, pointing at Harriet's new silver trainers.

'Oh, lord,' she said, 'do I look ridiculous? Tell me Kate,
you must know about these things.'

'No, you're perfectly gorgeous, like always,' said Kate,
'and so *thin* I can't bear it.'

'You're thin, too,' said Harriet, slipping into their familiar routine.

'I'm *not*,' said Kate, grabbing a handful of her belly,
floppy, like a cat's, 'I've got middle-aged spread, look, all
wobbly and disgusting.' And it was true, she was a stone
heavier than when Pete had left her five years ago, but she
didn't really care any more: at least, not enough to turn
down Bella's home-made shepherd's pie followed by apple
crumble and double cream. (Anyway, Isabel, who was a
psychiatrist and therefore knew about this stuff, had often
said that the only men who were attracted to painfully thin
women – skinny waifs, like Kate used to be – were repressed

28

homosexuals or sadists; though to be honest, much as Kate would have liked to label Pete as one or the other or both, he had shown no signs of being either, as far as she could tell; shown no sign of being anything but his unruffled, unreadable, unknowable self.)

'How was your Christmas?' said Bella, as she dished out lunch for the four of them.

'Oh, you know, low-key,' said Kate. 'How about yours?'

'Lovely,' said Bella. 'Everyone came – Paul and Becky and the twins – gosh, how they've grown . . .'

'Ten going on eighteen,' said Harriet.

'And Isabel – she's so tired, poor lamb, she really needs that holiday – and Harriet, of course, and Julian and Jessica and the children.'

Kate was gratified that at the mention of Jessica, Harriet pulled a small face (it was comforting not to be the only one who curdled at the thought of her). 'Jess-*sick*-a,' said Harriet, drawing out the syllables, 'says that Ralph Lauren is desperate for her to be his new consultant – apparently Ralph is longing to base a new campaign around her and her lovely home – but she thinks not, it would be too disruptive for the family.' Harriet stuck her fingers down her throat and made retching noises, which was practically the most cheering thing that had happened to Kate all week.

'Darling,' said Bella, 'don't be horrid.'

'Jessica, Jessica, always knows best,' said Harriet. 'You know, when I bought their kids some clothes for Christmas, Jessica asked for the receipt so she could take everything back to the shop, because she doesn't want them wearing stuff from the Gap. It undermines her taste, apparently, and her authority in the family. She's clearly deranged.'

'Julian might drive over later,' said Bella, ignoring Harriet, 'but only if he doesn't have to go and pick up Jessica and the children from her parents' house.'

'For God's sake, he's such a spineless sap,' said Harriet. 'Why can't Jessica drive herself home? It's only thirty miles or so, and they've got two cars.'

'Three,' said Kate. 'The Land Rover, the Mercedes estate, and a new sports car for Julian. He told me the new one was a present to himself on Christmas Eve.'

'I can't bear it,' said Harriet. 'I think I may actually have to be sick.'

'To them that have shall be given,' said Kate.

'What does that mean, Mum?' said Sam. 'We have a car, so why can't we be given a new one? A racing car – that's what I'd like. We need a new one, anyway – our car has got a scratch down the side, and it smells like sick.'

'It does not smell like sick,' said Kate. 'I cleaned it only yesterday.'

'Come on, Sam,' said Harriet, 'shall we go out into the garden and climb the oak tree before it gets dark?'

'Do be careful,' said Kate.

'Don't worry!' said Harriet, and took Sam's hand.

After they had gone, pursued by the yelping dog, Kate helped Bella load the dishwasher (no more Mrs Cox; though her arthritis had not prevented her from making half a dozen pots of Seville orange marmalade for Bella). 'I've got a lovely cleaning lady who comes every morning now, from the village,' said Bella, 'but she's poorly today, and of course, Charles doesn't even know how to switch on any domestic machinery . . .'

'Where is he?' said Kate.

'He went into Cambridge this morning,' said Bella, 'to catch up on some college paperwork, but he'll be back by tea time – he's so looking forward to seeing you, darling, and Sam. I thought I'd do a chicken casserole for dinner – Sam would like that, wouldn't he, but I'll feed him first, if that's OK with you? And lemon meringue pie for afters? I made the lemon curd yesterday, with some wonderful fruit from the Belvoirs' conservatory. I don't know how they manage to grow citrus trees in this climate, but somehow they do – I suppose it's an advantage having that glasshouse on a south-facing wall.'

Bella was as soothing as ever – she seemed to have no rough edges, no sharp points to avoid – and Kate remembered what she sometimes forgot when she was away from Elverson House, which was that she loved it here, that she belonged, even though she feared she did not. True, she had been an odd number – an only child, one, just one, not one of four or six – but she was part of the life of the house, nevertheless; and now there was Sam, which made two of them.

Yet much as she loved being lulled by Bella, she could not help wondering why her aunt was so invariably calm. Did she occasionally feel dread in her blood as midnight approached? Did her dead twin's voice ever speak to her from the back seat of a car? Did she dream, as Kate often did, of her foot slipping onto the accelerator instead of the brakes, of her hands losing grip of the wheel, the car spinning on black ice, over the edge, out of control? 'It's the anniversary of Mum's death this month,' said Kate, after they'd finished a second cup of tea. 'I was just . . .'

'Yes?' said Bella, when Kate's pause had become uncomfortable.

'Oh, I don't know,' said Kate. 'Do you ever think of her?'

'Often,' said Bella, 'but we have to move on, you know.'

'I do know,' said Kate, 'but sometimes the dead come with us.'

'One mustn't be morbid,' said Bella, and reached out to touch Kate's hand, briefly, before standing up. 'Now, my darling, I thought you'd like to sleep in the blue bedroom, with Sam next door. Would that suit you?'

'That would be lovely,' said Kate. 'I'll take our stuff upstairs now.' Bella led the way, graceful, yet swift as she ever was – really, she wasn't old at all – and then left Kate in the bedroom to unpack. (It was unthinkable that she would not unpack, even though they were staying for just a few days; unpacking was part of the Elverson routine.) The bedroom was one of four on the first floor at the front of the house, with a view south across the lawn to the oak tree, where Sam and Harriet were perched together, his hair like flames against the bare branches of the tree.

She smiled, to stop herself from sighing. Be mindful of the joy in little things, she reminded herself. Be thankful for small mercies. She shivered, even though the radiator in the room was warm. For an instant she imagined her mother's face – broken into tiny pieces, like china, the porcelain pattern smashed – and then put her middle fingers to her temples, and pressed hard, to make the picture go away. She had read somewhere, a long time ago, that if you pushed hard enough, the delicate bone of the temples would break; but what would lie beneath? Cold nothingness, she thought; just empty space – like the void that her uncle gazed into in search of the truth.

Four

At quarter to four, as dusk descended over Elverson, a car came up the drive: a fast, low-lying black car that purred, rather than roared. Kate had dozed for a little while, but stood up and went to the bedroom window again. Out of the car stepped her cousin, Julian. He did not know she was looking at him through the glass; could not see her seeing him, as he ran his fingers through his hair. It was still thick, like his father's, and cropped short at the neck, dark against his skin. Julian looked as solid as ever – a solidity that Kate could not help but admire, because what would be more disconcerting than a man with reed-like limbs? (Reid, reed, read, scrawled an unseen hand across the sand in her sleepy head; wake up, whispered her mother's voice inside her inner ear, wake up and face the day . . .) The smile on his face, thought Kate, was that of a man pleased with himself and what he saw before him: a smile that would remain, like the Cheshire Cat's, when everything else had gone. He was wearing jeans – expensive jeans, not frayed at the bottom like Kate's – and a thick navy pea coat, pure cashmere, she guessed, that looked similarly costly. He was six foot one, clear-skinned, broad-shouldered and apparently content. Bloody Julian. Bloody hell. Bloody New Year.

She bit her hand and turned away from the window. Lipstick, a bit of lipstick never went amiss. She put some on, then rubbed most of it off – Sam might notice, otherwise – and went downstairs. Julian was in the hall and came towards her, smiling still, arms wide open, as if to hug her. But she held back, chin down, unwelcoming. 'How's Jessica,' she said, looking over his shoulder to the front door, 'and the kids?'

'Marvellous,' he said. 'You should have come and spent New Year's Eve with us . . . We had an immense bonfire and fireworks in the garden – it was great fun.'

'Oh, well, maybe next time,' she said.

'There's always next time,' he said, and raised one eyebrow slightly.

Soon after, Charles arrived and Bella ushered them all into the drawing room, where a fire was burning and the red velvet curtains drawn against the dark outside. 'Tea and cake and presents,' she said, lighting real candles on the Christmas tree – from the Elverson woods, as ever – in the tiny burnished silver holders that Kate remembered from her childhood.

Sam's cheeks were glowing as he opened his presents, flushed with excitement and the warmth of fire after the afternoon's fresh air. Charles and Bella had bought him a telescope, to look at the stars, and Julian gave him a model aeroplane kit and an envelope with thirty pounds inside. 'Thirty squid!' said Sam, astonished, before collecting himself sufficiently to hand out the presents that Kate had insisted they make together (crumbling chocolate fudge,

34

cooked in the empty days between Christmas and New Year's Eve, and translucent chunks of coconut ice, pale pink and nestled against green peppermint creams).

'I'll help you make the plane after tea,' said Julian, who prided himself on his ability to charm all children, 'and then we'll set up the telescope in your bedroom and look at the moon.' Sam was, inevitably, completely bewitched. That was the thing about Julian: he took it for granted that everyone would adore him and, on the whole, they did.

Everyone except for Kate, that is. 'Why are you cross with me?' he said later, when they found themselves alone together on the first-floor landing.

'I'm not,' she said.

'You are,' he said. 'I can tell.'

'I. Am. Not. Cross.'

'Yes. You. Are.' He reached over and kissed her on the cheek, his butterfly lips brushing against her skin, very briefly. 'You look lovely,' he said, softly, 'as ever.'

'I don't. I'm worn out.'

'You need a good husband, like –'

'– you need a slap, you smug prig . . .'

He turned away from her, before she could turn her back on him (and who knows whether he heard her sigh). So she resolved, then, to be as charming as he was; to be light and bright and self-sufficient, instead of brittle and icy and inexplicably wronged. Before dinner Charles poured them generous glasses of wine and Kate felt herself beginning to thaw at the edges. Harriet had given Sam a bath and now he was in his pyjamas, finishing the model aeroplane with Julian on the kitchen table, sticky-fingered from the glue. 'Do you remember,' said Kate to Julian, touching his hand, 'when you were Sam's age, you had all those Airfix models hanging on thread from your bedroom ceiling? And you made me jump off the top bunk, because you said we were bailing out of your Spitfire? And I hurt my ankle?'

'What a fiend I was,' said Julian. 'I bet you wouldn't do that, Sam, would you?'

'I wouldn't push,' said Sam. 'Did you push my mum off the top bunk?'

'I didn't push,' said Julian. 'She jumped, all of her own accord.'

'Bedtime,' said Bella, and miraculously, impossibly, whisked Sam up to bed – at only eight o'clock! – and settled him, without complaint, before the adults ate dinner.

'How did you manage that?' said Kate, when Bella came back into the kitchen a few minutes later. 'Sam's got into the habit of terribly late nights in the Christmas holidays.'

'I let him have the dog on his bed as a special treat,' said Bella. 'But he's no trouble, anyway – just like you, when you were small, such a good child, so sweetly eager to please.'

Over dinner, Harriet and Charles sat at one end of the table discussing computer models of chaos theory. Kate had no idea how Harriet could understand any of it – she seemed to be suggesting that chaos, in fact, had a pattern all of its own; that chaos was not chaotic – while Julian and Bella sat at the other end, talking about his children. Kate, in the middle, kept half an ear on each conversation, which threaded together as the soft red wine took hold.

'Like father, like son . . .' said Julian.

'Could history repeat itself?' said Harriet.

'There is no sign of the random,' said Charles, 'yet the pattern may still be coincidental . . .'

'And Rafael looks just like you,' said Bella.

'But we know that the underlying principle here is the concept of symmetry . . .'

'I always thought she had my mother's eyes . . .'

'It may be abstract, but the manifestation of symmetry is real enough . . .'

At half past eleven, Julian stood up, clearing his throat, as if to go. 'You can't drive home, darling,' said Bella. 'I really think you've drunk too much.'

'Well, I suppose Jessica isn't coming home from her parents until tomorrow,' said Julian, 'so maybe she wouldn't mind if I stayed the night here, but it might be too late to ring her . . .' His voice trailed away and Kate made sure not to catch his eye; this diminished man (though how could she despise a good husband?).

'Look, it's snowing,' said Harriet, peering out of the French windows. 'Come on, let's go outside!' They went out onto the terrace, gasping for a moment in the clear, cold air and yes, she was right, snowflakes were falling – real ones, white magic out of nowhere, a gift – an answer – from the swirling clouded sky. Harriet put one arm through Kate's, the other through Julian's, and laughed out loud, opening her mouth to taste the snow, sticking the tip of her tongue out, as they'd all done together, in those Elverson winters of their childhoods, when the snow fell deeper on the ground. 'A new year, a new beginning,' said Harriet, drawing her cousin and her brother closer to her, 'but just like the old days, as well.' Out of the corner of her eye, Kate saw Bella reach for Charles's hand; but, absent-minded, he seemed not to notice and walked a few feet away, examining a snowflake on his sleeve, as if for the first time.

'Midnight, the witching hour,' said Bella, looking at her watch, though she didn't need to, because inside the house, the clocks were striking, not quite at one with each other (eleven, twelve, thirteen . . .). 'Bedtime, Charles?'

'In a little while,' he said. 'I just need to write a few notes . . .'

Bella kissed her children, and Kate, and put her hand to Charles's cheek. 'See you in the morning,' she said. 'Sweet dreams.'

After Bella had gone, Charles went inside, as well, to his study, and the others retreated to the warmth of the kitchen, for glasses of whisky and wedges of leftover Christmas cake.

'Do you think they are happy?' said Harriet, finishing the crumbs from her brother's plate.

'Who?' said Julian.

'Mum and Dad.'

'Of course!' he said. 'They're the happiest couple I know.'

'I'm not so sure,' said Harriet. 'It can't be easy being married to Dad.'

'What on earth makes you say that?' said Julian, sounding almost affronted, as if it were his own marriage that was being discussed.

'Well, he gets distracted . . .' said Harriet.

'In what way?' said Julian, glaring, bull-like, thought Kate.

'Oh, never mind,' said Harriet, letting a smooth dark curtain of hair fall across her face.

'Go on,' said Kate, 'I'm listening.'

'When your mother died . . .' said Harriet, eyes still hidden, 'I mean, do you mind me talking about this?'

'No, it's fine,' said Kate.

'After she died, I was the only one still living at home, and it was so awful, of course, so sad, and once I went into Dad's study, to tell him that dinner was ready, and he was crying . . .'

'And?' said Julian.

'And I didn't expect that.' said Harriet. 'That's all . . .'

'What's so odd about that?' said Julian.

'But it was him that was crying,' said Harriet. 'Not Mum.'

Nobody said anything (and what was there to say?). In the silence, Kate cut herself another slice of Christmas cake and then felt suddenly too tired to sit up, or swallow, or smile. 'I think I'll go to bed now,' she said, and leaned over to Harriet, hugged her; and then waved, absurdly, at Julian, a small, childish wave, that only he could see. Twenty minutes later, after she had brushed her teeth and climbed into a pair of clean flannel pyjamas – like unpacking, pyjamas were an intrinsic part of Elverson, though not the rest of her life – there was a knock at the door. It was Julian, as she had half expected (but he was always capable of doing the opposite of what she anticipated, as if to win some unspoken game; except that neither of them knew the rules, or what the prize might be). He sat down on the end of the bed, while she pulled the covers up to her neck.

'So, are you seeing anyone?' he said.

'It's none of your business,' she said; though she was tempted to say yes, *yes* she was; to invent an imaginary boyfriend, a successful accountant, perhaps, or a tax lawyer, with a large house in Hampstead, several million in the bank, and a mathematical bent. The truth of the matter, in fact, was that in the five years since she and Pete had separated, she had slept with two people: Pete, in the first year of their separation, occasionally, for comfort (and revenge, because his new girlfriend didn't know that he was being unfaithful to her, as well); and even more occasionally, an ex-colleague from the newspaper where she used to work a few years before Sam was born. (He was a clever, amusing man, but a disaster on the commitment front – always waiting for the perfect woman, which Kate manifestly was not; and though she pretended indifference when he made it clear he did not – would not – love her, she did care, a great deal, especially when he told her about his other romantic entanglements, as if she were simply a friend.) There had been two other half-hearted offers she had refused: the husband of an acquaintance, who arrived at her house one evening with a bottle of wine, saying he was 'just passing'; and a famously rakish actor she interviewed for the magazine last summer, who almost certainly asked everyone he met to have sex with him (man, woman, sheep, no doubt). But she didn't tell Julian about any of them: not him, with his cosy marriage.

'Jessica is being incredibly difficult at the moment,' he said, leaning back on the bed with a sigh. 'She's always bad tempered – in private, at least.'

'Don't you realize how *predictable* it is for you to be talking like this?' said Kate. 'That's what men always say about their wives, and I don't want to hear it, OK?' She knew as she spoke she was lying: because of course she wanted to hear Jessica's faults, or at least a bit of her did –

though it was a bit best ignored (because God would notice her mean streak; Sod's Law, He would, even though He managed to miss everything else). So she decided to change the subject. 'I know this sounds superstitious, but I do feel something will happen this year,' she said, 'something important, because big stuff is meant to happen every seven years. Sam was born seven years ago—'

'Nearly eight, actually—'

'All right, but he was born in my twenty-eighth year, which is when Saturn returns, I think. And you married Jessica at the same time. And we're both going to be thirty-six this year, which feels like a turning point, doesn't it? Closer to forty than ever seemed possible, inescapably grown-up . . .'

'Saturn returns?' said Julian. 'What on earth does that mean?'

'Nothing on earth – or maybe it is, I'm not quite sure, exactly. It's something to do with astrology, Saturn returning to the place it was in the skies when you were born, so please, whatever you do, don't tell Charles what I've said, he'll get into a terrible grump – you know what he's like, he thinks that horoscopes rot the brain. I'll have to ask Harriet in the morning – she told me about it last year when we got drunk one night and I said I needed a sign that things were going to get better . . .'

'Magical thinking,' said Julian. 'Not that there's anything wrong with that.'

'But Charles would still disapprove . . .'

'Even though your astrology seems no more incomprehensible to me than his physics. Last time I asked him about his plans for next year, he said that there was no such thing as the passing of time; that the future was a subjective concept, like the past.' They both laughed, and she forgot to hate him, in that instant.

'Maybe this moment is all there is,' said Kate; but she didn't believe it – and anyway, she *knew* that time passed – she had only to look at her child to remember (although her mother, perhaps, floated between past, present and future, and wound them together in a skein). Julian took her hand, laced his fingers through hers, and then let go, and she closed her eyes until he had gone from the room. (He was always *going* somewhere else, out of her reach, when they were little; and then to Oxford, when she was at Cambridge; and to Jessica, whom he had met the summer after leaving university.) She wished she had a sleeping pill to take – the oblivion would be so welcome – but she had none, so she tried to think instead of small, familiar things: the glass bowl of frail papery narcissi, planted with Sam last autumn, that would be blooming in her bedroom when she got home; the sweet-scented jasmine that grew, protected, by her back door, entwining the climbing rose with green, all through the long winter. And then her mind turned into water, and she was dreaming; she was on a train with Julian, going to the coast, and the carriage filled up with water, it reached their ankles. But no one seemed concerned, even though the railway tracks had disappeared and they were floating on some sort of river, down towards the sea. A guard arrived and put a plug into a neat, circular hole in the floor of the carriage. Soon they reached the coast and climbed out of the train, and there was a funfair on the shingle beach. Above the beach, high on the cliffs, were houses – big houses, with uncurtained windows, like eyes.

'That's where the stars live,' she told Julian. 'They built those houses years ago, before we were even born.' But he was gone – disappeared – and then she found herself in a kitchen with Jessica. 'Jessica,' she said, 'I would never, ever have an affair with Julian. I want you to know that. I don't approve of people who have affairs with married men.'

'But what were you doing with him in the water?' said Jessica, who was holding a baby in her arms.

'Nothing,' said Kate, 'I promise . . .'

And then she was awake again, but it was still dark outside, and her flesh crept with something; but truly, there was nothing, nothing at all.

Five

Tap, tap, tap, there was a tapping in her head; no, on her head, her head was tapping. 'Mum,' said Sam, who always woke her this way, with gentle fingers rapping on her skull, 'it's morning, and look, it's snowing, Mum, look!'

Kate surfaced from the currents of forgotten dawn dreams and sat up in bed because she was good at waking fast – she'd had to be, since Sam was born; there was no one else to hear him – and then followed him to the bedroom window. And he was right, there was snow on the ground, and snow still falling: swan-white, angel's feathers, casting an unearthly light in the winter dawn. God had answered her prayers – heaven sent, this had to be – except what had she promised in return? She couldn't remember right now, but she said out loud, trying not to sound ironic, 'Thank you, God.'

'Does God make the snow?' said Sam.

'I don't know,' said Kate.

'I think he does,' said Sam. 'I mean, who else would?'

'Why don't you climb back into bed with me and have a cuddle in the warm?' said Kate.

'But I want to go out!' he said, wide awake after his early night. 'Let's make a snowman and have a snowball fight! I want to see if all the snowflakes are different, like my teacher says. She says she doesn't know if God makes them all – she says there might be lots of gods, there might be fifty.'

'Sam, it's only half past seven,' said Kate.

'No it's not, it's twenty-seven minutes to eight,' he said, and started hopping up and down. 'Is it time to get up now? It must be eight o'clock!'

'It's *not*,' said Kate, 'it's twenty-six and a half minutes to eight.' But even so, she started getting dressed, double layers (like her mother, she always felt the cold). They went downstairs together, and while she made herself a cup of tea in the kitchen, Sam ran outside with the dog. She drank the tea too fast, scalding her tongue, readying herself for the day, and then put on her coat. On the front lawn, somewhat to Kate's surprise, Charles was already making snowballs with Sam; a willing victim for her child's as yet uncertain aim, both of them laughing (Charles laughing? She'd never remembered him doing that). Julian appeared soon after, his bag packed, ready to go. 'I've got to get off,' he said, 'and pick up Jessica and the kids before the snow freezes.'

'But I wanted to fly my new plane with you!' said Sam, small mouth drooping; and Kate felt the sting of rage in her eyes that Julian was hurrying back to his children, while Sam's father was carefree on the other side of the world, photographing a fashion shoot with a pouting starlet in Barbados.

'I'll fly the plane with you,' she said to Sam, wanting to make everything right when it was teetering towards wrongness, 'after you've finished your snowman.'

'When *we've* finished,' he corrected her, and so she started rolling a ball for the snowman's head, without looking at Julian. (It was tiresome, and confusing, this eternally unfinished business, but it seemed impossible to reach any conclusion.) She waved goodbye, briefly, too late, as he drove away in his stupid car, and then concentrated on the head in her hands, resisting the impulse to smash it and stamp it back into the ground.

When at last the snowman was finished, blind coal eyes in a frozen face, she coaxed Sam into the kitchen for breakfast as Harriet emerged from bed. It was already snowing again, covering over the footprints Kate had made earlier with Sam and Charles, obscuring the tyre marks left by Julian's car on the drive. The day stretched out before them, and surely it should be as perfect – as hopeful – as the snow, but somehow her spirits lowered like the heavy sky.

While Harriet and Sam unearthed an old sledge from one of the outhouses, and Bella told Kate that no, she didn't need any help with the cooking, it was already taken care of, Charles retreated back into his study. All was as it should be in Elverson, quiet and peaceful, the world beyond silenced; but it was then that Kate did the unthinkable, and disturbed her uncle. Really, she didn't mean to be disturbing – she'd spent thirty years behaving well for Charles, attempting to present a polished, impassive exterior to match his – but now she couldn't help herself; there was nothing else to be done. He was sitting by the fire reading, when she went into the study (knocking first, though not waiting for an answer). 'Charles, I need to ask you something,' she said quickly, gazing at the ceiling; anywhere other than his grave face. 'I don't know how to make it sound right, so I'm sorry,

I'll just have be blunt. Did my mother kill herself?' There, she had spoken the unspeakable, out loud, in her uncle's private space. But he said nothing, just stared at the fire, impossible to read, as ever, so she tried again. 'Was my mother unbalanced, in some way, when she drove away from here the night she died?' It sounded ridiculous, stumbling, though phrased with such formality – as if she was a policeman, not his niece; like a bad detective story.

'Goodness, Kate, these are big questions,' said Charles.

'But you deal in big questions,' she said.

'Who knows what passes through another person's mind?' he said. 'How can we answer for others?'

'I'm just asking, that's all,' she said. 'It's been seventeen years since my mother died. The anniversary of her death is next week, and I want to know – I really need to know – whether it was an accident.' The words sounded absurd to her, again, like they had been badly translated from another language, but she was speaking the truth.

Charles looked at the book on his lap and started talking, or was he reading aloud? 'Aquinas wrote that "an orderedness of actions to an end is observed in all bodies obeying natural laws, even when they lack awareness . . . which shows that they truly tend to a goal, and do not merely hit it by accident."'

'Is that my answer?' said Kate.

'It's an answer,' he said. She started laughing, but her uncle did not smile. Still, she could not stop, and laughed and laughed – too loud, savage and disordered – until there were tears trickling down her cheeks. 'Would you like a cup of tea?' he said, aghast at the broken noises she was making. 'A sherry? Can I get you anything?'

47

'It's OK,' she said, 'I'll do it myself,' and slipped out of the room, closing his door behind her.

The snow seemed to have deadened the sounds of everything now, inside as well as out; Kate could hear nothing except the grandfather clock in the hall. 'Hickory dickory dock,' said her mother's voice in her head. 'The mouse ran up the clock. The clock struck one, the mouse ran down, hickory dickory dock, tick tock, tick tock, tick tock.'

'Thank you very much,' said Kate, 'that's very helpful.'

'Talking to yourself is the first sign of madness,' said the voice in her head.

'You can talk,' said Kate.

'Look who's talking,' said the voice.

'So who's using clichés now?' said Kate. 'Anyway, I've had enough – I'm going to find something to eat.'

'How can you be hungry if you've had enough?' said her mother. 'Comfort eating won't help, you know.'

'Shut up!' said Kate, and slammed the kitchen door behind her. Things were not looking good; adolescent arguments with her dead mother – no, not good at all. (Maybe she should ask her cousin Isabel for psychiatric advice when she got back from holiday next week?) She started rummaging for a biscuit in one of Bella's striped blue and white china jars; but then her aunt came into the kitchen and Kate took her hand out, like a guilty child. 'Lunch is nearly ready,' said Bella. 'You wouldn't be a darling, would you, and lay the table?'

'Of course,' said Kate, and bit her lip, for want of anything else to bite.

Lunch would have been a silent affair, were it not for Harriet and Sam, elated from their morning in the snow. 'It was brilliant, Mum,' said Sam, between mouthfuls of spaghetti. 'We played this game where there was a bear in the woods, but it didn't catch us, and we escaped on the sledge, we were faster than a spaceship!'

'How fast would a spaceship go?' said Harriet.

'A thousand miles an hour,' said Sam, 'or maybe 1,500. Did you know a jaguar can run as fast as a car – seventy-five miles an hour!'

'That's very interesting,' said Harriet.

'Yes,' said Sam, 'and there's a bird that can go even faster, twice as fast, two hundred miles an hour.'

'What bird is that?' said Kate.

'I can't remember,' he said, 'but I read it in a book at school. It's a very good book, it's called *Five Hundred Questions and Answers* and it answers nearly every question there is. Some of them are quite easy, like, "Did King Kong climb the Eiffel Tower?" The answer is no, of course.'

'Well, of course,' said Harriet.

'Do you have any questions, Mum?' said Sam, politely.

'I don't think I do,' said Kate, 'except, "is it too greedy to have a second helping of spaghetti?"'

'Go ahead, it needs to be finished,' said Bella, so Kate kept eating, which seemed not quite to fill a gap. After lunch, while Charles showed Sam how to set up his telescope, Kate sat on her bed and tried to make a start on her piece for the magazine. 'Forget grunge or hippy chic,' she wrote, 'the new look for this year's heavenly Hollywood girls is polished perfection. Shiny, happy, glossy, buffed . . . and totally empty-headed.' She chewed her unmanicured thumbnail and crossed out the last bit. By a quirk of fate – or maybe it was simply down to good food in childhood,

reliable dentistry and plenty of fresh air – several of her contemporaries at Cambridge had become successful actresses.
(One A-list, one B-list, and several teetering on the way out,
or were they in again? It was hard to keep up . . .) Once
upon a time, Kate had been quite friendly with these
women, but it was more or less impossible now. They called
her when they needed something – a good write-up, an
introduction to a flattering photographer (her ex-husband,
for example) – and that was that. She couldn't ring them
and say, 'I'm feeling lonely and I need someone to talk to,
apart from my dead mother.' This was the thing about these
actresses: there was a strict equation, ruling all social
exchanges, which defined the limits of friendship. Only the
stars could be friends with the stars; everyone else was there
to serve, to ask respectful questions, to orbit their celestial
sphere. The non-famous couldn't speak about themselves to
the famous, even if they had been friends before stardust
had settled, like heaven's confetti, upon the shoulders of the
chosen ones. That was the way of this world – as hierarchi-
cal as a medieval court. Not that she was jealous of the
actresses – in fact, whenever she spent time with them, she
came home happier than before, grateful not to be defined
by the span of her waist or the lustre of her skin, and
amused that their birthdays seemed to have shifted by several years. Admittedly, she did sometimes envy them their
houses – such space, and with gardens as big as the playground at Sam's school – but the downside was the nervy
neurosis and constant halitosis, due to the inescapable
Hollywood starvation diet (no wheat, no sugar, no carbo-
hydrates, no nothing, really, except for celery juice and cig-
arettes and the occasional line of coke).

The strange thing was that her cousins (except for Julian, who refused to be impressed) thought that she was somehow touched by the glamour of what she wrote about and whom she had brushed against. 'So, tell me about all the incredible parties you've been to this week,' Harriet used to say, even though it was manifestly obvious that Kate's life in Crouch End was not glamorous, in any shape or form. True, that actor she'd interviewed last year did take her out to dinner once, before suggesting they had sex in his somewhat depressing Chelsea flat (depressing because it was filled with magazines featuring him on the cover, stacked beneath unwashed coffee cups edged with smudged lipstick stains). As she had told Harriet at the time, a half-hearted invitation to sex with the famous actor was more of an insult than him not making the offer; he'd never dream of propositioning another famous person in such a humiliating manner. ('I expect you'd like to go to bed with me now?') Anyway, Kate knew that the invitation was in fact no such thing: simply a tease, for if she had said yes, he'd doubtless have sneered.

Kate sighed and stared at her two incomplete sentences. Her cousin Paul's wife – Becky, who had written nothing since a university dissertation on the cookery contained in nineteenth-century literature (Tolstoy's porridge, for example) – would sniff if she ever came across anything as shallow as this piece (if Kate ever finished the sodding thing, which seemed unlikely). Becky expended a great deal of waspish energy discussing which contemporary novels had 'literary value' – very few, in her considered opinion – and made it clear that Kate's journalism was beyond contempt. Kate sighed, again, which turned into a yawn. Perhaps what she needed was a little sleep?

Sleeping in the afternoon: was this a sign of depression, of the threatened genetic inheritance she had evaded so far? Perhaps she should force herself out, exercise those leaden limbs, breathe some fresh air (the kind of healthy activity the magazine's beauty editor had suggested in this month's article about how to detoxify for the New Year; though Kate felt that the toxins that inhabited her body were more persistent than those referred to in the magazine). She looked at her watch: twenty to three – just enough time, if she got a move on, to walk to the graveyard and visit her mother before dark; not that her mother inhabited the grave; but still, it was the thought, or walk, that counted.

Kate left the house without telling anyone where she was going – Bella would only fret – and slipped across the side lawn, past her favourite lilac tree, not yet budding, and through the wooden gate that led to the church footpath. There were just a few snowflakes falling now, no drifting; hers were the only footprints on the white ground. It didn't take long to reach the church – ten minutes, walking briskly, without a child to herd – but she stopped, briefly, to pick up some pine cones from beneath a fir tree. Coming to a grave without an offering, however small, seemed churlish, even if her mother wasn't there; though for once, it seemed as if that maternal ghost might be flitting out of Kate's head and back to the headstone where she belonged (if the dead belong anywhere, that is). The grave was in the corner of the churchyard, beside some of Charles's dead relatives: a little gathering of the in-laws, huddled together against the cold as if at a chilly wedding party, waiting for the service to begin, or end, waiting for the feast.

'Hello, Mum,' said Kate, arranging the pine cones in a

circle at the foot of the headstone, brushing the snow from the carved words on the stone. 'Judith Mary Linden. 15 July 1939 – 12 January 1984. Rest In Peace.' Not enough words; not enough life . . . Forty-four seemed almost young to Kate, not so very far away.

'Don't get cold,' whispered her mother's voice inside her ear, or was it the wind sighing in yew trees? Kate shivered, and tried to button up her coat, but her fingers were too clumsy for the task, numbed without any gloves. 'Go home,' murmured her mother, as the leaves rustled, 'but thank you for coming . . .'

'Thank you for having me,' said Kate. She turned and started running back along the path where the shadows were turning into dusk and the dark between the trees was spreading. Before long, though, she had to stop, because her heart was hurting. 'Heavy-hearted, ill-starred,' she muttered to herself, and then she heard Sam's voice, high and clear from the Elverson garden. 'Mum!' he shouted, and his cry looped up into the empty sky, 'Mum, where are you?' Kate started running again, and her heart pounded, steady this time, and she was through the gate, faster than the wind, strong enough for both of them, arms around her child. 'I was missing you,' he said, lips against her ear, so no one else heard. 'I'm here,' she said, 'I'm right here beside you.'

'I couldn't see any stars in my telescope,' he said, leading her back into the house.

'Don't worry,' she said, 'we'll find some later, or tomorrow, maybe.'

'Do you promise?'

'I'll do my best,' she said.

Six

In bed that night Kate tried to remember her mother. But it was hard to fit the fragments together. Her face – what did her face look like? No, not smashed into pieces; stop shuddering, remember her face: her eyes, her mouth as she kissed Kate goodnight, as she kissed Charles, no not Charles; as her mother kissed her father. *Her* father. Her father, Sebastian.

Judith Mary Linden. Lips like roses, hazel eyes and creamy skin, pretty as a picture – that's how the story went, at least. What did her mother look like when she came to fetch her from Elverson House, the summer that Kate was seven? Well, she didn't come, did she? Kate's grandparents came to fetch her at the end of the holidays, to take her back to London. The end, the very *end*, mark you; and what kind of mother would leave her daughter for a month or more? 'You left me,' whispered Kate. 'I had no choice,' replied the soft voice in her head (whose voice? Kate's, perhaps . . .).

Kate's grandparents – Mr and Mrs Michael Scott, that's what Judith wrote on the envelopes containing her letters to them – brisk, they were, very brisk. You wouldn't cry in front of them, even when you were saying goodbye to Bella and Charles and the cousins, all of them, after the long summer. Bella had packed Kate's bag for her, with her doll at the top, bald Brigit, denuded and glassy-eyed; more surprised-looking than ever. (Kate and Harriet had chopped off Brigit's locks two weeks previously, on a hot August afternoon when the bees buzzed and so did little girls' heads.) Kate had chewed Brigit's nails, nibbled away the tops of her fingers. 'What a way to treat your baby!' said her grandmother. Poor Brigit, poor Kate; into the back of Mr and Mrs Michael Scott's big black car. 'Thank you for having me,' she said, peering out of the window, as her cousins waved goodbye and Julian ran behind the car down the drive, but he couldn't keep up with her, and then they were gone, she was gone, through the gates and onto the road.

'Why not have a little sleep?' said her grandfather, who was driving. 'When you wake up, you'll be back home in London, like magic.' Kate nodded off, in the car, in her bed; seven-year-old and grown-up self, melting, almost, into one; nearly thirty years binding them together, like a ribbon, like a bow. She'd learnt to tie a proper bow that summer. Isabel had taught her; so that Isabel's name had forever been written in Kate's mind like a bow, looping, tying. Tied in knots, she was, to all those cousins . . .

Kate dozed, and dreamt of her mother. She was in the car, hot leather seat under the backs of her knees, returning to London, like magic, long-ago London, where the sun shone and the swallows flew across the pale sky and there were no traffic jams and she walked through the park to school in the blue morning, over the dew-covered grass, past the chestnut trees where the squirrels lived. The squirrels were called 'Come-along'. 'Come along, come along,' Kate's mother called. Her grandfather had led her out of the car and up the stairs to the flat where her mother was. Her mother was waiting. But what did she look like? Porcelain face, and cool lips, and arched eyebrows. She could raise one eyebrow, like Julian, but Kate couldn't, not then, not now, not never. 'Hello, Kate,' her mother said, and Kate's heart felt too big for her body. Sometimes she thought her mother might be a wicked witch – well, no, that was a wicked thought, don't think it, only bad girls do; but it was as if her mother had disappeared, and the witch took her place, her face, her voice. At night Kate ran and ran in her dreams, away from the witch mother who said that Kate belonged to her.

Still, her mother had never done anything bad. She had never done anything, really, that stuck hard in Kate's mind, after the separated summer (except there was that Halloween when Kate had come home from school, and her mother had scooped out an orange, filled the hollow with lemon jelly, and carved a crooked smile and slit eyes on the side). What did they do, alone, together, Kate and her mother? Kate had watched her, for signs of something, not knowing what she was looking for, but nothing came clear. She seemed like a shadow mother; a wax figure, though Kate knew that mother love was there, warm enough to melt the wax; burning, perhaps. And then she had gone, leaving Kate behind, and the questions, like smoke. 'What did you do?' Kate asked her mother now, wherever she might be, in the shifting place between memory and dreams. But it was too late for an answer, for Kate fell into the deep; sleeping, oblivious, in the black space that she cherished. Blessed oblivion; for she was her mother's daughter.

Tap, tap, tap, came the fingers on her skull. Tap, tap, tap, went the little fingers. She woke with a start, in the dark, fearing the worst – though had it not already happened? – but it was Sam, the boy with the blue eyes, crying now. 'I had a bad dream,' he said, 'about a ghost outside the window, trying to get in, and I thought it was you, a ghost that looked like you, trying to scare me . . .' She put out her arms to him and he climbed into the bed with her, curling up close, toes resting on her knees, head against her shoulder as she stroked his hair. Soon he was asleep, breathing evenly, ghosts gone (nightmare mother banished, back into the night, where she belonged, along with the rest of her kind); but now Kate was awake, mind buzz-buzzing in the cold night. What was it her uncle had said at dinner? Time did not flow; simply *was*. We only imagined it moved. And though she had laughed when he said it, he was right, for now time was still, stagnant in the dark; time stuck like when she was a wakeful child, eyes open in the night, watching out for dangerous things, eyes closed, again, in case she saw them. Kate lay beside her son and waited for the dawn; for the world to turn again, as it must . . .

Seven

Morning broke. What a strange phrase, thought Kate, in the grey dawn – as if the day were like glass, waiting to shatter. Her eyes ached, but she could not sleep again – only yawn, uselessly, as the wasted night slipped away. She got out of bed and started packing. Time to go home.

She was still yawning after breakfast and three cups of tea. 'Darling, are you sure you have to leave now?' said Bella. 'You look a bit washed out.'

'Sam's got school tomorrow,' said Kate, 'and I've got to get a few things ready before then. Ironing, you know . . .'

'You never iron anything,' said Sam, truthfully.

'Well, I'm going to begin tonight,' said Kate, 'in a fresh start to life—'

'Surely you've got more exciting things to do?' said Harriet, who was still in her pyjamas, though she too was going back to London today.

'I always found ironing rather soothing,' said Bella.

'I like the idea of it,' said Kate, 'smoothing the creases of life away, but I suppose it always seems too much of a struggle, in practise.'

Charles was nowhere to be seen – 'Out walking, I think,' said Bella vaguely – and Kate thought about writing him a note, but was uncertain how to begin. Finally she settled for a sentence from Sam. ('Thank you for my telescope, it is grate, see you soon, and the man in the moon!!') As Kate climbed into her car, Sam buckled up in the back, Bella put something into her hand, then closed her fingers around it. 'For you,' she said, 'a late Christmas present. This was your mother's – I've been hanging on to it for years, but you should have it now.' Kate looked into her hand, which held something heavy, sharp-edged. It was a bracelet, a gold bracelet, covered in charms – a horseshoe, three stars, two hearts, three crosses. 'Look at it later,' said Bella. 'Drive safely, my darling.' Sam waved out of the window as Kate steered the car slowly down the drive and Harriet ran behind them, blowing kisses through the air.

Kate drove west, along the gritted roads, peering through her smeared windscreen, screwing her tired eyes against the sunlight. The fields were still snowy – iced over, improbably white, masking the turnips and potatoes and the heavy soil. 'Did you have a nice time?' she said to Sam, catching his eye in the rear-view mirror.

'Yes, lovely,' he said. 'Can we go back next weekend and find some stars?'

'Maybe,' said Kate, 'maybe in a month or so.'

'How long is that?' said Sam. 'Thirty days?'

'About that,' said Kate, trying not to remember her own childhood need for precision.

'OK,' he said, gazing out of the window as the fields began to grow trees. 'Mum, do you miss your mum?'

'Sometimes,' she said.

'What was she like?' said Sam.

'Well, she was very pretty, like Bella—'

'But Bella is quite old.'

'Not really. Anyway, they were young, then.'

'When?'

'When I was little. And they were pretty, like I said. Twin sisters—'

'Like princesses?'

'Perhaps. But very kind, not haughty.'

'What does haughty mean? Naughty?'

'No, sort of high up.'

'In towers?'

'Well, not exactly.'

'Stuck up?'

'Yes, that's right. Anyway, they weren't like that.'

'But what was your mum like by herself, without Bella?'

'It's hard to remember, Sam.'

'Are you going to die?'

'Not for a long time.'

'Before me?'

'When you're very old, probably.'

'I don't want you to die.'

'I'm not going anywhere,' she said, keeping her eyes on the road.

They were back in London by one, and her head was aching, though the snow glare was gone in the city, leaving only gritted slush. The cat was waiting on the pavement – like she always did, as if she knew five minutes before they turned the corner that they would be home – and Sam got out of the car and scooped her into his arms. 'Little kitty, did you miss me?' he said, and then lost interest, running to find his best friend instead, who lived three doors down from them. 'Can I go to Robbie's house and play?' he said, as Kate got the bags out of the boot. 'His mum says I can, is that OK?'

'That's fine,' she said, and breathed deeply, because it felt as if she had been holding her breath for miles and miles. 'I'm just going to unpack and make myself a cup of tea.' Inside, the house was warm – she'd kept the heating on – and her neighbour Maria, Robbie's mother, who'd been in to feed the cat and water the plants, had also left the post on the kitchen table. Two bills, a leaflet from the local pizza restaurant, some junk mail offering instant prizes and a real letter with unfamiliar handwriting on the front. She'd leave that for a moment (like saving the solace of chocolate for later) and check the answer machine instead. Three messages: one from Bella, to ask if they'd got home safely, and two from the features editor of the magazine, requesting Kate's overdue copy. She went back to the kitchen table and opened the post. Red bills – so much for her fresh start to the year – and then the letter; no, not a letter, an invitation – on expensive stiff cream card. An invitation to a birthday party next weekend, from someone called Helena Vickers-Green. Who the hell was she? On the back of the invitation was a note. 'Dear Kate,' it said, in neat italics written in proper ink, not scratchy biro, 'it would be marvellous to see you after all these years. You may remember me better as Helena Mott. My husband Henry works with Julian, who gave me your address. Do please come!'

Helena Mott, Helena Mott . . . the girl who used to live in a big white house around the corner from the flat where Kate grew up; a wedding-cake house, incredibly grand – an icing-sugar palace for a princess, that was how Kate had thought of the place, as a child. Helena Mott had one brother, one father, one mother; an abundance of good luck and blonde hair, and an Afghan hound, on top of everything else. She and Kate had been friends – until Helena had gone to a smart girls' private school on the far side of the park, while Kate ended up at the local comprehensive, where she pretended to be tough-skinned and streetwise, sneering while shrinking inside.

According to the address on the invitation, Helena had stayed on the expensive side of the park – another white wedding-cake house, Kate guessed, just down the road from the zoo. Doubtless Mr Vickers-Green, like Julian, had prospered greatly, thrown the right dice and fast-forwarded, smiling as he overtook those less fortunate in the game ('losers' Julian called them, his contemporaries who had lost their jobs or their confidence; 'loser' – he made it sound like a playground taunt). Kate imagined Henry and Helena would be proud parents of two blond cherubs, with an equally golden future – pink-cheeked children, confident that the world would always welcome them, like their parents, that their voices would not go unheard. Kate couldn't decide if the prospect of meeting the adult Helena was tormenting or not . . . Well, it might be good for her to get out to a party. She could wear the new black silk dress that Harriet had given her for Christmas and a pair of perilously high heels, the red satin stilettos that always raised her spirits, along with everything else. And the charm bracelet – her mother's bracelet; hers now, handed down.

Kate rummaged in the bottom of her bag and fished it out, fingering the sharp points of the little stars glinting in her hand. Was her mother wearing it on the night she died? Her hand on the wheel, the bracelet encircling her wrist, the gold harder than the flesh, not splintering like her mother's bones. Kate shook her head to shake those thoughts away – she wanted this bracelet to be lucky, not ill-charmed – and examined the two small hearts attached to the chain. They were lockets, complete with tiny hinges and clasps. The first opened up easily to reveal a faded colour photograph. Kate's mother smiled out at her, and a child – herself, in a picture she had never seen before, head resting against her mother's shoulder – seven years old, perhaps, Sam's age, or maybe eight. Mother's and child's eyes met hers, a steady gaze, not blurred by time or tears.

She closed the locket and rubbed it between her thumb and forefinger, not that she needed to see her reflection on the outside of the heart now that she knew what lay within. (Her mother's photograph offered some comfort that she had been real – not half-invented, as Kate sometimes feared; as if her memory might be cloudier than the picture.)

The second heart was harder to part, the hinges stiff with disuse, and she cracked two fingernails, cursing, before the locket opened. Inside this one was something else: a little lock of hair, though at first she could not tell what it was because it was somehow colourless, lost against the gold. (When Kate was six, her mother had taken her to see the Egyptian exhibits at the British museum; 'We're going to see the mummies,' Judith had said, and Kate had expected pictures of mothers – or maybe the real thing – but had been horrified instead by the shrunken bodies, laid out behind the glass, for all the world to see, hair still attached to their dead heads; real hair, but dead, too, as it had always been;

because dead hair grew on living people, that was what her mother said, but it stopped growing when they died.)

What colour had this hair been, locked away in the bracelet for all these years, shut up in the cold metal against the light? A fine, fair baby curl of Kate's, perhaps – or a snip of Bella's honey hair; unless the lock of hair had faded, like the photograph, from dark to light. Sebastian had been dark . . . like Charles, like Julian. Kate walked over to the mirror above the fireplace in the living room and stared at herself. Cropped feathery brown hair, pale winter skin, hazel eyes, like her mother, but greener in the daylight, with strange flecks of amber in the iris. 'O, beware, my lord, of jealousy. It is the green-eyed monster which doth mock the meat it feeds on,' she whispered, and then stuck her tongue out at herself, despising what she saw.

'That's my copy of *Othello* on your shelf,' her mother's voice whispered back at her – from where? Behind the mirror; or inside it, in a cold and fragile space . . . Surely not, she must be making it up; for mirrors had no memory, forgot what they reflected, as soon as it was gone. 'Pull yourself together,' said Kate to her reflection, to herself. 'Together,' came another whisper – an echo, from who knows what place.

Eight

Saturday 12 January. Kate's mother died on this day – that night – all those years ago, but was it a Saturday that she died? Kate couldn't work it out, couldn't quite remember. She counted the years in her head, but the line wouldn't run straight, it curved and turned inside itself, impossible to grasp. Kate remembered the date, of course – that, at least, she wouldn't forget – and marked it, as she had done since first moving into this house when pregnant with Sam, by planting lily bulbs in the garden. Not white waxy lilies – those ones she didn't want to remember, sweet-scented like the inside of a hearse – but tiger lilies, flame coloured like Sam's hair when they flowered in the midsummer sun. She planted the bulbs every year and some survived several years but gradually diminished, as new ones grew.

The day was a dark one, even at noon, the light scarcely filtering through dense cloud; the air grey like the bruised sky. Sam helped her with the planting, crumbling the clods of earth in his fingers, which made her shudder (she hated the feeling of bare earth against her skin; it was even worse than the memory of chalk on a blackboard, or unglazed pottery against her teeth). After they had finished, she washed her hands, though she had been wearing elderly gardening gloves, and then packed an overnight bag for Sam to take to his best friend's house. Kate almost hoped that he would change his mind about going, so that she could cancel her party outing and they could stay in together – as they usually did on Saturday nights – curled up on the sofa, eating chocolate raisins and watching some mindlessly soothing television or a rented video. But no, Sam wanted to go to Robbie's, as soon as possible, which meant that Kate was left with no alternative but to get ready for the party. She ran herself a bath, with the expensive scented oil that Julian had given her for Christmas (he was generous, there was no doubt about it) and lay there for longer than usual, soaking in the silent house. Afterwards, having dried herself, she opened the bottle of body lotion – another present from Julian – and rubbed it into her dry skin, parched from the winter. It was a long time since she had prepared herself with such care – plucking and smoothing and preening, like a chicken, or a teenage girl, she thought, with a mixture of amusement and disgust. Not that Kate had gone in for much adornment as a teenager; she had retreated, instead, into layers of black, torn in many places, the rips held together with safety pins; eyes lined with dark kohl, no need to powder her skin because it was already white. When she tried to remember that time, it was as if she had been in a shroud – muffled against the outside world, her body a shard to be protected against further breakage. (What a pain she must have been to live with, Kate thought now, hoping that Sam would be less prone to adolescent angst; though Judith had seemed not to mind, not to notice, even, which was perhaps a mark of sensible mothering, rather than negligence, or maybe Judith was simply muffled, too). Her country cousins – healthy, glowing teenagers, untroubled by spots or fits of despair – had nevertheless admired Kate. 'Cool,' said Harriet, 'you look so wicked, all in black,' even though Kate knew herself to be not cool, but half frozen.

Tonight, the black frock she wore would expose some skin – not too much, for the sleeves were long and the neckline modest, though the back dipped low. No need for layers – just the silk dress, sheer black tights and her red satin shoes. Oh, and the bracelet, of course. She slipped it on, last of all, after painting her lips, and then looked at herself in the mirror. The face that stared back at her was blank – the lines covered over, the cracks disappeared. She almost expected to see another face beside her, or floating just behind her – her mother's face, faded as the photograph Kate had found in the heart-shaped locket; but of course, there was no one else. Just Kate, tonight; she was alone.

She decided to drive herself to the party – it would save on taxi fares and stop her drinking too much. At half past eight she parked the car outside Helena's house, took a deep breath – it was still scary, sometimes, going out, unhusbanded (not that husbands were necessarily the antidote to social anxiety) – climbed the stone steps and knocked. Kate braced herself to smile at the first stranger, but the man who opened the door was . . . Julian. 'Hello,' he said, in his heartiest tone of voice – the one she found most infuriating.

'What are you doing here?' she said, ungraciously.

'I work with Henry, we're great friends – that's why *you're* here, in fact, because I was talking about you to him and Helena just before Christmas.' She gaped at him and did not move from the doorstep. 'Come in,' he said, more gently, 'you'll catch your death of cold out there.' Julian took her coat, and the birthday bunch of flowers she was clutching, and handed them to a waitress (a waitress! Such grandeur). He looked at Kate and said, very quietly, 'You look beautiful.' All at once she wanted to cry. 'Are you all right?' he said, his hand on her shoulder, and she wished she could put her head against his chest and rest there, like she did the night her mother died. That was the night . . . oh, God, it was impossible to face it herself, let alone talk about it with Julian . . . the night that she remembered like a dream, a nightmare, the night they . . . oh, spit it out, the ugly, stupid words – the night they slept together. Was it incest to have had sex with your cousin, and not just any cousin, but the son of your mother's twin sister? There were mitigating circumstances, of course . . . but what a mess, what a stomach-churning mess; though at the time it felt like he had saved her.

'What's wrong?' he said.

'Oh, you know, it's the anniversary of Mum's death. Dates shouldn't matter, I suppose, but somehow they do.'

'I'll never forget that night,' he said, his hand slipping down her arm now. 'You know, I . . .' As he hesitated, Jessica walked towards them, purposefully, Gucci steel stilettos clicking on the parquet floor.

'Hello,' she said, eyes flicking over Kate's dress, apparently unimpressed, 'and how are you?'

'Good,' said Kate, and leant forward to kiss Jessica's cheek.

'Darling,' said Jessica, turning away before Kate could

touch her, and taking Julian's hand, 'I really want you to meet an old friend of mine.' As she led him away, Kate watched their retreating backs: Julian, not much taller than willowy Jessica in her high heels, dark heads close to one another, like twins, almost. Julian and Jessica; Jessica and Julian – they were made for each other. He did not look back at Kate.

The waitress who had taken Kate's coat now offered her a glass of champagne, which she drank, fast, before taking another one from a silver tray and heading towards the sound of the party. There were lots of people in the ground-floor living room, their voices spilling out into the hall; laughter rising, like cigarette smoke, wreathed around the antique crystal chandeliers and up towards the high white ceilings, towards the open mouths of little plaster angels in the cornicing. Kate wondered if she would recognize Helena – she hadn't seen her for over ten years – but there she was, standing in front of a silvery Venetian mirror, unmistakable, blonde and bosomy and resplendent in an elaborate claret velvet dress, like an Edwardian society beauty. Beside her was a fair-haired, ruddy-faced man who could only be Henry – a stocky stockbroker, just as Kate had imagined him – and someone else, his face turned away from her. Kate swallowed a large gulp of champagne, and walked towards them, fixing a smile on her face. 'Kate, darling, you haven't changed at all,' said Helena, embracing her with clouds of perfume.

'Neither have you,' said Kate. 'It was so kind of you to—'

'Now, let me introduce you to my husband. Henry, this is Kate, my sweetest, oldest friend, you know, Julian's cousin, I've told you about her.'

'Pleased to meet you,' said Henry, bowing slightly, stiff in a black tuxedo and bow tie. Kate stifled a giggle (bowing, waitresses – Jesus, this was over-the-top) and tried to get a grip on her mounting hysteria.

'And this,' said Helena, turning to the second man beside her, 'is Adam, who is our tremendously useful builder – or are you an architect? Well, we'd be lost without you, whatever it is you are!'

'Hello,' said Adam, smiling slightly – but a real smile, so that the lines around his eyes crinkled.

'Now, I'm simply dying to catch up with all your news,' said Helena, 'but Henry and I must do a little circulating first. Come on, sweetheart, do your best.' And she propelled Henry forward, in the same brisk manner that Jessica had moved Julian away earlier. (Was this what good wives did, wondered Kate? Perhaps that was where she had gone wrong in her marriage – being too passive, rather than taking this firm stance.)

'Useful?' said Adam. 'I'm not sure I like the sound of that. It sounds rather boring.' He was as tall as Julian, but leaner, maybe, more weather-beaten; brown hair cut close to his head, like a soldier's, dark, with a few stray flecks of grey. 'How curious,' he continued, looking at her, steadily, 'we seem to have exactly the same colour eyes.'

'Yellow,' said Kate, 'that's what my son says, anyway.'

Adam laughed. 'My daughter calls them cowardy-custard eyes, which is even less flattering, I suppose . . .'

'How old is your daughter?' she asked.

'Rose is seven,' he said, 'eight in April.'

'Oh, just like Sam.'

They slipped into familiar friendly territory – schools,

parks, babysitters, bus routes; tracing the threads that linked friends of friends of friends, weaving them together like a cat's cradle. Although they had apparently never met before, Adam lived quite close to Kate, which made the conversation easy – London was made up of villages, after all, and they both inhabited the same one, with its comforting common ground. Neither mentioned a husband or a wife; neither asked about the other's. She liked him. She liked his hands – short nails, broad-fingered, workaday, capable-looking hands. 'I'm supposed to have given up smoking for the New Year,' he said, lighting a cigarette. 'Do you think January could begin again tomorrow?' He was wearing jeans, unlike the other dark-suited men in the room, and a faded-blue plaid shirt, untucked, and beaten-up brown leather walking boots. He was unshaven, but she liked that, too, as he rubbed at his stubble, searching for the right words. He looked at ease with himself, though when he talked, he rocked slightly, from foot to foot, apparently without realizing, like a father does with a restless baby, to soothe it to sleep.

'I like your boots,' she said, which was true, she did, very much.

'Mephisto,' he said. 'That's the label on the boots, I mean. Not that I have cloven hooves, I hasten to add.'

She laughed, and liked him more; more than the other men in the room; more than anyone for ages. But after ten minutes or so Helena swooped back upon them and said, 'Darlings, *darlings*, I must introduce Adam to my neighbours, who are simply longing for you to do them a conservatory like ours, romantic minimalist, that's what my gardening lady says, v. *World of Interiors*. Katie, sweetest, could you bear to lose him for a moment?'

'Of course,' she said, determined not to be caught blushing, and turned away, swallowing another glass of champagne for courage, hoping to find a familiar face in the room, but she recognized no one. 'Having fun?' breathed a voice in her ear, warm against her skin, and there was Julian, creeping up from behind. 'I've come to rescue you,' he said, pouring her more champagne.

'I don't need rescuing.'

'Don't you?'

'You really are insufferable,' she said, but looked him straight in the eyes, her cousin, *hers*, and she couldn't stop smiling. She finished her glass, down in one, and the bubbles filled her, lifting her up, lighter than air, turning her into gossamer, and she longed to kiss him, there and then, on his mouth, still tasting of the wine.

'Kate,' he said, 'I miss you, Kate.'

'You know where to find me.'

'Do I? I sometimes feel I lost you, after your mother died.'

'You found Jessica, remember?'

'She found me. I simply did as I was told.'

'It's strange how acquiescent you are with her, for someone so bullish in other areas of your life.'

'I know . . . I'm not sure why.'

'Well, it must suit you that way.'

'Perhaps . . .'

She closed her eyes, but he would not disappear. She saw him, behind her eyelids, his face, above hers, warm lips, on hers, muscles taut and arms encircling her, pulling her closer to him, on her narrow college bed. 'We belong to each other,' he'd said. 'Go away,' she said now, eyes still shut. 'Just leave me alone, please.' When she opened her eyes, slightly dizzy for a second in the light, Julian had gone, back to Jessica, laughing too loudly, arm around his beautiful wife, his treasure, in her pewter silk sheath dress.

'OK,' she said to herself, 'say thank you and goodbye; get your coat and go.' But she couldn't face Helena and Henry – better to disappear, and send some more flowers tomorrow, given that the ones she'd brought tonight were probably languishing, wilting like Kate. It was easy to leave unnoticed – the room was full, the party flowing, like the champagne; the voices slurring, blurring around the edges. Had she drunk too much to drive? No, she would be fine. Fine, she was fine. She fumbled for her car keys in her coat pocket, and went down the wedding-cake steps to the black gate that opened onto the road, the park beyond, dark trees and shadows, no stars or moonlight. Her mother . . . what was her mother thinking of as she climbed into her car that final night, all those years ago? Did the road curve before her, like a bow, her fingers slipping, the knot untied?

As she unlocked the car, she heard a voice behind her. 'Kate, hang on, don't go without me!' For an instant, she thought it was Julian, but no, this was a different voice, a less familiar one. She turned to look, and there, at the gate, was Adam. 'I was wondering if you could give me a lift home?' he said. 'I mean, only if that's convenient . . .'

'Of course,' she said. 'It'll be nice to have someone in the car with me. Actually, I wonder if I should drive – if I'm safe, that is? I might have drunk a bit too much.'

'I haven't,' said Adam. 'Why don't you let me drive you home?'

And so he did – a silent driver, a swift journey, as she

73

pressed her burning cheek against the passenger window –
and for that she was very grateful, though she did not realize how lucky she was until she was safely at home in bed,
guilty and appalled, while the room was spinning around
her (champagne never suited her – how could she have forgotten? How could she be so foolish, so *irresponsible*?).
Adam had parked the car dextrously, taken her to the door,
said goodnight, and disappeared. 'See you,' he said, over his
shoulder, as he walked away, in his devilish boots.

'See you,' she said, in a small voice, like a child.

Nine

Sunday morning: sick stomach, thick head, foul tongue. Kate lay in bed, unable to go back to sleep, unable to get up, cursing herself, cursing the day – still dark outside, January gloom, drizzly misery, impossible climate. Eventually, at half past eight, she heaved herself out of the bed and ran a bath. Sam wouldn't want to come home yet from his friend's house: they were probably still asleep after late-night secrets shared, along with midnight crisps. So she drank a cup of tea, and another one with sugar in it, and ate several slices of buttered toast, gazing, disconsolate, at her flabby belly, before having a quick bath (no need for scented oil today; no need for anything). Afterwards, drying her hair, and clean, at least, but uncomfortable in a pair of too-tight jeans (Kate's very own hair shirt), she mooched about the house, picking up discarded toys: a piece of a jigsaw, though not one she recognized; several batteries, presumably dead; and odd bits of Lego, covered in grey house dust, with no particular home.

At quarter to ten, just as she was going to collect her son, the phone rang. 'Hello,' said Julian, sounding faintly amused. 'How are you?'

'Fine,' said Kate, 'but I can't talk – I'm in a bit of a rush.'

'Do you have company?' said Julian.

'Yeah, right, my new lover.'

'Henry's builder – a bit of rough; I thought as much when you left together. Terribly unreliable, builders, I think you'll find.'

'But very good with their hands. Anyway, like I said, I must get a move on.' She put the phone down abruptly, feeling slightly more cheerful. Yes, her tone had been sufficiently ironic to cast doubt on the likelihood that she would ever have another man in her life, but even so, she knew Julian well enough to guess that he had been needled, teased as well as teasing. And what did Julian matter, anyway? Now was the time to move on; or if that was impossible, to show a semblance of maturity, at least. Stoic: that was the thing to be, perhaps; stoic and rooted, like the passion flower in the small pot beside her front door – root-bound, frost-touched, but still alive. 'Passion flower?' she muttered to herself, as she locked the door behind her. 'That has got to be the most *pathetic* thing you've come up with for ages.'

Down the road, Robbie's mother, Maria, was still in her flannel dressing gown, surrounded by drifts of Sunday newsprint, her black hedgehog hair flattened by sleep. 'So how was last night?' she said, beady eyed, pouring Kate a stewed cup of tea from the pot on the kitchen table.

'Oh, you know . . .' said Kate.

'No, I don't know,' said Maria. 'Was it fun?'

'Not very. I drank too much and got driven home by a man who seemed a bit disgusted by me.'

'Disgusted? Did you vomit over him or something?'

'No, *no*, of course not. But I think he disapproved of me.'

'How do you know? Are you sure you're not imagining it? Maybe you're just feeling a bit black-dogged?' The latter was Maria's shorthand for her own periodic depressions – brought on, she said, by overwork (she was retraining to be a teacher at the age of thirty-seven, now that her youngest daughter had started school) and her husband, Eric, a haggard solicitor who seemed to spend most of his life in the office.

'Where's Eric?' said Kate.

'Working, of course,' said Maria, 'either that, or shagging his secretary, which seems unlikely, given he's too stressed to have any sexual urges whatsoever. He just sighs in the middle of the night from time to time, in a martyred way, before prodding me with one outstretched finger, like I were a pork chop past its sell-by date. But don't change the subject. I want to hear about your new boyfriend.'

'As if . . .' said Kate. 'Where's Sam, anyway?'

'Very Freudian,' said Maria, who had a degree in psychology. 'I ask you about your new boyfriend and you reply with a reference to your son.' Just then – the point in the conversation when Kate might silently have taken offence, still smiling all the while – Sam and Robbie appeared in the kitchen, and she was able to forgive everybody everything for the split second that her son kissed her on the forehead.

'Hi Mum,' he said, already halfway out the door again, 'can me and Robbie go skateboarding? We'll stay on the pavement outside the house.'

'OK,' she said, and stood up to leave at the same time, ready to slump at home in Sunday torpor, keeping gloom at bay with shortbread biscuits and bad television.

'Stay,' said Maria. 'I'm sorry I was spiky. It's just I'm feeling sort of miserable myself. I don't know, maybe I need a higher dose of Prozac.' Kate squeezed her hand, unsettled by the single small tear trickling down Maria's cheek, but said nothing. What was there to say? Depression was infectious, and the whole neighbourhood was probably afflicted by now, passing it on like the interminable cold doing the rounds at Sam's school.

'It's probably just the time of year,' Kate murmured, at last, when the silence between them became uncomfortable. 'January always seems so grim, like a forced march through a long tunnel, without an end in sight. But we'll get through it, we will – we'll just have to light lots of fires, and watch all our favourite films on video – and then before you know it, spring will come, and everyone will feel so much happier.'

'I'll still be living in a sexless marriage,' said Maria. 'I mean, is this it? Glum celibacy for the next forty years? The terrible thing is, I don't even feel like making love – Prozac destroys the libido, you know, that and the fact that Eric smells of old socks and stale garlic and whisky mixed up with leftover takeaway curry – but it would be nice if my husband showed even the *occasional* glimmer of sexual interest in me. Honestly, I sometimes think you and Sam live in the happiest household I know – just the two of you, no arguments, no tension . . .'

'We don't always get on with each other.'

'I know, but you do most of the time, and it's so simple, so uncomplicated – I envy you, in fact. And there's so much more room in your house without a bloody messy man cluttering up the place, spreading his stuff everywhere, all those scratched vinyl records and broken cameras and tennis racquets that he'll never use – and think of the joy of being alone in bed, no farts or unwashed armpits. I wish Eric would move out, I really do.'

'You don't, not really.'

'Well, maybe I should try it for myself – a little flat of my own, with white walls and no one else's junk in the corners – except I can't, of course. We've got two kids, and Eric adores them both, even though he's hardly ever at home, and I can't split us down the middle. So that's it, I'll just have to have a secret affair with someone else.'

'Apart from the fact that there are never any decent single men.'

'Who says they have to be single? There got to be plenty of married men out there, just longing for a secret affair, no strings attached.'

'Like who?' said Kate, feeling interested, despite herself.

'Like . . . I don't know . . . an ex-boyfriend, maybe, someone you lost touch with years ago, but you can remember how brilliant he was in bed – we've all got one of those men, lurking in our pasts. Or Steven, my lecturer at college – he's a handsome, honey-tongued Irishman, looks like he'd know how to sweep you off your feet for an afternoon of rampant sex. Oh, I just want to be *seduced* for a couple of hours a week – better than taking bloody boring anti-depressants.'

'Maria! You can't!' said Kate, suddenly flushed with unwarranted guilt. 'Think of his poor wife – there's no such thing as an affair without any consequences. Someone starts to want more, someone else always gets hurt.'

'Oh, don't give me all that sensitive, sisterly rubbish. His wife's probably screwing his best friend, anyway – that's what happens in your thirties, isn't it? Actually, come to think of it, I bet that's why your man last night looked a bit disapproving – he's bound to be married, so he was feeling uncomfortable about the fact that he fancied you, not that you did anything wrong at all.'

'Maybe,' said Kate, 'maybe he is married, but happily so. . . and was simply longing to get home to his wife.'

'Nonsense. Everyone knows there's no such thing as a happy marriage, except in fairy tales. If I hadn't given up on feminism five years ago – do you remember, when the boys were babies, I said we must never let them have toy guns? – I'd say that the idea of marriage is a simulacrum, constructed by the western patriarchy. Mind you, I can't bear new men, either – so wet, they're soggy in the middle.'

'Do you know,' said Kate, 'I've never quite understood what a simulacrum is? I don't even know how to pronounce it, not unless someone else says it first.'

'I rest my case,' said Maria, pouring them both another cup of stewed tea, and though Kate did not know what she was talking about (what did guns have to do with it, anyway?), at least they were both smiling – Maria triumphant again.

Ten

That evening, after Sam was asleep and Kate had washed up, she decided to ring her father for the second time in less than a fortnight; even though they usually went for weeks at a time without communicating, she felt as if he might now have something to tell her; something that she needed to hear. (What it might be, she was not yet sure, thinking only that she would understand when the right words were said.) The phone rang and rang, over the hills and far away, long enough to sound as if it were echoing in an empty house, unheard, or maybe unwanted, but she let it go on ringing anyway, telling herself she would count to another ten, or twenty, before putting it down. And then her father's voice answered, at last, sighing before he spoke. 'Hello?' he said, unnecessarily loudly, invading what she had thought was the space between them.

'Hi!' she said, with absurd animation, like someone else was talking instead of her, 'it's me, Kate!'

'Oh, you,' he said, heavily. 'Well, you'll have to be quick. I've just taken a sleeping pill, and it's due to start working in the next five minutes, at which point I shall, with any luck, lapse into complete unconsciousness.'

'OK,' she said, jaw tightening with tension as it usually did when she happened upon him like this, gripped by a mood so black and viscous that it came seeping down the wires into her mouth and ears. 'I'll, um, I'll get a move on – it's just I was thinking about Mum, and wondering, you know, when you first met each other?'

'Really, you are the strangest child, I can't think where you sprang from – not me, I'm sure. You know when your mother and I met – in our last year at Cambridge, and what a hellish disaster that was, what a fucking mess.' Sebastian sounded like he was grinding his teeth – or maybe it was a noise made by the phone, crossed wires, an irritable ghost in the machine – but he kept on talking, though Kate found it hard to hear everything he said, as if the other noise – the grinding, the buzzing – had moved inside her head. 'We were far too young,' he was saying, 'and my parents wanted me to marry a nice Jewish girl, not a snooty snitty Gentile from the Home Counties. And you can imagine what her parents thought about it, that bitch of a mother, and her father, a fucking bourgeois pig, a pig of a man—'

At last Kate interrupted him, fearing the grating violence in his voice, wishing she'd never started the conversation but not knowing how to end it. 'Were Charles and Bella already together by then, when you met Mum?'

'Maybe, yes, I think so,' said her father, his words more innocent now, but still he seemed to use them like he hated Kate, or was she imagining it? 'Charles left Cambridge the year before us, but he and Bella and your mother had all been friends since his second year – that unholy trinity.'

'Just friends?'

'Well, obviously, Judith and Charles had had a brief flirtation first – a neurotically immature affair, if that's what you're wondering – but it didn't last and he settled down with Bella soon afterwards, out of college and straight into marriage and babies and everything. Typical upper-class Englishman – absolutely no insight into his own emotions, or anyone else's, far too selfish for that.'

'But why didn't you tell me?'

'Tell you what? That Charles is a cold fish with a head stuffed full of numbers instead of feelings?'

'No, of course not. I meant, why didn't you tell me that he had had an affair with my mother?'

'I don't know . . . you never asked, I suppose. It never seemed relevant.'

'And that was it? The affair ended and no one ever talked about it again? Not even when Bella and Charles were getting married, or at your wedding, or when Mum died?'

'I told you, that's the English upper classes for you. Morally bankrupt and quietly mad, the lot of them, beneath that polite veneer. They tie each other up in knots of anxiety and then they can't escape from one another. And they had the fucking nerve to tell me that *I* was the one who was mad – those crazy bastards labelled *me* the lunatic!'

'They're not upper class, anyway,' said Kate, guessing where his conversation was going, if she didn't head him off; but knowing, too, that none of her words would do any good, that all of them were soiled and spoiled for him, or by him, perhaps.

'Kate, I'm not about to start debating the finer points of

class distinction with you right now – you've never been willing to engage with Marxist analysis, you've swallowed all that Capitalist crap, you must be losing your mind working for that inane magazine – although of course it's obvious to anyone but a halfwit that the three of them, Charles and the terrible twins, always despised me, at some level – High Anglicans are totally anti-Semitic, you know, Nazis, the lot of them.'

'Are they?' she said, feeling more and more adrift.

'Yes, they blame Jews for killing Christ. Me in particular,' he sighed. 'Look, Kate, I've got to go, or I'm going to talk myself out of the beneficial effects of this sleeping pill, and then I'll end up having a manic episode at five in the morning, brought on by sleep deprivation and hyper-anxiety, for which you will be held responsible.' Her father put the phone down before she had said goodbye – he'd never yet got to grips with the usual rules of social etiquette, which was one of the reasons he was so lonely; and that made her heart ache for him (for he was surely broken-hearted; surely he did not mean what he said, only spat the words out, to rid himself of them).

Kate looked at her watch. Ten o'clock: not too late to ring her cousin Isabel, who should have got home from holiday this morning. But Isabel's answer machine clicked on after one ring, as did Harriet's, and there was no way Kate was going to brave Paul's fierce wife, his gatekeeper; not that Kate had very much to say to Paul these days (but what was it about talking to her father that turned her back into a child again; made her want to lose herself in her cousins, though surely those days were lost to her now?). Julian – he was the one she missed most at this moment, she longed for him, for the forbidden – but no, that call was impossible: and tempting as it might be to shake his deep-rooted belief in his parents' marriage with the news that her mother had had an affair with his father, she could not do so. (Was 'affair' the right word, anyway? It depended on the timing, Kate supposed, and she was finding it hard to make sense of that; to pin down the past, like a dress-maker's flimsy paper pattern, as a template for something she was trying to make now.) Maybe Julian was right, rather than smug. It had all happened such a long time ago, and Bella and Charles *were* happy, they had to be; far happier than her father, whose version of events could never be relied upon, anyway. (He was sometimes unbalanced, after all; and she was heading that way, too, if she didn't get a grip – but what, exactly, was she supposed to hold onto? Where was the solid ground in all of this?)

Bed, that was the best place to be: bed and a sleeping pill, if only she had one, just one magical pill; surely there must be one discarded somewhere in the house? She scrabbled through the chest of drawers beside her bed, hoping to find a forgotten packet in the tangle of rarely worn tights and odd socks and baggy knickers that had seen better days. After a while she admitted defeat and made herself a useless cup of chamomile tea and read a gardening book that Bella had given her the Christmas before last, until she fell asleep, lulled by a rather long list of shade-loving plants that might survive in a dry east-facing border, at least with careful mulching . . .

Later, she dreamt her recurring nightmare: the one she skimmed in and out of on bad nights such as this. In the dream, her mother and father were living with her –

imposing themselves, unasked, into her house, complicit and united against her. Sometimes it was her real house (too small for extra adults) and sometimes a dream house, or rather a nightmare hellhole: a place she had been forced into buying, against her better judgement; a place that she had ended up in, without being consulted, without even realizing why. In this version of the dream – the one that infected her head tonight – Kate mourned the loss of her real home, the safe house where she and Sam had been happy, which had been replaced by something rambling and dilapidated. Last month the dream had taken place in a dark mansion with crumbling roof and floors and rickety staircases without hope of restoration; now the house she had been forced into was around the corner from her own, but in a street she did not recognize, beside a river – no, bigger than a river – the sea, crashing against flimsy plate-glass windows while incompetent builders stood in corners, never starting the necessary repairs. And all the while her mother stood there, the resurrected ghost, damn her, with just a flicker of a smile. 'I don't want you to live with me,' Kate said, but no sound came out; her voice had gone and she could only mouth the words.

Eleven

Kate's diary for the New Year was such a void that she was almost relieved when the features editor of the magazine rang on a Monday morning to summon her for a 'futures planning meeting'. (In fact, on her way into the office the following day, Kate imagined herself begging the magazine staff to take all aspects of her future, and features, in hand: to make her over and shape her into something more dynamic; someone with glowing prospects as well as glowing cheeks.)

Arriving at the offices of the magazine was, as ever, familiar and yet also intimidating. In some ways it was unchanged from the days when she had worked here full-time – the same chemical smell of perfume from the beauty department, mixed in with acrid anxiety and office intrigue; and though there were new girls, they always looked the same as the ones that had gone – blonde, glossy, expensive girls, Kensington and Chelsea cashmere girls, who arrived at work in black cabs, rather than on the bus from Crouch End (a name that sounded like a bad joke to them). They glanced at Kate, briefly, as she made her way through the open-plan office to the features editor's desk: not hostile, nor even very curious – but enough for her to regret her choice of shoes (two-year-old trainers) and jacket (second-hand sheepskin, which had looked fashionably bohemian in the mirror this morning). The features editor was dressed entirely in black Chanel – more bloody cashmere, thought Kate (those poor goats were being decimated for their wool, left hairless and shivering on the slopes of Nepal) – except for her snakeskin stilettos, which had a beautiful red sole. 'Gorgeous, aren't they?' said the features editor, an alarmingly self-possessed twenty-five-year-old whose name was Annunciata. 'A Christmas present from my new boyfriend. He's a total poppet – just whisked me off on a skiing holiday.' Annunciata was blessed in other ways, as well: a first-class degree from Oxford and an inheritance that included a flat in Notting Hill. Even her surname – that of a long-established City banking institution – was expensive; standing in front of Annunciata's desk, Kate felt like an odd cross between poor relation, lumpen schoolgirl and dowdy housewife.

Annunciata waved her elegant fingers at Kate to sit down on a stool beside her. 'So, Kate,' she said, suddenly sounding like a headmistress, 'I need your ideas for next April's issue – we're running terribly late, but I'm thinking spring fever, I'm thinking Easter excess.'

'Chocolate?' said Kate, trying to be helpful.

Annunciata shuddered. 'Hardly,' she said, examining her manicure. 'No, I'm more interested in the rebirth of luxury, the shedding of the old and the rise of the new. You like?' Kate wasn't sure what she meant, exactly, but nodded, anyway, because Annunciata was beginning to look irritable. 'Not that the new luxury piece is really *you*,' said Annunciata. 'You're not really a concept girl, more's the pity. But come on, Kate, it's your ideas I want, that's why you're here, isn't it?' But nothing Kate suggested met with her approval (no to a guide to dating agencies for single mothers; and no again to Kate's hopeful request for an interview with George Clooney. 'Honey, he won't do it,' said Annunciata, 'not with you, anyway.').

Eventually, when Kate was suitably crushed, Annunciata relented sufficiently to commission her to write about a new diet regime. '"Eat Fat, Get Thin",' said Annunciata. 'Maybe you should try it for yourself, sweetie. It might buck you up a bit.'

But neither the diet, nor the bucking up, took hold. By the end of January Kate had given up all hope of bumping into Adam, or hearing from him ever again. She'd looked out for him in the local playground on weekend mornings – the time when Crouch End fathers were most often out and about, noisier and more competitive than the every-day mothers, who tended not to organize games of football on the muddy, dirty grass – and entertained brief fantasies about meeting him at the greengrocers. (He would say, 'Kate, I've been looking for you everywhere!' And she would say . . . well, what exactly would she say?)

But now it was clear that Adam was never going to get in touch – so she had been right, Maria was wrong, he was happily married, and their encounter quickly forgotten. That was that, done and dusted. ('You're talking in clichés again,' murmured her mother, soft as the breeze in the leafless trees at the bottom of Kate's garden.)

'I don't mind clichés,' said Kate to herself, as she

considered her latest article for the magazine, late in bed
one night. 'I am a living cliché. Lonely single mother, letting
myself go, gobbling another packet of chocolate-chip cook-
ies while I gabble about how to lose weight on the no-carb
Hollywood diet.'

'You're not a cliché,' whispered her mother, or was it
just the tendrils of evergreen clematis brushing against the
bedroom window in the dark, when the rest of the street
was sleeping? 'You're not lonely, and certainly not alone.'

'You're keeping me awake,' said Kate, gazing at her bedroom ceiling, 'and you're supposed to be dead, remember?'

As for the rest of her social life – well, she'd had regular
cups of tea with a couple of other mothers at Sam's school,
and one extraordinary outing to Knightsbridge, sent by
the magazine as an unlikely last-minute substitute for
Annunciata, to a dinner party held by a famous French fashion designer in his new shop. (Parties in shops – that was the
thing these days, and very odd it was, too; waiters emerging
out of changing rooms, or so it seemed.) Kate had been
placed between a gay hat-maker, who was delightful,
though hardly likely to become her new best friend, much
as she longed for him to be, and a smoothly handsome
American investment banker whose wife's couture
wardrobe for the season almost certainly cost more than
Kate's house. 'What do you do, exactly?' she had asked him,
genuinely curious about a part of life where her education
had been woefully lacking. 'I'm looking at utility companies
right now,' he said politely, pushing a pale breast of chicken
around a porcelain plate, as if food was a distasteful vul-
garity. 'But I guess the main thing is to amuse myself. Isn't
that what we all do? I find making money amusing.' The

banker was thirty-two, and had already amassed a sufficient fortune never to have to work again. When in London he rarely ventured further north than Hyde Park or south of Chelsea, yet the world was now his for the taking. Kate wanted to know more about his life – his Georgian townhouse in Cheyne Walk, for example, and whether he owned a private jet, to fly back to his Upper East Side brownstone, and was he raised in one of those wealthy American dynasties, or had he sprung, fully formed, onto Wall Street? But it would have been rude to ask; and anyway, as soon as the pineapple sorbet was served, the banker – whose name was Harry Holder III – moved to another table to sit beside his wife, who looked like a supermodel, honey blonde hair halfway down her back, and golden, peachy skin that glowed in the warmth of her husband's wealth.

By the beginning of February Kate felt the need to get out of London for a bit, and rang Bella to ask if she and Sam could visit Elverson. 'Darling, of course,' said Bella. 'We've been having a terribly quiet time of it up here – why not come next weekend? I think Isabel might be driving over on Saturday, as well.'

Kate hadn't yet seen Isabel since she'd come back from holiday – they'd left each other rueful messages on answer machines, half-joking comments on the impossibility of ever speaking again. She always looked forward to being with Isabel, though there was an undercurrent of hesitation – not felt by Isabel, guessed Kate, but by herself. Isabel was older and, though kind, occasionally given to uncomfortably shrewd insights about Kate, and others. It was Isabel who had suggested, much to Kate's irritation, that she had chosen to marry a man who would let her down; that betrayal was sometimes sweetly familiar, hugged to her cheek like a soft baby's blanket. Kate wondered, too, if Isabel had guessed about the nature of her relationship with Julian: both its simplicity and its guile.

Right now Kate was trying not to think about Julian: that was her new resolution for the year; and therefore she was not returning the occasional calls that he made on his way home from the office. 'I'll get you,' he'd said, in his last message on her answer machine, last Friday night; only three words, apparently light-hearted, breathed into the ether, yet Kate thought she detected a hint of menace even though she knew this to be paranoid. ('Out of sight, out of mind,' she whispered to herself, over and over again, like a rosary.)

By the time she and Sam reached Norfolk on Saturday morning, Kate was trying to remind herself – for the twentieth time that week – to shut out the bad stuff and concentrate on goodness and hope and the many wonders of nature. There was no snow on the ground at Elverson this time, much to Sam's disappointment, but the garden looked as beautiful as ever, still touched in places by frost, though primroses were already growing on the sheltered, southern slope that led down to the orchard. Sam was mollified by a bicycle that Bella had found for him: a hand-me-down, though he was not to know it, as she had polished and painted it and pumped up the tyres before his arrival. 'Bella, you are an angel,' said Kate, as Sam took off across the grass, riding in wide circles, skirting rusty croquet hoops and looping around the trees.

Isabel arrived a couple of hours after them, in time for lunch, as did Charles, who had stayed the previous night at his Cambridge college. Kate often thought that, even in a lookalike brood, Isabel was the child who took most after her father: they had the same high brows and straight firm noses; thick dark hair – though Charles was greying now – swept back from their faces; smooth hair, unlike Kate's, which was somehow unruly. 'Icy eyes,' her father had once said, as part of a tirade against Charles; but Kate thought it a rare, beautiful blue, if slightly clouded today.

Charles seemed preoccupied at lunch, despite being courteous as ever. His courtesy – in such marked contrast to her father's social awkwardness – was nevertheless distancing, in a different kind of way. What did he really think, amidst all those mathematical equations? Did love entwine itself through the numbers in his head, softening their sharp outlines? More than once Kate found herself looking at him across the kitchen, studying his face for clues. Had her uncle loved her mother before Bella, or after? Or was that unproven suspicion a shapeless, groundless fear that had darkened her father's mind?

Maybe it had been unrequited love on her mother's side, unnoticed by Charles, whose thoughts lay elsewhere, out there with the cold stars, distanced from the messiness of daily life where nothing added up to anything. She did not envy Bella – her marriage might be as lonely as Kate's had been; indeed, Kate often felt far less alone now that Pete had gone. (Nothing could be more solitary than those nights when she had lain awake in bed when Sam was still a baby, waiting for her husband to come home; knowing, as dawn broke, that he had not rung, that he did not care, that he might have fallen over the edge of the world, but was more likely warm in someone else's arms.) What could be worse than being with a man whose mind was always elsewhere; who remained untouched by the woman who believed she had shared her life with him? Perhaps the American banker lived the right way: in search of amusement rather than anything deeper. At least money – like other numbers – could be counted and stored, relied upon, immutable. Was that the lesson that Charles had taught his sons? Julian made money, lots of money (something to do with futures trading, which Kate didn't quite understand), while Paul was a successful economist, an advisor to another big City institution. Neither had married a woman like Bella – apparently soft, accommodating yet nurturing – choosing instead harder, redoubtable wives; though Kate understood, too, that it was impossible to know the truth of a marriage unless you were inside it, and even from the inside, the real truth was sometimes hard to see.

As for Charles's daughters: they both stayed unmarried, contentedly so, it seemed: keeping men at a slight distance – though perfectly happy to have them occupy a containable part of their lives. Isabel was thirty-seven and lived alone in a large, book-lined flat in Highgate into which she welcomed her lover, from time to time. He was a Harvard law professor, still married to his wife, the father of two grown-up sons; Kate had only met him twice, even though Isabel had been involved with him for the last six years at least. 'It works,' was all she said, when Kate dared quiz her about their relationship. 'It suits us both.'

Kate wasn't sure how much Bella or Charles knew about Isabel's love life; it certainly wasn't mentioned today. Instead, they talked about Isabel's winter holiday. ('Glorious,' she said, avoiding any mention of her travel companion, 'with sand like velvet and the most perfect, tranquil sea.') After lunch Bella suggested that all five of them should go out for a walk, to enjoy the sunshine while it lasted. 'Can I ride my bike?' said Sam.

'I suppose you can, if we take the track down to the church,' said Bella. 'It's quite firm underfoot, because of the frost.' Sam went on ahead, following the dog, who led the way, doubling back occasionally to check that everyone was following her. 'She's like a little sheepdog,' said Bella, affectionately, 'fretting about keeping us in place. She reminds me of when you were children – I'd take the five of you for walks and worry that I'd lost someone along the way. I had a recurring dream that all of you were really tiny – like Tom Thumb – and I'd put the lot of you in my pocket, and realize later, with horrible anxiety, that one had fallen out.'

'Which one?' said Isabel.

'Now, darling, I'm not one of your patients,' said Bella mildly. 'And, anyway, I can't remember every detail of a thirty-year-old dream.'

The path was too narrow for the adults to walk side by side, and by the time they reached the churchyard Bella and Isabel were a little way behind while Charles and Kate had gone on more quickly, to catch up with Sam. They found him by Judith's grave, spelling out the words on the headstone, his bike in the long grass by his side. 'Was Judith your sister?' he asked Charles.

'No, Bella's sister – her twin,' said Charles.

'But why is she buried with your family?' said Sam.

'Well, Bella thought it would be nice for her to be here.'

'Did you? Do you like her being here?'

Charles did not reply; just smiled, in a noncommittal

way, and started walking back towards the church. 'Mum, where do dead people live?' asked Sam.

'That's complicated,' said Kate. 'Some people think that the dead live in our hearts, when we remember them. Others think that they live in heaven, or maybe they don't live anywhere at all.'

'Just in the air?' said Sam.

'No, just nowhere, vanished and gone.'

'What do you think?'

'I'm not sure, darling.'

'I think your mum lives in the sky.'

'That would be nice.'

'Yes, so she can still look out for you, like the princess in the tower, except better than that, because she's not locked away.' He picked up his bike, and rode down the path, towards Isabel, who stepped out of his way.

'Hello,' said Isabel, when she reached Kate, putting an arm around her. 'Are you OK?'

'Yes, I'm fine,' said Kate, not wanting to be hugged.

'You seem a bit preoccupied.'

'Just thinking . . .'

'About what?'

'Oh, the usual – love, death, the meaning of life.'

'The simple stuff, then. And have you reached any conclusions?'

'No, just going round in circles, like always – why did my mother die, and so on?'

'What do you think?'

'I don't know. That maybe she wanted to be dead, if only for that night . . . that she wanted oblivion, to stop feeling anything.'

'Why?'

'Maybe . . . oh, I'm not sure,' said Kate, looking at her mother's gravestone, rather than at Isabel. 'My dad just told me that she had had an affair with your father, before he married Bella.'

'That wouldn't surprise me.'

'Really?' said Kate, turning to Isabel for the first time, though still not meeting her eyes. 'I wondered if it was just another of his delusions.'

'It's always convenient to have a mad person in the family, to blame the uncomfortable things on. And maybe he did imagine it – but it wouldn't be beyond the realms of possibility that Judith had been in love with Dad, at some point. There's always so much that's left unsaid in this family, like most others.'

'Have you ever talked to Bella about it? Or Charles?'

'No, they'd be appalled. They'd see it as the most unspeakable lapse of taste – an intrusion . . . But maybe you should talk to somebody about it?'

'Charles?'

'Oh, good God, no. Someone outside the family – a therapist.'

'You think I need therapy?'

'I think most people need therapy at some point in their lives. It's like servicing a car – only far more interesting, because it's about the nuts and bolts of happiness. Or you could think of it as an intellectual exercise, an exploration, and maybe it won't seem so scary.'

'I don't know if I could face it.'

'You might find that life is easier to face afterwards.'

'You think I don't face up to my life?' said Kate.

'No, it's not that simple. But I think that you feel that things happen to you without you having very much control over them. Because that's what happened to you as a child – at the risk of sounding absurdly over-simplistic.' Isabel smiled and raised one eyebrow – something she had always been able to do, like Julian, like Judith. (No wonder Sebastian had felt threatened, thought Kate, by that dry, wry family; no wonder he exploded with anger in the face of their apparent self-control.)

They started walking away from Judith's grave, past the church, where Bella had been arranging a few flowers by the altar, fragile snowdrops that she'd picked from the Elverson garden. Charles was far ahead by now, striding home. They could see his footprints on the path, purposeful, marked out like a code in the frost. By the time they'd followed him back into the house, he was in his study, door closed. 'He's frightfully preoccupied at the moment,' said Bella. 'Some new theory about the meaning of time.'

'Pity he doesn't understand it at a simple human level,' said Isabel, 'so that he might at last grasp the fact that it would be a good idea to spend a little more time with his family for a change.'

'Hush, darling,' said Bella. 'He can't help it if his mind's on other things.'

'It takes two to make a marriage,' said Isabel, at which Bella stiffened before making her own retreat into the kitchen. 'And you always thought we were the perfect family,' said Isabel to Kate, after Bella had disappeared.

'It looks that way from the outside,' said Kate.

'But you're on the inside, with the rest of us, aren't you?'

Twelve

On Valentine's Day Sam woke Kate up at seven o'clock in the morning with a card that he had made for her at school the previous week and smuggled home in his rucksack. It was crumpled and lovely: exuberant red hearts in slightly smudged poster paint. She walked him to school, as always, after breakfast – five minutes, hand in hand through the drizzly grey, though as they crossed the road in front of the main entrance he shook her off, to make his independence clear (a fact she wanted to point out to Maria, or Isabel, as if they sat in judgement on her relationship with Sam). 'When can I walk by myself?' he said.

'When you're nine or ten, OK?'

'Good,' he said, and then came closer, to whisper the question he asked every morning, even though he knew the answer. 'Who's picking me up from school today?'

'Me. I'll be there at three fifteen.'

'You won't be late?'

'I'm never late.'

'You were once.'

'Two years ago. I'll be there, I promise.' Then she knelt

down, so that no one else could hear her, and whispered back to him, 'Have a lovely day, sweetheart. I love you.'

'See you later,' he said, embarrassed, yet comforted by the familiar ritual, before running inside.

Sometimes, walking home from the school, she tormented herself with the thought of an unforeseen accident or tragedy: what if something did happen to her, and she wasn't there at three fifteen? (Imagine the horror of Sam being brought up by Pete, if she were dead, dragged around in an errant father's wake, like a neglected puppy, or worse?) Or what if Sam was hurt, if the school was invaded by a psychopathic axe-man – because the teachers never locked the playground gates – or a plane crashed into the classrooms out of the sky? She'd have to kill herself if he died, because she would have failed him, failed everything; and how would she amass sufficient pills for a successful overdose? These were not healthy thoughts, Kate realized, to be occupying her mind at nine o'clock on the morning of Valentine's Day (or any day, come to that). But there they were, and she was in the midst of them, head down to the ground in the rain, the eternal infernal rain, when she bumped into Adam. Literally bumped into him, hard enough to make her catch her breath.

'Oh,' he said, looking irritated, 'hello . . .'

'Sorry,' she said, hoping her rising blushes were hidden by her lumpy oatmeal jumper and wishing she had washed her crumpled hair.

'Do you want to have a quick cup of tea?' he said, no less grumpy.

'Well, if you're not in a rush . . .'

'I am in a rush, which is why it will have to be quick.'

'Don't let me stop you.'

'Look, I'm sorry – it's just a bloody awful morning. But tea with two sugars might make it slightly better.'

'OK,' she said, still feeling embarrassed. They crossed the road to the nearest cafe – full, as usual, with local mothers and babies and buggies, in a warm maternal fug – but found a table at the back. 'So, what have you been up to?' she said, hoping to look cool but friendly at the same time (impossible – especially now her nose had started dripping – and why bother, really?).

'Oh, the usual. Trying to juggle being a single parent with building kitchens for horrible rich people . . .'

'You're a single parent?'

'Some of the time – Rose's mother is away filming this month. She's an actress. Very glamorous, unlike me.'

'Oh, I see,' said Kate, rearranging her face so that she didn't look disappointed. (It would have been so perfect – so well arranged – if Adam really had been a properly single father, instead of a married man whose fabulous wife happened to be away at the moment.)

'And you, how it's all going with you?'

'More of the same. Being a single mother whilst trying to earn a living.'

He nodded, and she couldn't tell if he was surprised. 'Doesn't Sam's father help out?' he said.

'Kind of. I mean, they see each other, but Pete's away a lot – he's a photographer, always in another time zone. And he doesn't live that close to us – he's got a flat in Marylebone, and a whole other life, I suppose . . .' Adam looked straight at her, as her voice trailed away, but he didn't reply. Kate found it impossible to gauge what he was thinking; he wasn't a man who smiled, or talked, just for the sake of social etiquette. 'I hate this time of year,' she said, eventually.

'I know – fucking February . . .'

'Or not, in my case.' (My God – had she really said that? How hideously embarrassing.) He smiled, at last, and she remembered from the party how much she liked that rare smile of his; it made his face light up.

'Would you like to get together some time?' he said. 'We could do something with the kids.'

'That would be lovely,' she said, trying not to sound pathetically enthusiastic.

'How about this Sunday? It's bound to be too rainy for the park, unless you enjoy struggling through a mud bath, which I'm already doing at work this week – so why don't I cook lunch instead?' Adam scribbled down his address on the back of a paper napkin, and then stood up to go. 'Take care,' he said, and disappeared out into the traffic-clogged street.

Kate stayed for a few minutes longer, finishing her tea, examining the napkin as if it might contain a hidden message, wavering between elation and uncertainty. A date – was this a date? She didn't approve of liaisons with married men; but no, this was simply a friendly social arrangement between two parents, with nothing else to do at the weekend. It was all very modern, she told herself; there might even be a magazine article in it ('How To Make Friends With A Man And Really Mean It This Time'). Speaking of which, she had to finish that bloody stupid diet piece by lunchtime today. Was it a sign of growing up, or growing old, that she didn't really care any more? And, more to the point, that the magazine's features editor didn't much care for her either. 'You know what?' Annunciata had said to her on the phone this week. 'You need to pull yourself together.' Pull what, exactly, Kate had wanted to reply, but she'd kept quiet, so that the unsaid words blocked her throat, and she felt close to choking.

Still, there was Sunday to look forward to . . . and what should she wear? Jeans and jumper, as ever – or something red, as in Scarlet Woman? Fat lot of good it was writing for a glossy girl's magazine when you wanted advice on the right look for a double date with your son and someone else's husband and child. Kate returned to the napkin, and regarded his handwriting again (sturdy-looking, like his hands) before folding the paper up, very carefully, and tucking it in her bag, next to the keys to her house.

Thirteen

'Mum, why do we have to go to a girl's place?' said Sam, truculent and white-faced on Sunday morning, after Robbie had stayed the night and they'd woken each other up at dawn. 'I don't want to play with a stupid girl. Why can't we ever do things I want to do? Why can't we go to Dad's flat instead?'

'Because Dad is in New York,' said Kate.

'Why?'

'Why's he in New York? Because he's working.'

'Well, why can't he be here?'

'I don't know, Sam. You'll have to ask him yourself.'

'All right, I'll phone him.'

'Darling, it'll be half past six in the morning in America. He's probably still asleep.'

'It's not fair. Everyone else's dad lives with them.'

'No, they don't. Ben's Dad doesn't.'

'He does!'

'He doesn't.'

'You think you know everything! You never listen to me!'

'Look, are you upset about something? Do you want a hug?'

'No, I hate you!' Sam ran out of the living room, up the stairs, and slammed his bedroom door. Surely seven was too young for adolescence? Or was it going to get worse than this: a bleak future of his recriminations and reprisals, him blaming her for everything that had gone wrong in his life? Kate sat down on the sofa and sighed. Sam was overtired, and she was overwrought. The lunch-date was clearly doomed. She wasn't even going to bother with make-up – no point trying to paint over the damage or compete with his glamorous wife; and her most unfashionable jeans would have to do – they were the only ones that did up round the waist, anyway, without making her stomach bulge – with one of Pete's old sweatshirts on top. (She should have thrown it out by now, she knew, but it was her favourite – a dark green slowly faded to the colour of a new leaf, soft from washing and comforting against the skin; quite unlike Pete himself had been.)

By the time they reached Adam's road – a quarter of a mile or so away, along quiet Sunday morning streets – Sam's mood was showing no sign of improvement and her heart had sunk as low as the sullen winter clouds. 'Who is this girl Rose, anyway?' he said. 'Is she at my school?'

'I'm not sure. She might be at Southview Junior – I think that's a bit closer to where Rose lives than your school.'

'I hate everyone that goes to Southview – I think they're evil.'

'No you don't.'

'Yes I bloody do! They're all bloody stupid.'

'Don't swear, Sam.'

'Why not? You do.'

'Well I shouldn't, and I'll try to stop, if you try to.'

'Why should I try? You don't try.'

'Sam, I do try. I try very hard.' He scuffed his trainers against the pavement, and said nothing, pulling his hand away from hers, rubbing his fist hard against his eyes. 'Sam, please, let's just go and have some lunch with these people and then we'll come home, OK?' He shrugged his shoulders.

Fortunately, Rose looked as miserable as Sam did when they arrived – so at least Kate wasn't the only one with a grumpy child – and Adam seemed anxious, too, or maybe it was a kind of wariness. But the children brightened up at the prospect of watching a new video, and Sam's mood was further improved when Rose told him that she had thrown away all but one of her Barbie dolls last summer. 'I just kept the one that looks like my mum,' said Rose, 'except my mum is prettier.'

Once the children were safely installed side by side on an admirably clean taupe linen sofa (was domestic life less stained when shared with daughters?), Adam and Kate retreated to the kitchen, where she admired the zinc-fronted units. 'Lovely flat,' she said. 'How long have you been here?'

'About a year,' he said. 'We were in a house over by the park, nearer your street, but then . . . well, you know . . .'

What? What did she know? He bent down to inspect a roast chicken in the oven. 'Not vegetarian, are you? I should have asked . . .'

'No, definitely not. Sam loves roast chicken, and so do I.'

'Good,' he said, looking serious. She couldn't work out

his face, couldn't read it like she usually did, with a glib journalistic eye: was it forbidding, or preoccupied, or something else entirely? Did he actually want her here? It was difficult to tell.

'I'm really glad you could come,' he said. 'Sundays can seem a bit bleak when it's just me and Rose, and she starts thinking that the rest of the world is having a lovely time in an ideal family.'

'Like Sam . . .'

'Do you want a drink? A glass of wine?'

'A cup of coffee might be better. Otherwise I'll want to go to bed after lunch.' He glanced at her, briefly, half smiling. 'I don't mean here!' she said, blushing, again.

'Feel free,' he said, and started making the gravy.

Honestly, he was impossible: all those mixed messages and quizzical, cryptic looks. Isabel was right – she obviously went out looking for risky propositions, with the danger of rejection inherent; she couldn't help herself – or maybe it was something else she sought, as if she had to prove she could win a difficult man over, having always failed before. Well, this time was going to be different. The question of rejection or incomprehensible emotional negotiation simply wouldn't arise; she'd make sure of it.

Steeled by this decision (another man, another resolution; but still, Kate thought, you had to keep trying), she began to find the conversation over lunch easier. Sam and Rose, though shy, seemed ready to answer questions from the adults – and the food was delicious (proper gravy and crisp roast potatoes that melted inside; at least he could cook). Afterwards, Adam played basketball with Sam in the back garden, while Kate and Rose did a puzzle together – an illustrated map of Britain – on the living-room floor. She'd forgotten how different little girls were, after all those years of a son. Rose wanted to talk, to confide, even; to show Kate her room and her toys, when they were choosing a puzzle, to have a conversation about pink glittery nail varnish and her favourite jeans. It was nice, although Kate felt as if Rose were examining her, in some way; as if both of them were aware that they were on their best behaviour, puzzling each other out, as absorbed in this as in the fragmented picture on the floor. (Kate knew, too, that she was looking for the absent mother in the child's face; for Rose was pretty, without precocity: long, glossy hair, a lighter brown than Adam's, and different colour eyes to his, an unusual shade of grey.) 'When does your mummy get back?' said Kate, after the puzzle was finished, and immediately regretted the comment, as Rose chewed at a nail.

'Soon,' she said. 'And I'm going to stay with her next weekend, in Manchester.' Rose pointed to Manchester on the map, keeping her thumb on London and stretching her forefinger, straining to bridge the gap. 'My mum is going to be on the television.'

'That'll be fun,' said Kate. 'You'll have to tell me when, and I can watch out for her.'

'I'll tell her about you,' said Rose, 'so she can watch out for you, as well.'

By five, as darkness descended outside, Kate started making noises about leaving. 'Stay,' said Adam, 'why not? We could have a beer, watch the new episode of *The Simpsons* . . .'

'My dad likes *The Simpsons*,' said Sam, staking out familial territory, as Rose had done.

'So do I,' said Adam.

'When I get a puppy, I'm going to call him Bart,' said Sam.

'Dad, I want a puppy,' said Rose, 'I really, really want one, a tiny little puppy called Lisa.'

'Do you know what the biggest wingspan is of a bird?' said Sam. 'I do! An albatross, and its wings measure five metres across. It says so in my *500 Questions and Answers* book.'

Adam caught Kate's eye, and smiled. 'How about that beer?' he said.

At seven, the four of them were still on the sofa together – Adam and Kate at opposite ends, divided by their respective children; but his arm snaked out along the top, so that his fingers rested inches away from her head. She sensed his hand, just out of reach, yet almost close enough to touch her. No one had stroked her hair for so long, it seemed impossible now, so she tried not to think about Adam's fingertips; tried hard to concentrate on the television instead.

'We should do this again,' said Adam, as the children's eyelids drooped, then struggled open.

'That would be lovely,' she said. 'Do you want to make a date?'

'I'll call you,' he said. 'I need to sort a few things out first.'

So much for resolutions, then.

Fourteen

In bed that night Kate whispered the starlight rhyme to herself, even though the clouds obscured the sky. 'Wish I may, wish I might, wish upon a star tonight,' she said, three times, five times, ten times, until the words turned into a lullaby. What was the story that her mother had been trying to write when Kate was a child? It was about the stars, she'd said, no more than that; but Kate had found a single page of it, handwritten and torn from a spiral-bound notebook, when she and Bella had cleared out the flat after her mother had died. There had been no beginning, no end, words missing either side; but Kate had kept it, of course.

At one in the morning, still unable to sleep, she crept downstairs to find it, folded in a brown envelope next to her passport and birth certificate in the bottom drawer of her desk (the desk her mother had bought for her when she was twelve, battered Victorian mahogany, familiar, immovable). Kate hadn't read this fragment of a story for years but she read it now, deciphering her mother's tiny, tightly controlled handwriting.

'She poured the starlight into a bowl,' her mother had written, 'and when the bowl was full the woman dipped her hands into it, and her face, bathing herself until she was silvery like the sky. And then she took her silver knife and cut her wrists, but no blood was drawn, because the starlight was magical.'

Kate paused. This, surely, was the same bedtime story her mother had told her as a child; but the written version was more Gothic, so that Kate almost wanted to laugh, were it not so very dark outside. 'No one could harm the woman now, and she could not harm herself, even as she plunged the knife into her heart and twisted it. And forever after she lived alone in her tower, without man or child or friend, without need of anyone, and only the stars were her companions. But in the grey house on the other side of the hill, the cold man wept warm tears; the man who had once loved her, lonely now, amidst his family – dreaming of his lost love, while his wife slept by his side . . .'

And there her mother's story ended, on this surviving page at least, except for some incomprehensible, scribbled-over sentences at the bottom of the page, obliterated by angry black lines. Kate stared at it until her eyes hurt, but there was nothing more, no message, no clue. 'Hardly conclusive proof, is it?' said a voice in her head, tartly (or was it outside, breathing into her ear?). 'Or are you still convinced that your mad mother betrayed her twin sister?'

'Who are you?' whispered Kate, as her skin crawled.

'I might ask the same question of you,' said the voice, mockingly.

'I think I need a shrink,' said Kate.

'Shrink-wrapped, shrink-to-fit, shrunken heads . . . better be careful out there, little girl . . .'

The following morning, while Sam was getting ready for

school, Kate rang Isabel for advice. 'I'm scared I'm losing it,' she said, very quietly, so that Sam could not hear her.

'Losing what?' said Isabel.

'The plot.'

'The plot of what?'

'Of my life, my mind, everything. I'm hearing voices in my head. At first I just thought it was my mother – or me imagining her, anyway. But last night there was a new one.'

'Kate, calm down. What is this voice telling you?'

'Nothing, it's just an unhelpful running commentary.'

'But most of us have those. I have one nearly all the time, telling me I've fucked up or I'm making a mistake. Some people call it a conscience, or the voice of intuition, or straightforward anxiety. It's not a bad thing, you know . . .'

'What if I'm developing something awful, like schizo-phrenia?'

Isabel laughed. 'Then you wouldn't be worrying like this, sweetheart, you'd just be certain that the voices in your head were genuine.'

Kate sighed, but started feeling a bit calmer. 'So you're saying mad people don't worry that they're mad?'

'No, it's a sign of sanity that you're worrying at all.'

'Well, I don't know . . . I had lunch with a man yester-day, maybe that's what started me off?'

'A nice man?'

'A man with a wife and a child.'

'Ah, so a familiarly risky proposition.'

'What's that supposed to mean? Familiar to you, or me?'

'Familiar, as in it runs in the family.'

'Look, Isabel, I've got to go, otherwise Sam will be late for school.'

'OK, but don't take offence – and let's talk again later.'

Kate was staying with Sam today, accompanying the class on an outing to a wildlife centre on the other side of Wood Green. (Wood Green – it sounded so sylvan, so unlike its true urban self . . .) Kate did not enjoy school trips (what if she lost someone else's child?) but hated even more the thought of Sam going without her to keep an eye on him. (If the double-decker bus they travelled on was going to crash into an oil tanker, then she was going to be there with him, holding his hand.) As the bus had crawled over the hill, past Alexandra Palace, she'd roused herself sufficiently to point out the view of London to Sam and his friends – the hazy City (Julian's realm) and its towers beside the snaking river Thames – but a kind of fog descended afterwards, as they were driven northwards, smothering the suburban streets in an odd yellow gloom, that seemed full of a sulphurous grit.

They got out at the last bus stop – the end of the line – and walked across the road to their destination, a mish-mash of shabby greenhouses and prefabricated, impermanent chalets, beside the council crematorium and around the corner from a secondary school that looked like a borstal. It was basically a garden centre, providing employment for physically and mentally disabled adults, but with a class-room attached which contained five stick insects (one alive, four dead and decomposing); a caged hamster; a discarded papery snakeskin; and a glass box filled with earth, which made Kate think of things she didn't want to think about, a graveyard or a coffin, a glass coffin for an absent Sleeping Beauty. 'That's where the earthworms live,' said the woman who was showing them round today, pointing at the box 'except you can't see them – they're hidden inside there.' As she spoke, her hands flew around her, making shapes in the air, and Kate suddenly realized that the woman, whose name was Heather, was also talking in sign language, perhaps from force of habit.

'Do you know how to sign?' Heather asked the children, with an enthusiasm that made Kate feel ashamed of herself. They shook their heads. 'OK, I'll show you the sign for butterflies,' she said, and her fingers flitted in front of her face, 'and this is the one for good boys and good girls. See? My thumb is up. Thumbs up means good in sign language.' Soon the children were signing too, remarkably adept at picking up this new language, and for a moment their breezy excitement filled the room, gusting through the broken glass windows and along the weed-lined path outside.

'Can you do it, Mum?' said Sam, as his little fingers skittered like insects.

'I'm trying,' said Kate, 'but my hands aren't as quick as yours.'

Afterwards, as they trooped around the largest greenhouse, which was filled with delicate passion flowers in every shade of purple (astonishing in their exoticism in these unprepossessing, dusty surroundings), the children's hands still fluttered in sign language, as they did on the bus home. Kate looked at her own hands, dried out from the cold, covered in a web of fine lines, and they seemed somehow stiff, arthritic almost in their inability to sign. She wanted to reach over to Sam, but knew it would be wrong to still his fingers with hers ('Don't hold my hand so tight,' he'd complained this morning on their way to school), and so she tucked her hands away, like stones, inside her jacket pockets. Never had she felt quite so lost for words.

Fifteen

Adam didn't ring the next day, or the day after that, and she'd promised herself she wouldn't call him (for she could not bear for him to hear the need in her voice, kept swallowing it back instead, washed down with cups of tea and digestive biscuits). But on Wednesday evening, just after Sam had gone to bed, the phone rang and it was him, asking her if she'd like to go out for dinner on Friday night.

'Without the children?' she said.

'Preferably. Anyway, Rose is going to be up in Manchester with her mother.'

In the split second before replying, she'd clocked his phrase – 'her mother'; not 'my wife' – but she was still uncertain quite what he was saying. 'Is that a good idea?' said Kate.

'A good idea that Rose goes to Manchester? Well, probably not, but there's nothing I can do about it. Clare is her mother, after all, even if I sometimes cast her as Jezebel.'

'No, I meant is it a good idea that we go out to dinner?'

'Why not? We're both single, aren't we?'

'But I thought you were married?'

'I am married, but we're separated – didn't I make that clear? We still see each other, of course, because of Rose – I mean, I try to keep things as civilized as possible, even if Clare is screwing her leading man right now, which I'd prefer Rose not to know.'

'Oh, it's just you said . . . I mean, I thought you said you were only a single parent some of the time . . .'

'Well, that's true, isn't it? Some of the time Rose is with Clare – not very often, these days – but when she is, that means I can go out for dinner with another woman, as opposed to sitting at home feeling sorry for myself.' He stopped, abruptly, as if regretting his words.

'OK, dinner, that would be great . . . I'll get a babysitter, or maybe Sam might go and stay with Pete for a change. See you then.' Kate put the phone down, still confused. Everything should have fallen neatly into place, but why then did she feel as if she was missing something? Was it his tone of voice, or his words? What was it that didn't quite fit? When the phone rang again, a few minutes later, she half expected it to be Adam cancelling dinner on Friday and telling her it had been a mistake. But instead it was Bella's voice on the phone.

'Just ringing to see how you are, darling,' she said.

'Fine, I think.'

'And what have you been up to?'

'Funnily enough, I unearthed something Mum wrote – a page from a story about the stars. Did you ever read it?'

'No, never, and I'm not sure she ever told me about it – she was terribly secretive in some ways.'

'I always thought twins told each other everything, shared everything.'

'We shared things in different ways, I suppose.'

Kate bit her lip, to stop herself blurting out the question she longed to ask ('so did you share Charles?') and forced herself to change the subject. 'I went to this strange little garden centre on Monday, with Sam, but it turned out to have the most beautiful passion flowers in the greenhouse.'

'How marvellous,' said Bella, clearly relieved to be back on safe ground. 'I always thought it was interesting that passion flowers make you sleepy – not passionate at all – when they're turned into a tincture or a tea.' Then they talked about the Elverson herb garden, about Bella's lavender borders and the hardiness of lemon thyme, passing another five minutes equably, until both could say goodbye to one another with the sense that balance had been restored.

'Don't read too much into things,' murmured her mother's voice, as Kate lay in bed later that night, drifting towards dreams.

'What about the starlight story?' whispered Kate, wondering if she was already asleep.

'Just a bedtime story,' said her mother. 'And not a very good one at that. I should never have spent so much time trying to write – better to live, instead.'

'But you're dead,' said Kate.

'Not to you,' replied her mother, 'not to you . . .'

'. . . to-you, to-you,' hooted the owl outside; though it surely could not be an owl, thought Kate, because didn't the owl live in the Elverson woods, instead of here? That was where the owl flew, through the woods on either side of the stream by the footpath to the church; the stream she'd dreamt about as a child, where her father pushed her down beneath the water, or was it her mother's face she saw in the water? Whose face did she see: her own pale oval reflection in the shadow of the trees, or someone drowning, her mother drowning, drowning in what? 'What were you doing with him in the water?' hissed her father. 'I saw you with him in the water.' The pale face was lying still beneath the water, blurred by the ripples of the stream, and she was choking . . . Kate was choking, she couldn't breathe for fear of what it was she'd seen, or heard, or done. Or was it just a dream, nothing but a dream? as her mother had said the next morning, the morning she was sent to Elverson for the summer.

Kate woke up sweating, tears pricking her eyes, heart jumping, bathed in sour fear, not starlight. 'What were you doing with him in the water?' she whispered, out loud, but her mother was gone, and there was only darkness. What was it that had happened? Why would nobody tell her, or was there nothing to tell? She rubbed her tired eyes, sure that they must have witnessed something, once upon a time, but what she had seen seemed to have disappeared to another place, like the path beyond the crack in the old willow-pattern plate. Yet it was close – she felt it so close – for it was as if in sleep she had followed that path, stepping into the picture and through it to another side, and now she could not remember where it was she had started from, or how she might return . . .

Sixteen

The dream had hung over her for a day or two, leaden like
a headache; and she was still trying to shake it off on Friday
evening when she met Adam at a local restaurant. Sam was
staying the night at Robbie's house – his father having failed
to return home from New York as promised. ('Sorry babe,'
he'd said on the phone to Kate that afternoon, to her considerable irritation. 'Something came up, OK?')

Adam seemed almost as preoccupied as she was, even
though both tried hard to be light-hearted. It was noisy in
the restaurant, which somehow amplified the silences in
their own conversation, and her hands felt empty, clumsy
. . . She wished she still smoked, just for something to do,
but in lieu of a cigarette she played with the diamond stud
in her ear instead, twiddling it round and round.

'Nervous?' said Adam, at last.

'No, not really. Just a bit anxious. Or does that mean
the same thing?'

He shrugged, and she felt somehow dismissed; but that
was stupid, foolish (and what could be more destructive
than falling apart in front of him?). 'I'm sorry,' he said,

reaching across the table as if to take her hand, but then pulling away, leaning back in his chair again. 'I'm not very good company, these days. It's not your fault. I don't want to feel like this.'

'Like what?'

'Angry.'

'With me?'

'No, of course not. With Clare, with myself.'

'Why are you angry with yourself?'

'Well, it's impossible not to take some responsibility for the end of a marriage,' he said, voice hard, like his face. 'It takes two, doesn't it, to bring everything crashing down? Even if it's easy to blame her for having an affair, I must have been doing something wrong, otherwise she wouldn't have wanted to leave me. Sorry, that probably sounds soaked in self-pity.'

Kate hesitated. This was probably the longest speech she'd heard from Adam in their admittedly short acquaintance: there'd been the kids before, interrupting, or other people at the party where they'd met. But though she wanted to respond with reassuring words, he'd somehow made her pause for thought. It was uncomfortable, realizing that perhaps Adam was right: you couldn't simply blame the supposed guilty party for everything that went wrong in a relationship; life was more complicated than that (and all of a sudden she remembered Pete, long ago, before Sam was born, saying to her that she always expected the worst from him, that her uncertainty weighed heavily on both of them; and she'd tried to explain to him that saying her fears out loud was just a kind of magic – that if she said the worst, then it would never happen; but he'd said no, it didn't work like that, it was a way of bringing those bad things to life).

'I didn't mean to talk about Clare,' said Adam eventually, breaking into her silence. 'I'd rather talk about you. I hardly know anything about you. Tell me about yourself, everything or anything – whatever you like.'

'My mother is dead,' she said without thinking, not meaning to start like that.

'Recently?'

'No, a long time ago – when I was eighteen. And I don't see much of my father, so sometimes it seems like Sam and I are this tiny little family, but then we're part of this bigger one, as well. I spent a lot of time with my aunt and uncle and their kids, in Norfolk. And what about you?'

'Oh, your classic dysfunctional family: divorced parents, one brother who still won't fully forgive my father twenty years after Dad left home for another woman, another accountant, like him. I always thought I was going to make sure it was different for my children, but I suppose the pull of the familiar – the family pattern – is harder to resist than you imagine at first.'

His words niggled at her, jogged at her memory of what Isabel had said last time they'd talked, and Kate felt the same sting of something . . . irritation, perhaps, but something else as well. 'But we don't do exactly the same as our parents did,' she said. 'We have to be more than a reflection of their mistakes.'

'I suppose so,' he said, pouring another glass of wine (and drinking it fast, so maybe he was anxious, too). 'And I'm not like my father, because I wasn't the one that left in the first place . . . Anyway, he's not so bad – he does his best, we see each other once or twice a year, and he never forgets Rose's birthday. He's building up a nest egg for her, he says – she's his only grandchild.' Adam smiled, and Kate wondered what his father looked like; wondered what Adam would look like in twenty years' time.

'And what about your mother?' she said.

'Oh, she's remarried, too, thank God, to a very nice man, a retired doctor – they're up in Scotland now, where he comes from, so I don't have to worry about her, either. Both my parents are much happier apart from each other – in fact, they're proof you shouldn't stay together for the sake of the children.'

'So not so dysfunctional, in the end?' she said.

'I suppose not. You know, just before my parents split up, when I was about fourteen and they were arguing all the time, hissing at each other, thinking we wouldn't hear, I started building houses in my head: trying to imagine the layout of the rooms, working out the exact floor plan, designing the shelves, the colour of the walls. I never told anyone, though – it seemed too girly, too embarrassing, like playing with a doll's house. But I guess it was a way of escaping them, living somewhere else, if only in my head – which is maybe why I ended up building other people's houses, and why I'm not an accountant like my dad. Not that there's anything wrong with accountants – tell me to shut up, will you, if I'm burbling. I don't normally talk like this . . .'

'I like it,' she said, remembering the first time she met him, remembering how much she liked him, even now, even though she knew that his face could be stormy, and would be so again. At least he tried to talk – at least he tried; and though he struggled, he was never glib, not that she could see. 'I'd love you to see my aunt and uncle's house,' she said impulsively. 'It's the house that I always imagined I was living in, even when I was away from it. Maybe we could go in the Easter holidays? Just for a couple of days? There's a dog that Rose could play with, and a big garden and woods and a stream . . .'

'Are you sure?' he said. 'I mean, it sounds wonderful. I feel like I haven't got out of London for ages – and it begins to seem like a jail, doesn't it? Even though I've always lived here . . .'

Afterwards they talked more easily, about very little at all – as if enough confidences had been shared for one night; as if nothing more should be given away yet. He walked her home and before she could ask him to come in, he held her face in his hands, kissed her on the lips, and said goodbye.

'Don't you want a coffee, or something?' she said.

'Another time,' he said, and waved, then walked away, as he always did, without looking back.

Seventeen

It was hazy the day they drove to Norfolk, fog hanging like someone's breath over the fields and coppices near Elverson. 'Sea mist, perhaps,' said Kate.

'See what?' said Sam. 'I can't see anything at all.'

'I meant a different kind of sea,' she said, but Sam had already lost interest in the conversation and was playing with the little lead figures in his hand, the ones he'd bought when they'd stopped to look around a nearby market town. They were odd things – half goblin, half soldier – quite old, paint worn away by other hands. He'd paid for them with his pocket money – just a pound from the junk stall, and of course Kate couldn't say no, even though they gave her a strange sense of foreboding; or was she simply mistaking that for the nervousness she felt about bringing Adam and Rose to Elverson. She still hardly knew them, it seemed, even after several Sunday lunches together and an outing to the cinema without the children. They'd seen a film about a mathematician – a handsome code-breaker in the Second World War – and she'd forgotten the complicated plot as soon as they'd left the cinema; though not what had followed. That was the second time Adam had kissed her: in her front hall this time, but no more, no further, though the kiss was enough to make her want him to stay (she remembered it in bed at night; tasting it over and over again, holding the memory to her).

Bella, of course, had been welcoming of Kate's tentative request to visit Elverson with Adam. 'Of course you must bring your friends,' she'd said when Kate rang several weeks ago. 'Whenever you want – you know, darling, you're all welcome here. Would you like to come on Good Friday and stay for the long weekend?'

So here they were, the four of them, delivered here today by the ribbon of the road: Adam and Kate and Sam and Rose – the right size to be a family, but not, of course not. 'Regency, *very* impressive,' said Adam, regarding the outside of the house. 'You didn't tell me it was going to be a mansion.'

'It's not,' said Kate. 'It's just a big, sturdy family house.'

'Not the kind my family lived in,' he said.

'Nor mine,' she said, wanting to stay on his side. 'I grew up in London, anyway, in a flat above a chemist's shop in Marylebone High Street.'

'Can I sleep in your room, Daddy?' said Rose, looking anxious. 'It's a scary house, like in a scary book.'

'No, it's *not*,' said Sam scornfully. 'It's brilliant here.'

Rose's lower lip trembled, but before she could start crying Bella came to the front door, followed by the dog. 'Ah, just the people I wanted to see,' she said, taking Sam by one hand and Rose by the other. 'I've almost finished making an Easter cake, but I need two very special children to decorate it with chocolate eggs. Could you do that for me?'

Later, while Bella helped the children to blow ducks' eggs and then paint them with watercolours, Kate took Adam for a walk around the Elverson grounds – through the rose garden, down to the orchard, and then into the acres of woods, dappled by milky afternoon sunlight now that the mist had dissolved. 'What a magical place,' he whispered, as if he wanted no one else to find them, and no one but her to hear. 'You'd never guess the house was there – you can't even glimpse it from the road – it doesn't announce itself, not like you'd expect.'

'It's full of secrets, still,' said Kate, as quietly as him. 'There are bits of the garden where you can escape from everyone else, thickets in the wood I've never been in before – and attics in the house that I didn't even know existed until I was a teenager.'

'With a madwoman locked up inside?'

'I hope not. But most families have a few skeletons in the closet, don't they?'

Adam reached a finger out to her mouth, and traced her lips with it. 'So much we still haven't told each other,' he said, and her mouth opened, a little, but she did not speak. He pulled her close to him, and they were kissing, she did not want him to stop, no words, just lips, his hands against her skin, the balm of his touch . . . 'Will anyone see us here?' he said, but still she said nothing, there was nothing to say, cradled in his arms, beneath the trees, only the birdsong breaking the silence, and as she closed her eyes it felt as if she had found the hiding place she'd dreamt of as a child, lost in the leaves, at last, at the end of the willow-pattern path.

That night, the two children safely asleep in the bedroom that Kate had slept in as a child (the little lead figures on the side table between them no longer sinister, simply travelling companions for the journey), she played Scrabble with Adam and Bella – just the three of them, for Charles was still in Cambridge. It was an easy evening: simple spellings on the Scrabble board ('hear' turned to 'heart', 'hop' to 'hopeful'); no undercurrents of tension, and Kate felt she had never been so happy in Elverson, so . . . what was the word she wanted? Complete, perhaps, or at least not searching for an unknown missing thing, the lost piece of a puzzle. Afterwards, in bed, she waited for Adam, sure that he would come to her, across the corridor from his room; and he did, slipping between her clean linen sheets, staying until the dark turned into dawn.

The sun was still shining several hours later when – fully dressed – Adam gently woke her with a cup of tea to drink in bed. 'You don't have to get up,' he said. 'Bella's already cooked breakfast for the kids, and she's taken them to see the hand-reared lambs at the farm down the road.'

'So there's no one else in the house?'

'Just you and me, unless there's a silent ghost.'

'I don't think I've ever been alone in this house before.'

'You're not,' he said, stroking her hair. 'I'm here.'

'I feel like a naughty teenager,' she said, feeling suddenly embarrassed about last night with this man, this stranger.

'Enjoy it while you can.'

'It's too good to be true, isn't it?'

Just then, as Adam was unbuttoning his shirt, a car came up the drive. 'Don't go,' he said, as Kate went to the window, swaddled in an eiderdown, to see who was crunching across the gravel outside. 'Just ignore whoever it is . . . don't answer the doorbell.'

'He's got keys,' she said levelly. 'It's Julian, my cousin.'

'So what? I'll lock the bedroom door. Come on, Kate . . .'

But she shook her head, feeling a hot blush spread up from her neck, and ran into the bathroom for a shower, leaving Adam to fend for himself. By the time she was dressed, the two men were sitting together at the kitchen table, drinking coffee, silently, as far as she could tell. 'Well, *what* a surprise,' said Julian, as she walked in.

'Didn't Bella tell you we were coming for the weekend?'

'Possibly. Possibly I wasn't paying attention.'

'So, where's your lovely family?' she said.

'On their way – we passed my mother on the drive, so she's taken the kids off to see the lambs, as well.'

'And Jessica?'

'Jessica is having her hair done and will be joining us after lunch. If her mood improves, that is. I'm in the dog-house.'

'Why's that?'

'Oh, don't ask. It's a long story. The usual trials of married life . . . Still, you know all about that, don't you? Or have you forgotten, in the first flush of blind romance?'

'Aren't you mixing your metaphors?' she said tartly. Adam cleared his throat and stood up. 'I think I might go out for some fresh air,' he said, and left the room without asking her to join him.

'Bob the builder,' sang Julian, quietly. 'Can he fix it? Bob the builder, YES, he can . . .'

'You are insufferable,' Kate said, irritation infecting her like a rash.

'I didn't say anything – don't be so touchy.'

'No wonder Jessica gets annoyed, having to live with you.' They glared at each other across the table, but neither made a move away. Julian opened the business section of the newspaper on the table, still humming to himself; Kate chewed a hangnail until it tore down to the quick.

'Not very friendly, is he?' said Julian eventually.

'Who?'

'Your boyfriend. Didn't hang around for long.'

'Oh, fuck off,' she said, and stalked out of the kitchen, slamming the door behind her. He was hateful, he really was; and he knew how to get under her skin every single time. She scratched herself as she went out into the garden, itchy with rage, not knowing where she was going until she found herself marching along the path to the church, as if in righteous indignation. But it was impossible to remain angry today; and by the time she'd reached the graveyard, she'd stopped cursing Julian – the sky was too blue for that, the colour of a baby's eyes; the new daffodils too hopeful – and rounded the corner of the church, to find herself face to face with Adam.

'We must stop bumping into each other like this,' he said, rubbing at his stubbly chin, his eyes creased in the sunlight.

'Sorry about my obnoxious cousin.'

'Julian? Oh, he was fine. You just looked a bit tense, so I thought I'd leave you alone. I've been having a peaceful time of it, anyway, mooching around your dead relatives.'

'Did you find my mother's grave?'

'I think so – that one in the corner? Was her name Judith?'

'Yes, she's there, surrounded by the in-laws, poor thing.'

'I didn't realize your father's relatives were buried here, as well.'

'No – sorry, I meant my uncle's relatives. My father is Jewish, not that he sees much of his family – but you wouldn't catch him dead in a place like this.'

Adam laughed, and took Kate's hand. 'Shall we go and find our children?' he said. 'Back in the land of the living . . .'

Eighteen

It had not taken long for Bella to win Rose over, but whether Kate would do so was far less clear. Rose did not look overly delighted to see Kate when they returned from the farm. 'Are you still here?' she said, rosebud mouth drooping slightly. 'I thought you'd gone back to London.'

'No, not till tomorrow, when we're all driving home together,' said Kate briskly. 'Now, what would you two like to do before lunch?'

'Go for a walk with my daddy,' said Rose, taking his hand.

Kate didn't argue with her – after all, why should Adam's daughter welcome a female interloper? She'd never particularly warmed to her own mother's occasional lovers after Judith and Sebastian had separated; even though part of Kate had wanted, desperately, for her mother to be taken care of by someone other than herself, none of the men who drifted in and out of their lives seemed up to the task. (There was that slightly sinister Persian doctor with whom Judith had smoked opium before passing out on the sofa; and an equally creepy Welsh engineer, whose nose sweated when he caught sight of Kate.)

Sam, on the other hand, who often longed for adult male companionship, displayed another form of family loyalty by asking Julian to watch him do a new skateboard trick on the terrace outside. Julian responded with alacrity, of course – which left Kate and Bella together in the kitchen. 'He seems terribly nice, your friend Adam,' said Bella, after everyone else had departed.

'He is,' said Kate. 'He's lovely.'

Bella was too tactful – or astute – to ask any more questions; but the silence that fell between them was not uncomfortable. 'And Rose . . .' said Bella, eventually, 'she seems like a sweet little girl, and pretty, as well – those great big grey eyes in that perfect heart-shaped face.'

'Like her mother.'

'You know Rose's mother?'

'No, actually, we've never met, but she's an actress and I've seen her on the television occasionally – that dodgy series set in a football club. She plays one of the footballer's wives.'

'Rose mentioned something about her mother living in Manchester for a few months. Did she and Adam separate a long time ago?'

'I don't think so, but I'm not quite sure – he's a rather silent man.'

'Oh, I know all about those,' said Bella, smiling.

'And how is Charles? Is he coming back here today?'

'I believe so . . . though he's getting even more silent these days. But I've never minded that – I find it rather restful, actually. Imagine living with someone who talked all the time.'

'Like Julian,' said Kate, and then stopped, blushing for the second time that morning.

'Poor Julian – I'm not sure he's having a very happy time with Jessica at the moment . . .'

Kate said nothing, much as she longed to find out more; and as Bella started peeling potatoes for lunch, Kate was reminded how often they had been together, like this, neither asking nor answering their unvoiced questions; yet surely aware of them, all the same. Was that how it had been with her mother and Bella? Side by side, yet distant? Kate knew that both of them were sent to boarding school at the age of eleven, separated into different classes and dormitories ('They'd needed to be shaken up,' her grandmother had remarked, once, in passing). Afterwards they'd gone on to Cambridge, but to different colleges and different subjects (Judith had studied English, Bella, history); and then came Charles. Had their reticence with each other extended to him, as well?

'Who met Charles first?' said Kate. 'Was it you, or my mother?'

'Gosh, that was a long time ago. What makes you want to know now?'

'No reason in particular – I was just thinking about her.'

'I seem to remember Judith befriended him at a garden party at the end of our first year. She was rather taken with him.'

'But then you came along?'

'Yes, I suppose I did, but not until our second year.'

'Did Mum mind?'

'Mind what?'

'Mind that you and Charles were together?'

'Not particularly. I think she'd already become involved with your father by then, or maybe that was a little later.'

'What was she like then? I was trying to remember a time when she seemed happy, but there was always something sad about her.' As Kate spoke, the memory of her mother's smile flashed by, and was gone again; and she wondered whether she was mistaken.

'I'm not entirely sure,' said Bella, and Kate tried to concentrate on her words, fearing she had already missed something. 'Judith had a streak of melancholy, it's true, but it was hard to tell, sometimes, what she was thinking. People always assumed that we were close – each other's other half – but it was more complicated than that. The darker she became, the lighter I tried to be – to compensate, maybe, so that we balanced each other out. And maybe she did the same.'

'So that the happier you seemed, the more unhappy she was?'

'Perhaps . . .' Bella shook her head, a small, impatient movement, as if to clear the conversation away, but for once she did not change the subject. 'The strange thing is, Jessica sometimes reminds me a little of Judith . . . But maybe I'm imagining things. With Charles in Cambridge so much these days, I end up spending inordinate amounts of time talking to myself. Not out loud, I hasten to add. Just sort of meandering around . . . I'm probably turning into a batty old lady.'

Kate was touched, yet also taken aback: Bella had never seemed anything other than eminently sane to her – entirely capable, practical, though without Kate's grandmother's brusqueness. To her family, Bella was cast in the role of sweet-natured domestic angel; but there was no reason why angels should not have moments of doubt.

'Easter should be such a hopeful time of year, shouldn't it?' said Bella.

'Should be – but sometimes it feels so sad, like nothing ever changes. Pete left me on an Easter weekend, you know? We'd gone to Wales for a few days, with Sam, on holiday. On the Saturday evening Sam was asleep, in this not very nice rented cottage – I'm not quite sure why we'd ended up there, it was horribly damp – and Pete and I had just got into bed, and he was staring up at the ceiling, I thought he was looking at the mildew, and then he told me he wanted a divorce. "Is there anyone else?" I said. "Yes," he said, and I felt like I couldn't breathe, like I'd swallowed a stone. But I didn't say anything, just waited to hear what was coming next. She was nothing to do with it, he said, the someone else – he loved her, but that wasn't why he was leaving me. He just didn't love me any more. "What about Sam?" I said, and I started crying and crying. I couldn't stop, which really irritated him, so he went and slept on the sofa downstairs.

'The next morning I woke up really early – earlier than Sam, even – and I got dressed very quietly and went for a walk. It was a beautiful morning – mild sunshine, like today, when you're hoping that winter might finally be over – but that didn't help. Anyway, I ended up in a little church, just outside the village – very ancient, built on the site of a Celtic burial ground, apparently. It was very simple – nothing grand inside, just a painted blue ceiling, I remember that, like a sky held up by the wooden rafters. Anyway, it was empty – far too early for the Easter service, but someone had already filled the nave with flowers. So I sat down in a pew and started praying.'

'To whom?'

'Anybody – everybody – God, my mother – I needed a streak of magic, a sign that someone was listening. I didn't close my eyes; I just stared at the stained-glass window above the altar, and there was a shaft of sunlight coming through – but it didn't seem like the sign I was looking for. I wanted a unicorn to come crashing through the glass . . .'

'So what happened next?'

'Nothing, really. I suppose I felt a bit better – I thought of all those people who had sat in the church before me, for hundreds and hundreds of years, praying for help in their troubles. And even though God hadn't talked to me, at least I knew that I wasn't alone, because everyone suffers, don't they? So I walked back to the cottage and made breakfast for Sam, and then Pete woke up a couple of hours later and we drove back to London in silence. No miracles there – he moved out the next day, Easter Monday. It was raining again by then, and when Pete drove away Sam put his head back and howled, like a dog. I'd never heard him make a noise like that before.'

'But you've both survived, haven't you?'

'Yes, we have – we're OK, me and Sam. But not born again . . .'

'I wouldn't expect divorce to bring about the finding of God.'

'I didn't mean that, exactly. But you hear people talking about divorce, and bereavement, as marking the start of a new life – a new beginning. But it never seemed like that to me. The old life always hung around. I couldn't just lose it.'

'Very few people can,' said Bella, 'even those that say they're rid of the past.' She shook her head, again, more firmly this time. 'Anyway, darling, I really must get a move on. Now, what do you think about lunch – mashed potatoes with the chicken, or would the children prefer roast? Time waits for no man, whatever my husband says.' As Bella turned her attention to the cooking, Kate found herself thinking again about her mother and how time had not waited for her. She wanted to say something to Bella, tried to frame the words in her head, but could not speak them, could not ask whether there was a moment – no, not even as long as that, a few seconds would have done – when the past caught up with the present, and Bella might have reached out to Judith, warned her of what was to come? Weren't twins supposed to sense when danger threatened the other? Or if not Bella, then someone – Kate, anyone – should have known, or should have guessed, that Judith was at risk on the last night of her life. 'Slow down' – those were the words Kate could have said to her mother before she drove into the dark (two words, such little ones, they'd take no time to say); but why did time move on, relentlessly, when we most needed it to hesitate?

Nineteen

In the end, Jessica did not arrive at Elverson – 'she's got one of her migraines,' said Julian, sounding genuinely concerned. And Adam, too, seemed preoccupied, after a long conversation on the mobile phone conducted out of earshot in the garden: with Clare, presumed Kate, though he said nothing. Bella, as ever, kept the day cheerful – setting up a treasure hunt for all the children, with handwritten clues that led them to a little chest of chocolate coins, hidden in the orchard. Even so, Julian left before dinner, looking downcast, though still playing the perfect father (a favourite role of his, which infuriated Kate). And Adam left the table soon after dinner, having made several fruitless attempts to settle Rose, who seemed unable to fall asleep this evening unless he stayed beside her. He was still there, sleeping himself, on the edge of the narrow single bed, when Kate looked in on them later; and though she lay awake, wishing and wishing that Adam would come to her room, if only for a moment, if only for a word, he did not appear.

How precious happiness was, she thought, and how fragile, how easily broken. One step in the wrong direction, one stroke of bad luck, one single error or lapse of concentration, and everything came crashing down. Why hope that joy would last for a lifetime? But how hard it was to stop hoping. A few days after Pete had left her, she had taken Sam to an old-fashioned steam fair that came to their local park every springtime, and they had ridden on the roundabout together, Sam in front, she behind him holding on for them both, wooden horses rising and falling, turning in circles and going nowhere. He'd wanted to stay on for another ride, and another one, but she was feeling dizzy and persuaded him off, and while they were deciding what to do next, she had put some money into a fortune-telling slot machine. When the coin dropped, a piece of card emerged in the jerky, painted hand of a wooden gypsy, promising her good fortune. Kate kept the card still, propped up on the mantelpiece in her bedroom beside a photograph of her mother, laughing, and a circle of cowries, collected on beaches over the years – her talismans of good luck. ('Interesting events are due to occur in your life during the next few months,' said the fortune card. 'Among them are to be found a marriage, a christening, a birthday celebration and a silver wedding anniversary. Truly a charmed list of happenings to which you may look forward. You are about to enjoy life as you have never enjoyed it before . . .')

Kate – wanting to believe in the magic of the prediction – did sometimes wonder if it were true: not that there was much in the way of charmed marriages or wedding anniversaries in her life, but even so, she was beginning to find pleasure in the smallest of things, given that the big stuff was a disaster. Or maybe the little bits and pieces of happiness were all that mattered. It was those that kept a life on course: moments of pure joy that weaved her messed-up world together. The day after the fair was Sam's second birthday – Pete was in New York, by then, photographing his new girlfriend for a *Vogue* fashion shoot – and although Kate knew that her marriage had been a failure, and her chest ached and her throat was raw, and it seemed as if the grey sky outside would never clear, she could not help but be filled with hope as Sam blew out the two candles on his birthday cake. 'Make a wish, sweetheart,' she'd said to him, not sure if he would understand. 'Make a special wish, but don't tell me what it is – it's your secret, just for you.'

It was on that night, gazing at the first star in the sky, the evening star that she sometimes half believed to be her mother, when Kate made a promise to herself that she would not repeat Judith's mistakes. Except it was more complicated than that, because in her mind Judith then was not Judith now. Her dead mother – the mother in the star; or beyond it, maybe, scattered like stardust throughout the night sky – was a more magical spirit than Kate's remembered, past-tense mother, that breakable being, the cracked doll who had wept real tears. Neither mother, though, seemed made of flesh and blood . . . which left Kate feeling insubstantial, almost imaginary herself. Sometimes, when she wrote the words to accompany the pictures on the pages of a glossy magazine, those two-dimensional shiny women seemed more real than she did, living in their world on the other side of the mirror, the looking-glass world where nobody wept.

Now Kate was reminded of that uncertainty again; not consuming her, as it once had done, but nibbling at the edges of her heart. On Easter Sunday she went to church with Bella and Charles in the morning, leaving Adam at home with Rose and Sam. Somehow – and this was unplanned – Kate found herself sitting between her uncle and aunt, and although there was a kind of natural order in this – the two ballasts of her childhood on either side of her still – she had felt uncomfortable, unable to concentrate on the vicar's sermon about resurrection and renewal. Back at Elverson, after the children had scattered around the garden in an Easter-egg hunt (chocolate and God, irrevocably linked), she found herself trying to ask Charles about his faith: if he had any, that is. 'I don't understand physics,' she said tentatively. 'I'm illiterate that way, I'm afraid.'

'Don't be afraid,' he said.

'But doesn't life simply prove itself to be chaotic – lacking in any order or pattern?'

'If God's not dead, He deserves to be, you mean?'

'Not that, exactly, but yes, I can understand if something terrible happened – the death of your child, say – you would feel that way. But the stars, as well – I want to believe in a perfectly balanced universe, like you do, at least I think you do, where accidents are part of the grand design – but surely the stars don't always do what we expect them to? They explode and collide and turn into black holes, there are accidents and meteorites and . . . and nothingness.'

'There is a beauty – a poetry – in the equations that govern the universe,' he said and then paused, drawing breath as if to start talking again, but then stopping, dropping back into silence, and she knew he did not have the simple language to say to her what he wanted to say – or what he felt to be true.

'I wish I could believe in magic,' she said.

'Physics is not magic, even if it sometimes looks that way. It is mathematical, logical, even if it seems impossible to comprehend.'

'And God?'

'God only knows . . . I don't.'

Afterwards, as they walked back into the house together for lunch, Charles rested a hand on her shoulders, briefly, like a benediction. She remembered how as a child she had longed to be singled out by him for praise; to feel his steady gaze upon her face. She had struggled hard with maths at school, trying, on his account, to understand numbers – the meaning of them, even when they seemed meaningless. The only time they made any sort of sense was when her father told her that Pythagoras – whose theorem tormented her – believed that numbers had special, mystical significance: ten, for example, being perfect, as the sum of the first four whole numbers. But she had never progressed far: the figures eluding her, as written words did in her dreams. (And still she could not read in her dreams – the letters dissolved on the page, like water, or turned themselves inside out, as if seen in a mirror; but worse were the numbers in her nightmares – unable to comprehend them on a phone pad, her mind could not see the figures and tell her fingers what to do, she could not even dial a simple 999 . . .)

At lunch they ate roast lamb, with early spring vegetables from the garden. 'Is this the lamb of God?' asked Sam. 'At school last week we read a book about Jesus being a shepherd. So why are we eating his lambs?'

'Jesus wasn't a sheep, stupid,' said Rose. 'He was just an ordinary man.'

'No, he wasn't,' said Sam, 'he's the Holy Ghost.'

'My dad says there's no such thing as ghosts.'

Adam looked down at his plate, and Kate felt a flash of annoyance. Who did he think he was, to stay silent at the table? Was making conversation beneath him? The passion she had felt for him yesterday seemed compromising now, almost distasteful. He was just another arrogant, difficult man; worse than Julian, even, with a false veneer of humility. She tried to avoid looking at Adam for the rest of the meal, appalled that she had believed herself to be falling in love with him (appalled, too, that if she caught his eye, the warmth returned, unwelcome now). But in the murmur of other voices around the table – Bella, soothing, drawing Sam and Rose together in harmony; Charles, telling Adam about the architectural history of the house – Kate heard her mother's voice, which had been quiet for so long. 'Now, now,' she whispered, 'don't be hasty on my behalf. It's the mention of ghosts that made you so cross, isn't it?'

'Roasts, ghosts,' spelt out a hand in Kate's head, unsteadily, in the writing that might have been hers as a child.

'Approach, encroach, reproach,' wrote her phantom mother. 'As for the Holy Trinity – well, I've never regarded three as a lucky number. You'll understand why . . .'

Kate chewed the inside of her lip, almost certain that she was making these riddles up in her head, a distraction from the more immediate problems at the table. 'Helpful as ever,' she said, not realizing she was speaking aloud.

'What was that, darling?' said Bella. 'Can I help you to some more roast lamb?'

Twenty

Kate was still confused about what, exactly, she felt for Adam when he drove them back to London on Sunday evening. The children were asleep in the back within a few miles of leaving Elverson, which meant she did not have to lower her voice when she told him about her mother's death as they approached the place where Judith had crashed. 'This is where her car came off the road,' she said, pointing out the oak tree that had become Kate's signpost for the accident.

'It must have been terrible for you,' said Adam, slowing down, 'not having a chance to say goodbye.'

'It seemed impossible – as if she had just disappeared off the face of the earth. I never saw her body – it was too smashed up, my uncle said. But it might have been better if I had, because then I'd know she was really dead, instead of this vanishing act. I still sometimes think I've seen her again – turning the corner on the other side of a street, or disappearing into a tube train as the doors close in front of me. There's a place on the Circle Line between Baker Street and Great Portland Street where the trains pass in the tunnel, going in the opposite direction to each other, and you can glimpse into the lighted carriages, the ones that are travelling the other way – and I'm always looking out for her. That's where she used to catch the tube, at either one of those stations, up the road from our old flat . . .' They'd passed the oak tree by then, but Kate imagined her mother sheltering behind it like a child playing hide-and-seek, coming out only when they were gone, watching the car disappear into the distance (and would Judith be frightened, then, all alone in the shadows, wishing she had been found?).

'I've occasionally imagined my parents dead,' said Adam, 'which is an awful thing to admit, as an adult, and entirely undeserved on their part. But I'm sure the reality of their deaths would be appalling – and the guilt.'

'That's the thing – the dead aren't really dead to us.'

'Like the living . . . even when we wish they were.'

'By which you mean?'

'OK – another awful admission – I felt today that it would have been better if my wife had died, rather than left me.'

'What brought that on?' said Kate, her stomach churning, looking at him while he kept his eyes on the road.

'Clare found out that I was with you this weekend and announced that she wanted Rose to live with her in Manchester.'

'But is Clare going to stay in Manchester for good? I thought she was just filming there?'

'She doesn't know where she'll be working in three months' time – it was just a way of getting at me.'

'But she can't mind about me? I mean, what is there to mind about? For all she knows, we're just friends.'

'I told her . . .'

'Told her what?'

'That I care about you.'

'Well, that's not such a big deal, is it?'

'Isn't it?'

'I thought she was having an affair with her leading man, anyway.'

'He's talking about going back to his wife.'

'So presumably your wife wants you back, as well.'

'Maybe.'

'How very predictable . . .'

'Is it?'

'Can you please stop saying, "is it?" and "isn't it?"? Yes, it is predictable. But anyway, how does this fit in with Rose going to Manchester? Are you all going to move up there together?'

'No, I don't think so. But Clare's coming back to London for a few days next week, so we can try and sort things out.'

Kate stared out of the window, at the wildwood. If it wasn't for Sam, she wished she could make Adam stop the car, stop everything, so that she could get out and slip into the dark. 'Sort things out' he'd said. What the hell was that supposed to mean? 'I don't quite understand what you're trying to tell me, Adam,' she said, when the silence between them became oppressive. 'That you care about me but you might resolve your marital problems next week?'

'I don't know what's going to happen. I don't know what to think. It's just a mess—'

'Well, I don't want to be involved in someone else's messy marriage, OK? I've been through my own, and that's enough for a lifetime. I knew it – I *knew* it, I should never have got involved with you.'

'I'm sorry,' he said, eyes still fixed on the road. She wanted to scream, to shake him, scratch his face, anything other than sitting quietly, pretending to be calm. But there was no escape; just say nothing, don't cry, there's a good girl, we're nearly home.

Twenty-One

Monday morning. Jesus had risen, but Kate just wanted to stay in bed. How was she going to get through today? (And the rest of her life – but no, don't do it, don't think about that.) After eating breakfast with Sam, she'd started sifting through the piles of paper on her desk, trying to find a red bill she'd forgotten to pay last week and her new chequebook that had arrived in the post not long ago. Both seemed to have mysteriously disappeared – lost, swallowed with the other vanished things. 'I am a loser,' she said to herself, scrabbling through the paper chaos, wishing she could shred it instead, hamster-like, and curl up to sleep in a ball. 'No cheque book, no tax return, no filing system, no husband, no mother . . .' She imagined ringing Charles and demanding that he come and inspect her study, so that he might see his theories of inherent cosmic harmony disproved.

Just as she was about to dump every single bit of clutter from her desk to the floor, the telephone rang. 'Kate?' said Julian.

'Yes,' she said.

'Are you going to be around later? I thought I might pop in.'

'Pop in? You live over a hundred miles away.'

'Well, I'm dropping the kids round to Isabel's at lunch – she's taking them to see a baby ballet at Sadler's Wells, or something, as a treat. And you're just round the corner.'

'Why didn't you mention this on Saturday?'

'I'm sorry – I just forgot.' He sounded so unlike his usual bumptious self that she began to feel concerned.

'Are you OK?'

'Could be better. Jessica's still prostrate with a migraine – we were supposed to be going out together today when Isabel had the kids.'

'So I'm a last-minute substitute. Thanks a lot.'

'Don't be like that. I'd love to see you – I can't think of anyone I'd rather be with than you – you're a blessing in disguise.'

'Disguised as what?' she said. 'Your grumpy cousin?'

'Kate—'

'OK, OK,' she said, cutting him off. 'Pete's supposed to be taking Sam out today, but don't count on it.'

'I'd be very happy to see Sam, as well, you know I would.'

'Fine.'

Unusually, Pete did arrive on time, with Easter eggs for Sam and a huge bunch of daffodils for Kate. He was tanned, as usual, but looked older than she remembered – more wrinkled than before, and sagging, slightly, like worn leather, from too much tropical sun. What on earth had they been thinking of, she wondered, having a child together? But they'd just been babies themselves – though you'd think they'd have both known better, at twenty-six, than to choose such mutually unsuitable partners. Not that they'd properly chosen – she'd simply got pregnant, by accident, five months after they'd met. ('Accidentally on purpose?' Isabel had asked at the time, but it was nobody's fault. 'Just a cock-up,' Kate had replied, with a smile; but Isabel said she did not believe in random events, and though Kate did not agree out loud, she half believed her.)

So they'd married in a flurry when she was six months' pregnant – a quiet registry-office wedding, she in an off-white linen dress, crumpled before the ceremony had ended; not the one in the Elverson church she'd imagined as a child, not the man she'd imagined, either – and then along came Sam, and a week after his birth Pete had departed for a fortnight to work in Los Angeles, and thereafter seemed nonplussed by his new role as a husband and father. She'd tried to make believe in Pete – wishing away his absences; but even when he came home, he seemed not to be there, impassive, empty-headed, perhaps, though she'd told herself he simply had his mind on other things; and, as it turned out, he did. (Maisy, wasn't that her name? Or was it Maeve? Kate couldn't quite recall which girl had been the first.)

But for all Pete's shortcomings, she could never wish away Sam. And Pete did love Sam, in his own way; and Sam loved his father. 'We're going to have a boys' day out,' Pete had said this morning. 'Skateboarding, burgers and the flicks. I'll have him back at nine-ish, OK?' And despite her doubts, she had to trust him (this almost-stranger, for all that they shared) that he would return their son safely tonight. 'Take care of him,' she said to Pete, as she waved goodbye to Sam.

'I will,' he said. 'I always do.'

So there it was – against the odds – an afternoon alone with Julian; the first they'd spent in how many years? She tried to dismiss the thought that there might be a price to pay for this encounter – an unknown, unseen calculation involving Sam's absence – but the uneasiness remained as she kissed Julian on the cheek when he arrived at her front door, just after Pete had gone.

'No Sam?' said Julian.

'No, his father made an uncharacteristically prompt appearance today,' she said. 'Can you remember the last time we did this?'

'I'm not sure,' he said. 'Is this a trick question?'

'Don't be silly. I just wondered when we'd had a day out together, without the kids or relatives and stuff.'

'There's always stuff that gets in the way, isn't there?' he said. 'Emotional baggage.'

'Babbage's baggage.'

'What?'

'Don't you remember that old picture your father had in his study of Mr Babbage, the famous Cambridge mathematician? Isabel made up a rhyme about him when we were little – "Babbage's baggage". He trailed lots of baggage . . . ate lots of cabbage – it was just a private joke.'

'I don't remember,' he said, 'not that that means anything – Jessica always says my memory appals her. But shall we leave our baggage behind today? Just go out, without having to carry it all – make up for lost time?'

'That's fine by me. Where do you want to go, then?'

They ended up, by mutual consent, at Regent's Park, walking through the rose garden towards the lake, with bread to feed the ducks, just like they'd done as children on the rare occasions Bella had made the trip to London. 'I always thought you were so glamorous, living near here, right in the middle of London,' said Julian.

' "*Were* glamorous"? And aren't I stylish now, ensconced in Crouch End?'

'Tremendously so,' he said, 'as ever.'

It was easy, she realized, to be happy with him when they steered the conversation away from difficult subjects (his marriage; her love life; what might or might not have happened in the past). It was like a holiday from the real world; or maybe this was just as real, this living in the present – not immersed in memory, or anticipating tomorrow. Perhaps this was what he meant by making up for lost time: not a catching up, just a kind of floating, free from counting hours and weighing words.

At the far end of the lake there was a little bridge to an island. The gate that led to it was usually locked, but today it stood ajar and they crossed over the water to the island, closing the gate behind them. 'There,' he said, taking her hands in his, stroking her fingers, 'we're king and queen of our own country. Never forget that.' Kate smiled at him as he spoke, but afterwards, she felt impatient, wanting to be away from him. Freedom: weightless and wordless, that was what she wished for herself; that was the place – the ungoverned island – she longed to be.

Twenty-Two

In the days that followed, Adam did not ring, and she forced herself not to call him – except once, in a weak moment, and a woman answered the phone. 'Adam's not here,' said the woman – the wife, it had to be. 'Do you want to leave a message?' 'No, I'll call back,' said Kate, vowing that she would not.

Instead, she rang everyone else she could think of for advice and distraction. Harriet recommended shopping: not Budgens, but Bond Street, which was out of the question, given Kate's current financial crisis. (She didn't know what she was spending her money on – surely nothing extravagant, just the usual stuff: orange juice and peanut butter, the endless loaves of bread – but cash seemed to slip through her fingers, disappearing into nothing; and anyway, why buy a new dress, without Adam to see it; why bother, really, with the pretence of everything?) Isabel suggested therapy, again, having reminded Kate of her announcement last week that she hated Adam, in contrast to this week's statement that he was the only man for her. Maria also repeated her earlier advice – her only advice, actually, regarding all matters of the heart – to have an uncomplicated affair with a married man. But the only married man that Kate could imagine having an affair with was Julian – which should of course be unimaginable, and therefore grounds for therapy; and there was no way that she was going to discuss this embarrassing business with a stranger.

Her father wasn't much help, either; he was preoccupied with a new, surprising plan to become a rabbi. 'But you don't believe in God,' said Kate, when her father asked if she might loan him £10,000 for rabbinical college.

'Of course I don't – I mean, you'd have to be insane to see divinity in the blighted world we live in – but that's not the point. I've decided I need some kind of structure in my life.'

'And have you been accepted to study at the college?'

'No, not yet – but I shall keep working at it.'

He sounded disappointed when she explained she did not have £10,000 to hand right now; and was not mollified by her promise to give it to him should she win the lottery. She did not, in fact, do the lottery, but perhaps now was the moment to start.

'You choose the numbers,' she told Sam, on their way to the corner shop after school.

'One, two, three, four, five, six,' he said.

'I don't think those numbers are going to come up, sweetheart.'

'Why not?'

'It doesn't seem to work like that.'

But maybe Sam was right – God's maths was unpredictable, incomprehensible – so why not go for this simple approach, a kind of counter-bluff? They bought the ticket, having marked his numbers, and as they were walking home, Sam planned how to spend his winnings ('a big house, big enough for you and Dad and all my friends to live in, with a skate-park at the back, and a swimming pool.'). Despite herself, Kate was caught up in his enthusiasm – believing in him, and in his simple magic; so much so that she could hardly bring herself to check the lottery results later that evening, not wanting the spell to break.

In the end, she had to tell him: they had not won; not a single one of his numbers was picked. 'Why not?' said Sam, incredulous at their loss. 'We're meant to win, I'm sure we did – someone must have made a mistake.'

'I don't think so,' said Kate. 'I think that's just the way it is.'

'Well, it's not good enough,' said Sam. 'Is it? Is it, Mum? Mum, why don't you answer me?'

Twenty-Three

Sam's eighth birthday was ten days after Easter Sunday this year, which caused him a certain amount of confusion. 'Why is my birthday – like Jesus's birthday – on the same date every year?' he asked. 'But the day Jesus died is different every year? Why's that, Mum? It doesn't seem very well organized to me.'

'It's something to do with the calendar,' said Kate, vaguely, muffled by a mouthful of toast.

'The thing you drain the spaghetti with?'

'No – the thing we have on the wall that tells us the days and the months in the year.'

'I know that – we learnt it at school. "Thirty days hath September, April, June and November. All the rest have thirty-one, except for February alone, which has twenty-eight days clear, and twenty-nine in each leap year." Is that why Easter leaps forward?'

'Well, sometimes it goes back. Last year we had an early Easter.'

'Like when the clocks go back?'

'Actually, the clocks go forward in the spring. Remember, we changed them a couple of weeks ago?'

'So why does Easter go back, when the clocks go forward?'

'Oh Sam – I don't know, I'm afraid. Maybe you should ask Charles next time we see him.'

'When are we going to see him?'

'I'm not sure.'

'You don't seem to know anything very much today. You do know it's my birthday tomorrow, don't you?'

'Of course I do,' she said.

He woke at dawn the next day and came running into her bedroom, bright-eyed, full of hope and certainty, his trust in her restored. He'd asked for – and received – a PlayStation: a joint present from her and Pete in a rare act of parental togetherness. Actually, Pete had paid for it, but she had wrapped it the night before, along with some other presents she'd bought (a skateboard t-shirt, Bart Simpson chocolates and the latest in a series of his favourite gruesome detective stories). Sam opened his cards first, sweetly, slowly, including one from Sebastian – a print of a medieval world map, the *mappamundi* in Hereford Cathedral (and Kate was reminded that her father loved old maps – the more misleading, the better – and this was one of his favourites, despite the figure of Christ that sat above the earth). 'An old map for you to examine with new eyes, now you are ten,' Sebastian had written inside, enclosing a ten-pound note. 'If you look carefully, you will see an angel on the left telling the blessed to "Arise, and come to everlasting joy," while on the right the lost sinners are being led away with the command, "Rise and depart to hell-fire prepared." Enjoy your birthday, your own day of judgement, my darling grandson, for you shall grow to see more clearly than the rest of us.'

'I'm eight, not ten,' said Sam, having read the card and looking faintly perplexed, 'but it doesn't matter. It was really nice of Grandad to send me the money.' He opened his presents then, very carefully, examining each with pleasure, his sureness that the world was all his today unshaken. It was a school morning, unfortunately, so he had to leave before the PlayStation was set up – but she promised it would be ready for him when he came home with his three best friends.

That was the theory, anyway, but the instruction manual defeated her. Presumably Sam would be able to do it himself – he knew how to work the video, for example, unlike Kate – but what if he couldn't? Pete's mobile was switched off – he was away again, and not back until the weekend – and Kate could not think of a single neighbour who might be able to help. Unless she rang Adam . . . It was an innocent enough request, wasn't it?

'I was going to call you,' he said, when he answered his mobile. 'How are you?'

'Fine – apart from the fact that I don't seem to be able to sort out Sam's new PlayStation, and it's his birthday today. I was just wondering—'

'Of course – I can fix that up for you at lunchtime. I'm working around the corner from you this morning.'

It took him five minutes to get the machine running – but he stayed a little longer, lingering in the hall. Kate had been prepared to stick with her new approach – the non-combative, smooth-surfaced one that had worked so successfully with Julian last week; the looking-glass way, perhaps – but Adam seemed to want to talk about Clare; to explain himself. She was back in Manchester, he said, having left after Rose's birthday at the weekend, but things were still 'unclear' between them. (For a second Kate imagined the two of them, Clare and Adam, standing facing each other, divided by a misted, smeared screen of glass; while she, the uncomfortable third, hovered to one side.)

'The trouble is, I think I'm already half in love with you,' he said as he was leaving, as if this would make everything clear.

'How very half-hearted,' she said, and closed the front door. ('Half in love': what was that supposed to mean? Which half? The half that didn't love his wife, or the half of Kate he liked?)

Aside from this uncomfortable conversation, the rest of Sam's birthday ran smoothly: he and his friends were delighted with the PlayStation, and then she took them skateboarding in the park, in the April sunshine, yesterday's showers gone, and no one fell off or grazed a knee, and afterwards they ate takeaway pizza and Sam blew out the candles on his cake, all at once, and nobody cried.

Later that evening, when Maria came round to collect Robbie, she stayed for a drink, and then another, apparently reluctant to leave. Kate didn't mind: it was nice having her there, while the boys watched cartoons in the other room, so they opened a second bottle of wine, and all of a sudden, midway through a meandering conversation about whether or not they should book in for a pedicure at the new beauty salon on the Broadway ('The thing is,' Kate was saying, 'my toes are looking hairy, like a gorilla's, so I'd have to have them waxed'), Maria confessed to an affair with her college lecturer; a confession unasked for, but she was longing to tell. 'He even loves my feet,' she said, 'and he's gorgeous – his name's Stephen – the Irish one I told you about—'

'The married one?'

'They're all married, Kate – all normal men of our age are married. Anyway, it's fabulous—'

'I thought you were looking unusually cheerful – I should have guessed, with that lovely glow on your face.'

'So you don't disapprove?'

'What would be the point of that? But do be careful, Maria. Don't let it end in tears . . .'

Maria, of course, was too elated to imagine any ending at all; and perhaps this was why Kate found herself recounting a story about Judith – and also because Maria's confession seemed to demand another in return, so that matters were more even between them. Kate did not go into detail – she had no detail to tell – but simply said that she had been wondering if her mother had had an affair with her twin sister's husband.

'What makes you think that?' said Maria, looking surprisingly shocked (which was the reaction Kate wanted, if she was honest with herself; not that honesty was necessarily her prime motive in telling what might have been a cautionary tale).

'I don't know,' said Kate. 'It's just this time I keep remembering, before my parents split up. My father was saying to my mother, "What were you doing with him in the water?" Over and over again, he kept saying it.'

'But that doesn't prove anything.'

'I know, but I also remember – or I think I do, though it could have been a dream, or a memory that got mixed up with a dream – my mother being in the water with my uncle.'

'What water?'

'I don't know – just water – but I had this burning feeling of shame, that they shouldn't be together there.'

'Have you ever told anyone about this?'

'No, never. You're the first. I've never thought it through before – but maybe I'm just imagining it all.'

Afterwards, when Maria and Robbie had gone and Sam was in bed, she worried about her confession. The image of Judith and Charles together – where on earth had that come from so suddenly? She had told Maria it might have been a memory – but if it was, she had never remembered it before; not until tonight when Maria had started talking about her own affair. And anyway, why had she told Maria about Judith's possible – impossible – infidelity, instead of confessing to her own with Adam? Blaming the mother for the sins of the child – wasn't that the phrase? But there was something else that was bothering her, too, something that Pete had mentioned to her on the phone earlier this evening when he rang to wish Sam happy birthday. He'd got hundreds of pictures of Sam, he said, taken on his new digital camera, and was going to go through them all, before sending copies of the best to Kate. 'The thing is,' he'd said, 'I've been thinking about getting rid of most of the digital photos – it's pointless storing them indefinitely – but you never know, you can take a picture that doesn't seem important at the time, and then it's only later, in retrospect, that you see it was the one picture – the only one – that had the crucial detail in it, the one that everybody was looking for later.'

'Like what?' she'd said, confused.

'Like that single frame of Bill Clinton kissing Monica Lewinsky. There was only one photographer who'd kept all his pictures from that day – the others dumped most of them because the President was just moving down a line of nobodies. But the photographer that hung on to his pictures – well, he got the magic one that everyone was searching for a year or so afterwards, of Clinton hugging Monica as she stood in line with all the rest of the onlookers. He's rich now, that guy – lucky bastard. But he was smart – he got the story . . .'

Was it the anecdote that had prompted Kate's memory, she wondered? Not her father's reference to seeing clearly, to judging and being judged – nothing as overt as the medieval map that he'd chosen to serve as Sam's birthday card – but this smaller nudge towards the detail that seemed not to matter at the time; the thing that no one else noticed. Charles and Judith together in the water. What were they doing in the water?

She wanted to sleep – it was too late to be thinking about this now, too late tonight, too late forever. But when she closed her eyes in bed all she could see was her mother – shadowy, in the dark, in the water, and a tall man standing over her – was it Charles? And her mother's arms were around his neck, dripping water, silvery water, running down her pale arms, like starlight, and they were kissing each other, in the water. And then she heard her father's voice. 'I'll kill you,' he hissed in the darkness. 'You're killing me, you're driving me crazy. You sit and pass judgement on me, but what about you, you bitch? What were you doing in the water? WHAT WERE YOU DOING WITH HIM IN THE WATER?'

She couldn't breathe, Kate couldn't breathe, her heart was muffled, her face was hidden, she was drowning in this, she was drowning in the water . . .

Twenty-Four

So she did it, she went to the therapist Isabel had recommended. The therapist was called Eve, a name which seemed to Kate to signify a neat beginning, a good omen for a fresh start. (She decided to forget, for now, Adam's similarly biblical name.) Eve lived in a big house not far from Kate's: at least, Kate presumed she lived there, unless she simply had a consulting room in someone else's home. It seemed ridiculous not to ask – but of course that was against the rules of psychoanalysis; Kate knew this, having tried – and failed – to have therapy once before (at university, after her mother had died: too hateful an encounter to contemplate today; awful, like a visit to a gynaecologist). As Eve led her into a room at the back of the house, on the first floor, with a view of the big radio mast at Alexandra Palace, Kate thought how much easier it would be if the ensuing conversation could somehow take place without either of them being present (through sound waves, or something; there must be something like that, something zippy and new, not the telephone). But she was here, and Eve – quizzical grey eyes, ash-silver hair, her mother's age, perhaps –

was waiting. (Her mother's age, if only she had lived; what made her think of that? Should she tell Eve? No, too obvious.) She told her instead about Judith and Charles, about the water – the thing that she hadn't remembered until now. 'But maybe I just made it up?' she said. 'Wouldn't that be terrible?' Eve did not reply, and Kate could not see her face because she was lying on a couch, staring up at the ceiling. They were quite annoying, these silences in therapy, from the unseen therapist. It reminded Kate of her dead mother, again: silent, but present in the room. She told the therapist this – it seemed unavoidable.

'I remind you of your mother's ghost?' said Eve.

'That's what I just said,' said Kate, irritably. 'I know that's the point – transference, isn't it? But I've already got one silent woman in my life.'

'I thought you said you heard your mother's voice at times?'

'I do, but sometimes she goes quiet on me. And she rarely says anything helpful at all.'

Eve said nothing. Kate's neck was beginning to ache – the couch wasn't quite long enough (did Eve only cater for short people, or was the discomfort designed to keep clients alert?) and her head was hurting, in this room heavy with other people's sadnesses, other turgid silences, unaired . . . 'I'm not saying it's definitely my mother's voice,' Kate said, after a long pause. 'I mean, I could be imagining it, couldn't I? Like the water.'

'Does it feel real to you?' said Eve.

'I don't know what feels real. Sometimes everything seems imaginary, doesn't it?'

'Does it?'

Kate was tempted to tell Eve that she found this repetitive echoing annoying, but she did not want to be rude to her therapist. Still, she cancelled her subsequent appointment and did not make a new one, even after Eve left two messages on her answer machine (something her mother never did, even though Kate almost expected her to – a crackly whisper, an imprint of a memory, a sound wave from the stars). So much for the new beginning, then.

It seemed wrong to feel like this in the spring, when everything else was growing and unfurling, the blossom like kisses; and she was . . . stuck. The past reached out to her, held her, not steadying, but leaden, deadening. And the future? She could not think beyond the end of each day. The quickening she had felt with Adam was over; now she was lumpen, and when she caught sight of herself in a mirror she was shocked – at the grey circles under her eyes, at the bagginess of her body. Nothing seemed to fit – neither her clothes nor her flesh; she was . . . what was the word her mother used to use? Discombobulated. Sometimes she felt dizzy, as if she had lost her sense of balance as well as everything else.

Still, Sam was there – and his presence righted her. She made him breakfast in the morning and sandwiches for his packed lunch; walked him to school, picked him up in the afternoon, cooked dinner for them both. She ensured that they had sufficient fresh air and clean clothes; she read to him every night, and tidied the house while he slept. Unlike him, she did not sleep well – waking every hour or so, listening out for the slightest of sounds. In the day she longed to lie down again, but forced herself to keep going. She managed to do some work – she had to, they needed the money – and wrote several very chirpy pieces about spring fashion. When the phone rang in the evening, she did not answer it. Sometimes she wrote down the messages on bits of paper, but forgot where they were.

Eventually, Harriet got hold of her. 'Hello, stranger,' she said, when Kate finally picked up the phone on a weekday lunchtime, fearing that it might be Sam's school to say that he was unwell.

'Oh, hello . . . Can I ring you back?'

'No – you never return my calls. What's wrong?'

'I don't know. I'm just feeling a bit low.'

'In what way, low?'

'Tired.'

'Well, why don't I come round and see you? Or we could go out together.'

'I haven't got a babysitter.'

'What, not ever?'

'Look, you needn't worry about me, I'm not depressed. Actually, I've just finished writing a piece about the pleasures of summer shift dresses.'

'That sounds like fun. Shall we go and buy some?'

'No – I've got a winter pot belly, which is *so* not a good look underneath sheer chiffon.' Kate tried to inject some jollity into her voice but without much success (she probably sounded demented, instead); which was why, she guessed, Harriet rounded up the rest of the family to ring her on subsequent evenings. Bella called several times, asking Kate and Sam for the weekend; Isabel left more messages; Julian sent an email ('Blue? Me Too. Love You.'). Even Paul rang, for the first time in almost a year, to invite her to Sunday lunch at his house in Wimbledon. 'Really?' Kate said, too tired to hide her surprise. 'I thought Becky didn't like me?'

'It's not you she doesn't like – she just finds my family a bit oppressive.'

'Well, it's not as if I'm your immediate family.'

'Of course, you are – you're far closer to them than I am.'

'I never think of it like that – I always imagine you as one big, happy family.'

'That's the fairy-tale version – the one my deluded mother propagates. We're just an averagely unhappy family, like everyone else.'

His voice was sufficiently sour for Kate to decide that a day with him and Becky might not be the most cheerful of prospects: a realization that was in itself cheering (she did not have to have lunch with them – hurrah!). She rang Harriet back, instead, and asked her to come round on Saturday night for a takeaway curry, and Harriet sweetly obliged, of course, arriving with two bottles of champagne, a box of chocolates and a new PlayStation game for Sam.

Around midnight, the two of them stretched out on the sofa together, head to toe like when they were children, Kate tried to explain herself, which was difficult, as they had finished both bottles of champagne and started on the brandy left over from last year's Christmas pudding. 'I'm stuck in a rut, I know,' said Kate, 'but, even so, everything seems unpredictable – completely random. It makes me feel unstable, literally, but you can't say that to anyone. If I said that, people would think I was mad.'

'The Uncertainty Principle,' said Harriet.

'The what?' said Kate. 'I don't think I'm uncertainly principled.'

'I don't mean that,' said Harriet. 'I meant the thing that made me give up physics when I was eighteen. Just when I thought I'd got to grips with it all – gravity, velocity, the classical laws that seem to make things run like clockwork – we had to learn about bloody quantum theory. It was that man's fault, you *know*, what's his name?' Kate did not know, but nodded, vaguely, wanting to seem companionable. 'Werner Heisenberg!' said Harriet, after a pause. 'He was to blame, wasn't he?' She seemed to be expecting some kind of response.

'Harriet,' said Kate, suppressing a hiccup, 'I'm afraid I don't know what you're talking about.'

'I'm not entirely sure that I do, either,' said Harriet, examining her recently pierced navel.

'So, go on, then. What about him?'

'Who?' said Harriet.

'Mr Heineken.'

'Oh, him. Well, he was this German physicist who decided that the act of observing alters the reality being observed. He had these terrible allergies, you see, so he went to an island to get away from the pollen, and that was when he had his big idea – the Uncertainty Principle. Personally, I never felt certain about trusting his uncertainty, because afterwards he went to work for the Nazis, on an atomic-bomb project . . .'

'Sorry, you're losing me – are the allergies something to do with the uncertainty? Was his vision blurred by hayfever?'

'No, I'm just trying to give you the *full* picture. What he said, this somewhat suspect Herr Heisenberg, is that if you're trying to measure the position of an electron, the energy of the measuring device will alter the momentum of the electron – and vice versa – so you can never know both at the same time. And without knowing the exact position and momentum, you cannot predict its future state . . .'

'That's the Uncertainty Principle?'

'Sort of . . . My memory of school physics isn't good enough to be entirely precise about it.'

'And your point is?'

'That uncertainty is inherent in the universe – so you're not mad when you feel that everything seems unpredictable. It's a scientific fact, until someone else comes along with another theory.'

'But why doesn't Charles think that?'

'I'm not sure what he thinks. His mind moves in mysterious ways. It may be that he prefers not to concentrate on the irrationality of the subatomic world – or perhaps he's found different ways of finding order within it. Wave theory or string theory or something like that.'

'String? Harriet, you're making this up.'

'I'm *not* – I promise; it's about strings of . . . everything. All joined up in a harmonious whole, stringing us along . . .' Harriet waved her arms in the air and nearly knocked over the lamp.

'Are you drunk?'

'Yes, absolutely. Aren't you?'

'A bit. I quite like the idea of this uncertainty whatsit, if it proves it's normal not to be sure about *anything*. Maybe it means I should stop worrying about whether my mother drove into a tree accidentally on purpose . . .'

'Do you think about that a lot?'

'Quite a lot. Speaking of which, you'd better not drive home tonight.'

'Time flowing backwards – there's a theory about that, as well, which would mean we could remember the future, instead of the past. A time-symmetric universe . . .'

'Why did you give up physics? You make it sound so interesting.'

'Far too creepy to follow one's father,' said Harriet, yawning loudly. 'History repeating itself . . .'

'I always wondered about that.'

'Maybe there are little patterns, rather than direct repetitions. You and Julian falling in love with each other, like your mother and my father.'

Kate stared at Harriet, suddenly wide awake, when she'd been on the verge of drowsiness. 'Is that true?' she said.

'You tell me,' replied Harriet.

'I don't know,' said Kate. 'I don't know about Julian and me – there's nothing to tell, really – and I don't know about my mother and Charles. I don't know if I ever saw anything, and if I did, I don't know if that altered the reality of what it was I saw.' Kate stopped, losing the thread of what she was trying to explain. 'What was I just saying?' she said to Harriet. 'I don't know what I'm talking about now.'

'Best not to try and pin it down. That's the point, perhaps – if we can't measure electrons precisely, why try to be precise about human emotions? We change our minds too often for that.'

'But you must have suspected something – about our

parents. Otherwise you wouldn't have said what you just said.'

Harriet shrugged. 'There was nothing, really,' she said, 'or just the tiniest of things. Things too minute to describe . . .'

'All I can remember is my father saying, "What were you doing in the water?" I know I heard that, but I think I've changed it to "what were you doing with Charles in the water?" That I've altered the reality of what I observed . . . Maybe that's it.'

'And what did you observe?'

'I'm not sure. Something to do with the water.'

'Poor Kate,' said Harriet, reaching out to stroke her cheek. 'You look so tired. Go to sleep now and I'll make myself a bed here on the sofa. Try to stop worrying, OK?'

Twenty-Five

She did stop worrying, for a while. The days were getting longer, and the tiger lilies flourishing in the back garden along with the buttercups on the lawn. After school, on sunny afternoons, she and Sam went to the local park, and while he skateboarded along concrete paths, faster every day now, she talked to other mothers, all nursing their paper cups of takeaway tea from the cafe beside the paddling pool. She knew their faces, if not their names, and wondered if, like them, her wrinkles were a little more visible in the early summer sunlight; her face more faded than last year. None of them seemed brimming with happiness, exactly, but they were not discontent: peaceful, they seemed to be, in the park, at four o'clock on weekday afternoons. She did not see Adam or Rose in the park or out of it. It was fate, she told herself (whatever that might mean).

Sometimes, at night, when Sam was sleeping and she should have been finishing an article for the magazine, she logged onto the Internet instead, and found herself searching for something, though she was not quite sure what, exactly, it was. She located cheap flights to exotic places, but could never bring herself to actually book them, to commit to the button marked 'Go'. Twice, she entered her uncle's name in a search engine, and was astonished at the thousands of entries that were listed on the Web. Some of these she read, staying up far too late, yet unable to stop, as if following the clues on a treasure hunt, scattered through screen after screen; but there seemed to be no conclusion, no answer to anything, and he, Charles Reid, remained incomprehensible to her. Still, she printed out a sentence from one of her uncle's papers, published on a distant website, which said: 'The interactions between different entities (e.g. electrons) constitute a single structure of indivisible links, so that the entire universe has to be thought of as an unbroken whole.' She meant to pin these words on the wall above her computer, next to one of Sam's paintings (her favourite – a square rainbow); but she never got round to it, and the sentence was lost, eventually, beneath a pile of receipts for her uncompleted tax return.

The days seemed fragmented, often, too many bits left unfinished; but she loved the moments when she allowed herself to lie down on her bed and doze, with the curtains open to the sky outside; the wide empty sky above the rooftops of her neighbours' houses; and eyes closed, she drifted for a little while, everything merging together, blurred and lovely and meaningless, until a dog barked or a baby cried.

She would not allow herself to lose faith, to give up seeing the point of anything (though what might 'the point' be, exactly? What did it mean? Sometimes she imagined herself searching for this point – the tip of a sharpened pencil, perhaps, or a broken needle – lost in her house somewhere).

Sam was learning his multiplication tables at school and she practised them with him, confessing that she had never been very good at remembering them herself. He was interested in numbers – counting the days in a week, a month, a year – and she found herself both moved and bemused. How hard he tried – as she had done, as everyone does – to measure the world, to give it form and structure and meaning. She sat at her computer, typing out the letters and the words, tap, tap, tapping, keeping it all going, as if it mattered, which it did . . .

What next? What would happen next? No point asking, but impossible not to care. She remembered a short story she had read at Cambridge – one by D. H. Lawrence, but she couldn't remember the title – and though the beginning of the story had faded in her mind over the years, the ending was still clear. A man and a woman, on a boat, disappearing into the darkness, out on the lake. 'What does it mean?' she'd asked her tutor (a man she'd liked; a man now dead). 'What's supposed to happen next?'

'We don't know,' he'd said. 'That's the point – to let them go, knowing that we don't know . . .'

One afternoon in early May she went to the park to watch the children in Sam's school run around it, to raise money for their shabby playground. They ran, all of them, even though the headmistress had said it wasn't a race, running as fast as they could, in a huge circle, back to the beginning again. As Kate watched them, Sam and his friends, doing their best, she felt tears in her eyes. 'Well done!' she cried at the finishing line. 'Well done, all of you!'

That evening she rang Isabel, and told her about the race. 'It's so touching,' Kate said, 'seeing them try so hard.

It makes you think, there must be some sort of meaning in life, even when it doesn't always seem that way . . .'

'Maybe it's a distraction, looking for the meaning,' said Isabel. 'Maybe the point is simply that you feel sad, sometimes, but you keep on going, doing your best, caring about your child.'

Kate said nothing – except the usual prelude to a goodbye – but inside she felt churned up. There had to be some sort of meaning, and even if there wasn't, we needed the search . . . She remembered stepping over the cracks in the pavement as a child – if she didn't touch them, the bears couldn't escape from beneath the slabs of stone, and her daddy wouldn't shout when she got home, no one would be angry – and she'd kept on counting the cracks, every single one of them, every day; day after day after day. It hadn't worked, though, had it? It hadn't worked, however careful she'd been.

Twenty-Six

Eventually, when she had given up imagining what Adam was doing, he rang. 'I've been missing you,' he said.

'I've missed you too,' she said. 'When are you going to come and see me?'

He arrived later that night, when she was almost asleep and not at all glamorous in a red plaid dressing gown. 'I deserve you,' he said, apparently undeterred by the plaid, and she wasn't quite sure what he meant; whether that was an expression of guilt or desire or something else entirely. But she said nothing, and they went up the stairs to her bed together, very quiet, so as not to wake Sam. It was so easy . . .

She locked the front door after he'd gone, and then drew back the bedroom curtains, so that she could see the sky. It was clear tonight and the stars were shining, but she could not remember their names; the names of the constellations that her mother had taught her, years and years ago. Mindful of what Isabel had said last week, she tried not to look for meaning in anything that had happened tonight; tried not to look ahead to the future. Surely it was

significant that Adam had returned to her when she had
stopped thinking about him? But no, that was the wrong
way to go about this: searching for significance when there
was none (or none that was yet clear). 'That way madness
lies . . .' Her father had said so, once, when she was seven
or eight. He had moved out by then, but had come visiting,
taking her for a walk in the park behind the flats. It wasn't
the big park – Regent's Park, a place of sunshine and
remembered roses – but the little one, shaded by tall trees,
that used to be a graveyard, though the ground was covered
in grass and asphalt now. She'd learnt to ride her bike there
two years previously, riding round and round the circular
path, past the old ladies on the benches, and the office
workers eating their sandwiches, past the grey mausoleum
with the worn stone angel on top, its nose worn away, eyes
blinded by the rain, lips blurred, silent, always.

This time, when her dad had come for a visit, they'd left
her bike at home and walked to the park together. She
didn't like to hold his hand; he didn't reach out for hers.
When you went through the iron gates into the park, the
swings and roundabout lay on the left; but she hesitated,
wanting to swing up to the sky, up above the streets, but not
wanting him to push her – and she didn't know which way
he wanted to go today. The path to the right led to the
mausoleum, and on the side of it there were words carved
in the stone, but they had faded too, like the angel, and she
couldn't read them. 'That way madness lies,' her father said,
seeing her glance towards the right. And his face was
unreadable, too, even though a tear trickled down his
cheek, and his teeth were bared, like a wolf, but ground
down at the edges, yellowing. 'You don't understand, do

you?' he'd said to her. 'You're like all the rest of them . . .
Well, never mind, never mind. I'm mad these days, so they
tell me. But in the kingdom of the blind, the one-eyed man
is king . . .'

What had he been talking about? Fragments that added
up to nothing, a faded map of forgotten lands, where rivers
flowed the wrong way and roads led nowhere, just dried-
up marshes: no stop that now, stop thinking about it, stop
trying to make it all fit together, like one of her uncle's
equations. Nothing equalled nothing. Let that be an end to
it . . . But with Adam, it didn't end. There was no proper
ending. Kate did not ask him about his wife, about where
his marriage was going, or not going; and the morning
after his midnight visit he'd rung and said, 'I love you,' but
he would not say more, he had to go, he said; indecipher-
able, as ever.

She sat down in front of the computer and forced herself to write an overdue piece on the semiotics of lipstick
(not for the magazine, but a broadsheet newspaper, that
seemed to like the odd bit of froth from Kate). High gloss,
red alerts, pink rosebuds, cupid kisses: she gathered them
together, mixed in with wry asides, but she kept Adam's lips
out of it. He was her secret, for now; like Julian had been.
The impossible thing about secrets, her father had once said
to her, was that in order to be concealed, they must also
have the potential to be revealed: there had to be clues. He'd
said it not long after her mother had died, and at the time
she'd brushed it aside as irrelevant, just another sentence in
one of his monologues about his current academic obses-
sion (Jacques Derrida, probably, or some other purposefully
obscure French philosopher). But it had stuck with her,

somehow, that thing he had said . . . Strange how words could haunt you, like people.

Speaking of which, her mother had gone very quiet on her these days. There had been a deathly silence since Kate's single session of therapy (not that death had entailed silence, on her mother's part, anyway; not until now, it seemed). What was her mother doing with herself, Kate wondered? Impossible to think of the dead doing nothing . . . surely they had something better to do?

She was drifting, she realized, staring at the computer screen instead of finishing her article. It had a beginning and a middle, but no end. An ending, that was what she needed: a conclusion, so that she could move on to something else.

Twenty-Seven

In June it was Kate's birthday. As a child she had often thought that this was the one well-organized aspect of her life – to have a birthday halfway through the year, exactly six months after Christmas, in fact. The parties themselves had been no less chaotic than any other little girl's – there were the usual infant tears, and adolescent disasters, and the time Judith had worn an embarrassing embroidered kaftan and Kate had told everyone that her mum was confused, she had thought it was fancy dress. But now Kate was going to be thirty-six (far older than her mother had been when she wore the offending article), and parties were not a consideration, thankfully; though Sam always insisted on some small ceremony – a birthday cake at least.

Token ceremony, however, was not what her family seemed to have in mind this year. First of all her father rang, saying that he wanted to pay her a birthday visit, which was unexpected, given that he generally forgot the date altogether; and then Bella phoned, asking her to come to Norfolk with Sam. When Kate refused, explaining that she'd already promised to see her father that weekend, Bella was undeterred. 'You can bring Sebastian, too,' she said, much to Kate's surprise. 'It will be lovely to see him after all these years.'

Even more surprisingly, Sebastian agreed to come to Elverson: which was why Kate found herself driving him there through the crimson sunset of a summer evening, Sam dozing in the back of the car, on the day before her birthday. Her father hadn't been to the house since Judith's funeral, and it seemed inexplicable why he should want to return now; but there he was, hunched beside her, apparently asleep, though every so often he opened his eyes, and sighed.

When they reached Elverson, at last, he looked more uncomfortable than ever; yet it was clear to Kate – and she was touched by this – that he had made an effort, with his semi-ironed cotton shirt and new corduroy trousers. 'I've bought you a present,' he said to Bella, before taking off his coat, and started rummaging through the collection of plastic carrier bags that made up his luggage. Finally, after much teeth-grinding, he located a bottle of cherry brandy, which he handed over without a word.

'Sebastian, how very kind of you,' said Bella, taking his hand and leading him down the corridor, as she might a child.

'And I've got a present for Kate, too,' he said.

'That's lovely, Sebastian,' said Bella. 'Shall we save it for the morning, do you think?' But he had already produced another bottle out of a different plastic bag – this one of Bailey's Irish Cream, leaking, slightly, from the screw-top lid. 'How very delicious,' said Bella, as Kate gave her father a kiss (and saw, to her horror, that his hands were shaking).

'I'd like to go to bed now,' he said, 'if that's convenient.'

'Of course,' said Bella, and took him upstairs as if this were the most ordinary of encounters. Kate put Sam to bed soon afterwards and fell asleep beside him, tired after the journey, the road still swooping behind her eyes, until she woke up with a jolt, certain that her hands had slipped from the wheel, that the car was skidding, out of control; but no, they were safe here, and it was night time.

The sun shone for her birthday and they ate breakfast on the terrace – Charles and Bella, Sebastian and her – while Sam practised cartwheels on the lawn. Her father blinked in the light, tortoise-like, but he seemed happy enough, eating a great deal of toast spread with Bella's home-made strawberry jam. Sam had already presented Kate with a picture that he had painted at school, a portrait of Kate, with a wide smile on her face, and stars in a turquoise sky above her. 'Nice to see he has such a positive image of his mother,' said Sebastian, before returning to his toast. And Bella gave her a beautifully wrapped box, inside which were diamond earrings, elegant little hoops. 'From Charles and me,' she said, but Kate knew that Bella had chosen them, and they were perfect, of course. She hugged Bella, and Charles too, and then her father, so that he didn't feel left out, and then sat there smiling at them all, unable to quite believe the gathering at this table.

After breakfast she and Bella went to pick lettuce from the garden, leaving Sebastian explaining to Charles, at some length, his newfound interest in medieval Jewish cartography. 'It has the imaginative scope of the old *mappa-mundi*, with some mythic elements,' he was saying, 'but I think you'd find it to be scientific, as well – far more so, perhaps, than your imaginary maps of the universe, your curious mystical physics.'

Charles was nodding, not rising to the bait, not yet, anyway. (And why should he? Kate had never heard him argue with anyone, not even his children when they were at their most provocative.) It wasn't long before they would be leaving for the beach – Bella had organized a picnic lunch with Julian and Jessica and Isabel and Harriet – and Kate went upstairs to put on a summer dress, the first she'd worn this year. It was an old one she'd found last August on the jumble stall of a Norfolk fête – 'vintage' was the fashionable term for such a dress, these days – and she'd washed it carefully by hand, so as not to shrink the thirties chiffon, and hung it out to dry, so that the faded pink fabric roses fluttered in the breeze. 'What a beautiful dress,' said Sebastian, when she came back downstairs in it. 'A tea-dress – isn't that what they used to be called? You look just like your mother did at a Cambridge college garden party.'

'Except I'm middle-aged now,' said Kate.

'Nonsense,' said Bella. 'That's what I am . . .'

And that was the odd thing about the passing of the years: when Kate had looked in the mirror this morning, she did not feel very much older than when she had been a student herself, even as she fingered the fine lines on her forehead and those around her eyes. Would it be the same when she was Bella's age, she wondered? At what point did you see a reflection not of yourself but an unrecognizable old lady? And if time did not pass, as Charles maintained, then why did we age? Did we pass through time, perhaps? She wondered whether to ask Charles, but he had disappeared again – and anyway, whatever his answer, she still wouldn't understand what he was talking about.

They reached the beach at noon, meeting at the same spot they always came to, despite the immensity of the sands. Harriet and Isabel were already there, having driven straight from London, and Julian and Jessica arrived soon after, with their children – Jessica, perfectly bronzed all over, stripping down, rather alarmingly, to a black Gucci bikini, without an inch of fat or cellulite on her smooth, hard body (like an impenetrable alien, thought Kate, but she was jealous, too). Bella had packed a picnic big enough for everybody – ham rolls, cucumber sandwiches, flasks of tea, cartons of juice and a chocolate birthday cake for Kate, with candles and everything. Jessica had also brought food, sufficient for her immediate family, in a wicker hamper. 'No cake, darling,' she said, as Rafael reached out for a slice. 'We don't eat sugar in our family, do we?'

'We do,' said Sam.

'My mummy says that's why you're fat,' said Rafael.

Sam was not, in fact, fat: solid, certainly, but where was the harm in that, thought Kate, furious by now. Jessica appeared not to have heard – she was lying on her back, elongated in some sort of yoga position – but Bella had been listening. 'What nonsense,' she said, briskly. 'Sam is a lovely strong boy—'

'Probably end up playing rugby for England,' said Harriet.

'I like football,' said Sam, who had brought his ball to the beach. 'I'm going to practise my skills now.'

'Can I come?' said Rafael.

'No,' said Sam. 'You're too small and puny.'

At this, Jessica sat up looking disapproving. 'Sam,' she said, 'that's not very nice, is it?'

'Too bad,' said Sam. 'Rafael's not very nice to me.' And he ran off with the ball, leaving Harriet smirking and Kate hiding a smile behind her hand.

'How about making a sandcastle?' said Bella. 'Do you remember those marvellous ones we made when you were little? With moats and turrets and everything?'

Julian, who had remained silent so far, got to his feet, taking each of his children by the hand, and then started marking out the shape of a castle, a little further down the beach. Jessica was supine again, eyes closed, as Kate followed Julian with a couple of buckets and spades. 'Sorry,' he said, when she reached him.

'What for?'

'Everything.'

'You've got nothing to apologize for – honestly, it's fine.'

'Fine,' he said, making the word sound leaden. 'That's such a catch-all, isn't it? Mum rings me every Sunday morning and says, "how are you, darling?" And I say, "fine". Even when I'm not . . .'

'Well, I really am fine,' said Kate. 'And it's such a glorious day – blue skies and everything.'

'And I've got you a present,' he said, reaching into his pocket. It was another small jewellery case, inside which were two gold charms: a key and a heart.

'They're beautiful,' she said. 'They'll fit my mother's charm bracelet – how did you know?'

'You were wearing it at that party in January,' he said. 'And they seemed appropriate – my charmed girl, with the key to my heart.'

She looked away, embarrassed, and then glanced at his face to see if he was teasing her. And maybe he was, because he was smiling, but it was not a taunting smile. 'Come on,' she said, 'let's build our castle in the sand.'

'There must be some sort of metaphor in that,' he said.

'Let's not look for one,' she said. 'That's my birthday resolution – to stop searching for patterns or false certainties. To just . . .'

'. . . be?' said Julian.

'Bee,' said Madeleine, tugging his hand, 'bzzz bzzz bee.'

Soon after, Sam came to help with the sandcastle, and so did Bella and Harriet. Isabel and Charles had gone for a walk along the water's edge, and Sebastian was perched on top of a sand dune, writing notes in an untidy exercise book, while Jessica guarded the picnic spot, her tan deepening as the afternoon went on. The tide was still a long way out, and it was hard to make out where Charles and Isabel might be, amidst all the other figures in the hazy light, blurred beside the shimmering, shifting water. Kate stood up and stretched, eyes squinted, looking at the point where the water met the shore. 'In what way,' she asked Harriet, who had come to stand beside her, 'might my act of observation change the reality of what I am now observing?'

'It depends how you look at it,' said Harriet. 'What are you observing, anyway?'

'I was looking for Isabel and Charles. And say I saw them – or I thought I saw them – in the water, or beside the water – how might my seeing change what I saw?'

'Maybe if they knew they were being watched,' said Harriet, 'they might adjust their behaviour accordingly.'

'I'd never thought of that,' said Kate. She started digging

the moat again, picking out the pebbles from the sand, and then when that was finished, she built a small stone circle beside the castle.

'What's that?' said Rafael, who was obviously longing to knock it over.

'Fortifications,' said Kate.

'Bob the builder,' sang Madeleine, 'he's not here.'

Twenty-Eight

For the rest of the weekend Kate waited for a moment when she might talk to her father alone and ask him about that long-ago quarrel she'd heard, so that he might provide a simple explanation of what those words had meant (to turn the water, perhaps, into something more solid). But it never seemed to be the right time; time twisted and slithered this weekend (or was her father simply avoiding her?). Jessica and Julian had driven back to Suffolk straight from the beach; Harriet and Isabel had left after breakfast the following morning – yet despite the quietness of Sunday (just Charles in his study, Bella in the garden with Sam), Kate could not pin Sebastian down. He had been out in the woods, walking and reading, he said, when at last he returned (mysterious as ever, she thought, like an elderly tree elf); and they did not set off for London until the early evening, when the shadows were lengthening. She waited until Sam had settled down in the back of the car, eyes glazed, listening to his favourite story tape on headphones – this was not a conversation that she wanted her child to overhear – and then she asked her father, seizing her chance when they were just out of the woods where her mother had crashed.

' "What were you doing in the water?" Is that what you heard me say?' said Sebastian, examining his fingernails as if they might be dirty.

'I think so . . . It was the night before I came to spend the summer at Elverson, when you and Mum were splitting up.'

'It was such a long time ago,' said Sebastian, tearing at his nails now, 'and I was in the middle of a mental breakdown. People kept telling me that I was hallucinating, that I was paranoid, schizoid. I don't know – maybe I was – I don't like thinking about it now; I've left it long behind me. But I thought I had seen your mother with Charles, kissing him in the water. Or somebody told me they were . . .'

Kate was confused: the argument had taken place in London – so how had they all been by the sea? 'It wasn't then I was talking about,' said Sebastian. 'It was another time – maybe the summer before, when you were six. And it wasn't the sea, it was somewhere else.'

'Where?' asked Kate.

'I can't remember,' said her father vaguely. 'A stream or a river or something, perhaps, near the house, near Elverson.' He closed his eyes, as if the conversation was now finished, and Kate felt a curious sense of anticlimax. Was that it? She'd waited so long for a conclusion, and yet this was so inconsequential. She'd imagined that her father's words would be the clue to unlock the secrets of her family, but they seemed not to offer any answers at all. She felt clueless; foolish to have cared. 'Have I disappointed you?' said her father, as if reading her thoughts behind his shut eyelids.

'A bit,' she said, 'but it's not your fault.'

'In this, or in general, or both? It's hard for parents not to be trying, in both senses of the word . . .'

'I know,' said Kate, hoping that she was looking affectionate but not wanting to take her eyes off the road. Up and down, around and about, she'd come along this road, over the years, for years and years, miles and miles and miles. It would be comforting to think that she was getting somewhere in these journeys to and from Elverson – growing up, gaining wisdom along with a thicker waist. That was the point, wasn't it? (the getting of wisdom, not the waist). She yawned and forced herself to concentrate. It was darkening, slowly.

'So, what did you make of Charles and Bella, after all this time?' she asked her father, to lighten the silence in the car.

'Same as ever,' he said. 'Her circling him, like he was the sun.'

'But he'd be lost without her, wouldn't he?'

'Maybe . . . maybe not. And what about you? Who are you in love with these days?'

'Nobody, really,' she said. And it was true – she loved Sam, he was the only certainty. Everything else could wait.

Except her father: he didn't want to wait; he wanted to drive back home tonight, in his own car, to his own house, over the hills and far away. He left as soon as they arrived back at Kate's house, not wanting a coffee, just wanting to go, exhausted by them all. She didn't mind: she was happy to say goodbye, happy to be able to breathe again after that long drive. Sam was sleepy and went up to bed without a fuss, and Kate watered the plants in her dry back garden.

Life could be very peaceful, like this; no one to argue with, no one to disagree. She sat on her garden chair, on the little patio, a glass of wine in her hand and the cat purring beside her, and tilted her head up to the sky, up to the stars, to the place where her mother was watching, wordless. 'Goodnight,' said Kate.

'Goodbye,' said her mother. No, she didn't speak – Kate knew she was imagining it; but her mother's ghost did seem to have bid her farewell. Perhaps that was a step forward, for both of them. Perhaps that had been her mother's problem, in life as in death – not letting go of the past.

'What codswallop,' said her mother sharply, tart as an apple fallen in the Elverson orchard. 'Incidentally, I wasn't kissing Charles in the water. I was crying, because Sebastian was having a breakdown and my marriage was a mess, and anyway, there we were, and Charles was wiping away my tears, and he gave me a quick peck on the cheek. Which made me want to cry even more, of course.'

'But what were you doing with him in the water?'

'Looking for tadpoles. With you, in the stream at Elverson. That's why I was trying to stop crying – because you were watching. Otherwise I might have been really howling.'

'You're making this up.'

'No, I'm not – you are.' And with that her mother was gone; if, indeed, she had ever been there at all. (But what was that scent? Just the jasmine flowers, white in the shadows, or something else, a half-remembered perfume lingering in the still evening?)

Tadpoles? Kate wanted to laugh, but it had the ring of truth – or at least the sound of something she wanted to believe in, a bedtime story that she could tell herself. Her mother had been crying and Charles had wanted her to stop – he could never bear the sight of tears – and she, Kate, had seen it all. But then how had her father known about the water? Had he been watching, too, or had she – a guileless little girl – told Sebastian that she had been in the water with her mother and her uncle, that her uncle had kissed her mother better? She began to laugh, at last, out in the garden, in the darkness; it was all so ridiculous – too absurd for words.

Perhaps it was time to put it away now, this fragment of a story, like her dead mother's bit of fairy tale safely stored in Kate's desk drawer. At university, and for several years afterwards, she had hoarded old postcards and invitations, like brittle autumn leaves, thinking – childlike – that she might one day make a scrapbook. But when Sam was born, she started throwing things away, all those dusty bits and pieces, though she could never bring herself to discard the glass jars of shells and stones that she had collected since she was a little girl. There weren't so many – she'd always been careful to select only those that had seemed to her most important, cowries, never cockle shells, and her favourite sea-worn bits of coloured glass, all sharp edges smoothed away by the waves. Those had been her mother's favourites, too. After she had died, and the funeral was over, Kate had gone to Judith's flat with Bella, to clear it – that was the word they had used: it had to be cleared. It had taken a couple of days – unbearable, because neither of them wanted to sleep there, even though it was the place where Kate had grown up. But they had spent one night there together – Kate in her old room, Bella sleeping on the sofa, because she could not bring herself to get into her dead twin's bed. The next morning Bella looked exhausted, ashen in a way that Kate had never before seen her. 'What are we going to do with these?' Bella had said, gesturing at the jars of glass and pebbles that Judith used as bookends on the shelves. 'We can't throw them away.'

'I'll take them,' said Kate, and had put them in a cardboard box. She'd kept very little – some books, with her mother's tiny italic handwriting in the margins and between the printed lines; the single page of Judith's story; and a silver ring, too large for Kate, that she'd worn on a chain around her neck for six months before hanging it on a hook on the wall, beside a bunch of dried lavender. Bella seemed to want nothing at all, though she must have taken the charm bracelet. They packed the clothes away in bin liners for a local charity shop, which made Kate shudder (other people fingering her mother's things – but what else were they to do?). And everything else – well, it seemed to disappear, like her memory, like her mother . . . All Kate could remember was the feel of the dust on her dry hands, and the faint smell of Judith's soap, and a list she had left, torn from the same notebook, perhaps, in which she had been writing her story. 'Things to do' she had written at the top and then underlined. 'Tax return, Kate's student grant forms, car MOT, FINISH BOOK!' It could not possibly constitute a suicide note, so why had Kate suspected that her mother's death had not been an accident? They'd spent Christmas together, and Judith had seemed depressed – 'I've been feeling a little bit bleak,' she'd said – but no worse than usual, and happy enough to pick up the pieces of conversation with Kate over their modest lunch. (Judith hadn't eaten much, but then she never did, for her food was always mixed up with frugality and asceticism.) And yet Kate's doubts could not be swept away, though it was impossible to tell Bella her fears as they sifted through Judith's belongings on that cold January weekend. Bella's face had been a mask – like her mother's in Kate's nightmares – that had only cracked when the box filled with glass and shells split apart on the street outside. The cardboard had given way and the glass jars smashed, spilling their contents everywhere – shells scattered across the grey London pavement, coral splintered like bits of bone. Bella had fallen to her knees, weeping, trying to gather up the broken things, cutting her hands on the glass. 'Just leave it,' Kate had said, taking her aunt's hands in her own. Where had Charles been, when they needed him? It was Bella who had driven Kate back to Cambridge, her poor wounded fingers gripping the steering wheel. Afterwards, when they had kissed each other goodbye and Bella had gone to meet Charles at his college, Kate realized that her aunt's blood was still on her hands. She'd gone upstairs to her room and washed them in the basin. It was very cold that winter – there was ice inside the window of her college room because the heating had been off for several days – and her hands were sore; the water made them worse.

And that was it – that was the end of it. She'd fallen asleep waiting for a sign from her mother. But there was none; only the snow falling from the grey Cambridge sky, settling on the stones, obscuring everything . . .

Twenty-Nine

In the weeks after her birthday, the sun shone most days, and how could she be unhappy in the sunshine? She had craved it all winter – counting the weeks away – and here it was at last, and her body loosened in the gentle warmth. She painted her toenails red and bought a pair of pink flip-flops decorated with glass beads, like jewels, and wore them every day. Part of her regretted the passing of the longest day, the summer's waning, the roses fading – and August was a month Kate feared a little, remembering its melancholy emptiness in previous years – but this one was going to be different; not like the time when Sam was a baby and Pete was away working, and it seemed as if she and her child were the only people left living on their street, amidst the dust and the discarded ice-cream wrappers. (She'd taken Sam down to the river then, in search of something – fresh air and people, laughter in the summer city – but it was quiet there beside the Thames that August morning, just the mournful seagulls overhead. Sam had fallen asleep in his pushchair and she'd stood looking at the muddy water; high tide, and the rising smell of London, rubbish carried by an invisible current, west towards Vauxhall Bridge. She'd felt confused, she remembered that – because surely the river should have been flowing in the other direction, east towards the sea?)

The summers since then had been easier – even the first one after Pete had left, because in some ways it was the same as ever, except people had been kinder now that Kate was officially a single mother. But this year she had decided that they would spend the whole of August away from London, and to do so she had worked late into the night, most nights, until Sam's school term ended. Each word she wrote, Kate told herself, would pay for a little more August freedom, and so she did it willingly, everything the magazine asked of her (even the piece about thirty-six being the new twenty-six, which was blatantly not true in her case, despite the red toenails). Sometimes Adam rang while she worked; sometimes she took his calls, sometimes she ignored them. She knew no more about the state of his marriage; though she guessed that his wife was back in Manchester, and when Rose had visited Clare there one Saturday, Adam stayed in London (and in Kate's bed, until she made him leave before Sam returned home from Robbie's house). He was much better at sex than talking, she decided; and there seemed no point in arguing with that, though she couldn't help, pointlessly, wishing that he might explain a few things about his life to her after they had made love, and his silence draped over them like an invisible mosquito net, keeping irritant questions at bay.

Her friend Maria, meanwhile, had given up on her lover. 'I knew I had to put a stop to it when he started lecturing me in bed about teaching practice,' she'd said at the end of the summer term. 'It's too much of a weird power thing – a bit creepy, like having an affair with your boss – and anyway, it's boring enough being a mature student, without having extra tuition on your days off.' So Maria and Robbie and the rest of the family were going to Devon, which she seemed rather cheerful about ('Nothing like guilt to revive a flagging marital sex life,' she said, with a sly smile). And Kate and Sam were on their way to Elverson, for a whole month – for two weeks of which they would be alone, in theory, while Bella and Charles went to Italy. 'Are you sure you'll be all right by yourself?' Bella had said, repeatedly, in July. 'Do have friends to stay, darling, whenever you like . . .'

Adam, in fact, had already rung to ask if he might come with Rose for a few days (and without her, too, while his wife took Rose to stay with friends in Cornwall). 'I'm not sure,' said Kate, staring out of the attic window where she was sitting at the time, phone in one hand, the other resting on the computer keyboard.

'Why aren't you sure?' said Adam, from wherever it was he was.

'Because you're not sure about me.'

'Kate, I thought we didn't have these sorts of conversations.'

'Well, I try not to, but sometimes it just happens.' She knew he wanted their relationship to be straightforward – uncomplicated by recriminations or contrariness – but she also knew that ordinary life wasn't always as simple as that, however much Adam wanted it to be; and to make it seem that way took hard work and the imposition of silence when complaints might otherwise be heard. It was the method, she guessed, that Bella had employed to make her marriage work, and quite possibly the very opposite of how her mother and father had operated. But though her parents' marriage had failed, she did not want to pursue the alternative approach: the quiet unspoken understanding of certain rules. (*The Rules* – she vaguely remembered that book coming out at about the time Pete had left her, prescribing the correct behaviour for a woman to win, and keep, a man. Never ring back, never talk back – wasn't that the instruction? But rules were just asking to be broken . . .)

One of the main complications, of course, was Sam – or what he might think, if he were to know about Adam; and then there was Rose to consider. People talked about happy blended families (like a sort of delicious healthy fruit shake), but what was the point of trying to blend the children together when she and Adam were still mixed up, in entirely the wrong way? Kate could not contemplate letting Sam see her share a bed with Adam; not yet, anyway – and as for Rose, the poor child doubtless wanted her parents reinstated in marital harmony.

So she went to Elverson without plans; just her and Sam and three large bags (but no baggage, she told herself on the way there, nothing to encumber a clear mind and a free heart). Oh, the summer, the lovely summer . . . they would eat picnics on the grass, and no evil PlayStation for Sam, simply the trees and the sky and the fresh air blowing London away.

And it was almost like that: sufficiently happy – despite Sam's wasp sting and her mosquito bites and the occasional morning of grey boredom or a rainy afternoon – to ensure that one day, she hoped, this time could be retold as a con-

soling family story. ('Do you remember?' she imagined herself saying to Sam in an unknown future, 'that summer when
you were eight and we spent a month at Elverson? The sun
shone every day, and we picked raspberries and you learnt to
fly a kite on the beach . . .') After the first two weeks Bella
and Charles departed for their holiday abroad, leaving the
dog behind ('You're her babysitter,' said Bella to Sam, much
to his delight) and a larder full of provisions. It was the sight
of Bella's freshly baked bread (three loaves) and cakes (one
cherry, one lemon), as well as the two dozen scones, that
encouraged Kate finally to ring Adam. That was what she
told herself, anyway – and him, as well. 'Bella has left far too
much for us to eat by ourselves,' she said, when she rang half
an hour after her aunt and uncle's early-morning departure.
'I'll either have to organize an impromptu garden fête or
you'll have to come immediately for tea.'

'Just tea?' said Adam.

'Don't push your luck,' she said. 'What more could you
ask for than cherry cake?'

He arrived that evening, and Sam – starved of the company of other children for the last fortnight – seemed so
pleased to see Rose that he invited her to share his bedroom
(the one that Kate had slept in as a child with Harriet and
Isabel; the same twin beds side by side, though the truckle
bed had gone and the pink walls were now painted blue).
'OK,' said Rose, 'but where's my Daddy going to sleep?'

'In the room next door to you,' said Kate, 'like last time
you came to stay, and I'll be across the corridor. Is that all
right?' She could not tell if that was a look of relief that
flickered across the little girl's face (though it was surely not
disappointment).

And so the children were settled, and sleeping at last, and Adam kissed her, covered her in kisses. 'I've missed you,' he said, undressing her. 'I've missed you so much.' And she said nothing, wondering if she was his secret, as he was hers. But the days that followed felt open, easy – blessed by sunshine, as she had hoped they would be, and uncomplicated by children's arguments. On the beach together, she guessed that they looked to others like a happy family; and though she and Adam were careful never to display physical affection openly, Sam and Rose seemed to enjoy it when other children assumed that they were brother and sister.

Slowly, in jigsaw bits and pieces, she pieced together what might have been happening between Adam and his wife. One morning, while Adam and Sam were repairing an old tree house in the woods – not used since her cousins had left home – she stayed behind with Rose, who wanted to play interminable hopscotch on the terrace (and Kate did not mind, even enjoyed hopping with her as she had done with Isabel and Harriet on the same stones, where the creeping chamomile grew, all those long summers ago). 'I don't know if I want to go to Cornwall tomorrow,' said Rose, balanced on one skinny leg, stork-like, her other leg tucked up under her skirt. 'I like it here.'

'I'm glad you like it,' said Kate, 'and I love you being here. But I'm sure you'll have a lovely time in Cornwall, as well, and your mum will be missing you . . .'

'I don't like her friend,' said Rose. 'He's called Rob and he's got a stupid nose.'

'In what way, stupid?'

'It's not very big, but he rubs it against my mum's cheek – how disgusting is that?'

Kate did not reply immediately, wary of the dangerous ground on which they might be venturing. 'His tongue is disgusting, too,' said Rose, still one-legged, but wobbling now. 'In Manchester, when they thought I was asleep, I saw him put it in my mum's mouth. It makes me feel sick.'

'Have you talked to your mum about it?'

'No, because I wasn't supposed to be looking.' Rose looked anxious, and her right eye twitched a little, like Kate's did when she was very tired. Kate paused, again, wanting to say the right thing, but still unsure as to what that might be. (What would Bella have done? How could she be to this child as Bella had been to her?) In the end she simply put an arm around Rose's shoulders and stroked her hair. 'It's hard, isn't it?' said Kate. 'Grown-ups can be very confusing.'

'Do you get confused?'

'Often – especially when Sam asks me to help with his maths homework. I'm hopeless at it – no help at all . . .'

'You should ask my dad – he's really good at adding things up and taking them away.' She slid out from under Kate's arms, skipping across the chalked hopscotch stones, looking less troubled. 'Look,' she said, 'there's a car coming up the drive.' It was Julian's car, and Julian was driving – though Kate could not yet see if he was by himself. She took Rose's hand, without knowing why.

'Hello,' said Julian, stepping out of the car, alone. 'I just happened to be passing – thought you might need some company now that Mum and Dad are away – but I see you have some already. I remember you,' he said to Rose, with his usual charming smile, 'you were here at Easter, weren't you? And where's your Dad today?'

'In the woods with Sam,' said Rose, still holding Kate's hand.

Kate offered to get Julian a cold drink, and he followed her into the kitchen, leaving Rose on the terrace hopping alone for a moment. 'So, what brings you here?' she said.

'I was just passing, like I said . . .'

'Julian, you live in Suffolk, and you work in the City. Where're Jessica and the kids, anyway?'

'They're staying at her parents for a few days. I've just dropped them off there . . .'

'And why aren't you with them?'

'Lots of work to catch up with before we go to France.' His face gave nothing away, though oddly, like Rose's, his eye was twitching slightly.

'You look tired,' she said, for something to say.

'I'm always tired at the moment – the kids have been waking up at dawn, and I try to spend an hour with them before driving into work.'

'That's very noble of you.'

'I like it. And Jessica has them for the rest of the day, so I feel I ought to do my bit.'

'Look, I'd better get back outside – I don't want to leave Rose by herself for too long.'

'So, it's on again, is it, with the handsome builder?'

'He's not a builder – he's an architect, who also knows how to build.'

'OK, OK – I was just asking.' She was about to go when he reached out and grabbed her hand. 'Don't be angry with me,' he said. And as he looked at her she saw what might have been tears in his eyes – but, no, she must have been imagining it; for she had never seen Julian cry; not him, letting words flow instead.

Outside, she suggested to Rose that they walk over to the woods, to see how the tree house was progressing. She did not invite Julian to come with them, but he did, anyway (and she reminded herself that it was his house, his garden, more than hers). 'Have you ever lived with a depressed person?' he said, in a low voice, as Rose skipped a few yards ahead of them.

'I don't know . . . well, my father, of course, and my mother always veered towards the melancholic. Why do you ask?'

'Because Jessica went to our GP and he says she's clinically depressed. *Clinically* – that doesn't reflect very well on me, does it?'

Kate stopped herself from telling him not to be so narcissistic, and simply murmured the usual platitudes. But they didn't seem to help – of course, they didn't – and as she walked beside him on the path through the woods, his unhappiness was palpable.

'I've always thought of myself as cheerful,' he said, swinging his hand at the leaves, swiping them away, 'so why am I making my wife depressed?'

'It might not be to do with you. People feel unhappy for all sorts of reasons – maybe she's suffering from a form of chemical imbalance.'

'Why now?' said Julian. 'She didn't seem depressed before we got married. And I'm worried about the children – it can't be good for them living with a mother who's miserable all the time.'

'Children are very resilient . . .'

'Well, I'm not – this is not what I expected . . .' His voice sounded strangled, almost, and then Kate realized that he was fighting back tears. 'I thought everything was going to be perfect – no, not perfect, but OK, you know? Like my parents – a good marriage.'

'Julian, I'm sure it'll get better – it's not like she's been depressed for years, it's just a phase, you're just going through a bad patch – everyone does, you'd be abnormal if you didn't.'

'I feel blighted,' he said, rubbing at his face, harshly, as if he were trying to wipe something away. 'Like your parents . . . but it should be you.'

'What's that supposed to mean?'

'I don't know. I just feel that maybe you could make things right again, even though it's gone wrong for you, that you might know the answer . . .'

'There aren't any answers,' she said. 'That's the point—' But before she could finish (though she didn't know where her sentence was going), he had taken her face in both of his hands and was kissing her on the lips, and his tears were on her cheeks, warm, warmer than his skin. She pulled away from him (for where was Rose? Kate didn't want anyone else to witness this; but did she want it to happen? It was impossible to tell.) Rose was nowhere, and Kate felt the sour taste of panic in her mouth and started calling the girl's name. 'Rose!' she cried, spinning round, running now, 'Where are you?'

'Coo-eee,' came a distant answer, 'I'm playing hide-and-seek with Dad and Sam . . . You'll have to find us.' Julian seemed to have disappeared, walking back to the house in the other direction, she guessed, as confused as she was; and there was no one to be seen, just a rustling in the trees, but that could be the wind. She stumbled off the path, into a bramble patch that scratched her bare legs and arms, and then slid down to the stream, panicking, fearing what she might find there. 'Got you!' said Sam, jumping out from behind some bushes, pointing two fingers at her like a gun. 'Come on, come and see the tree house.' Her face was burning – calm down, she told herself, just calm down – as Sam led her to a ladder at the bottom of an oak tree. Rose's face peered down at her, but where was Adam? And then she saw him – higher than Rose, up in the branches above the tree house, motionless, dark face camouflaged against the bark.

'Hello,' she said, waving up at them both. 'Hello!' said Rose, waving back, but Adam said nothing. Had he seen her, now or before? What had he seen, if anything?

Thirty

Adam didn't say anything, of course. And Julian had already gone, driven away, before she could speak to him. Rose seemed preoccupied – but then she would, wouldn't she, with the prospect of the trip to Cornwall ahead of her? And that must have been on Adam's mind, as well, which could explain his silence. He was often silent, anyway, wasn't he? These questions harassed her, chasing each other around in her head – so that she was grateful when Sam started asking her different questions: ones that might have an answer. Could he and Rose have some ice cream, the raspberry ice cream he'd made with Bella, with the berries he'd picked from the vegetable garden? Yes, they could, of course, she would get it out of the freezer right away. When were Adam and Rose leaving? Well, tomorrow morning, she thought, but he'd have to check with Adam. Where was Adam? He'd gone for a walk. Could they go and find him? No, she wasn't sure where he'd been headed.

He was wearing those boots of his she liked – the Mephisto boots, the ones that reminded her not to expect people to be angels (or devils, either). What had he seen, face gazing down from the sky? (No, not the sky, the tree – he was not all-seeing; no one could be.)

'We should talk,' she said when he returned, an hour or so later, the dog at his heels.

'About what?' he said, not smiling, but with no apparent tension in his face.

'About where we're going – I mean, about when you're going.'

He put his arms around her and pulled her to his chest, so that she could breathe in the smell of him that she loved. 'I'm not going anywhere,' he said, 'not just yet, anyway. I'll drive Rose back down to London tomorrow, to meet Clare, and then I've got to check up on a couple of jobs. But I thought I might come back here for a few more days – unless you want some time alone . . .'

'I'd rather be with you,' she said.

'So Julian didn't stay long,' he said.

'No, he just dropped in.'

'Rose told me. Shame I didn't see him.'

'You didn't see him?'

'Well, only from a distance.'

He let his arms fall away from her as the children became audible in the kitchen, struggling with the ice-cream scoop, squawking at each other. 'I'll go inside and sort them out,' he said. 'Would you like a cup of tea?' And that was it – another inconclusive conclusion to their conversation. She never seemed to *get* anywhere with him, yet she thought he loved her – he had said so, last night, in bed, whispered it in her ear, once, twice, three times, and her limbs had felt honeyed, as he stroked her, stroking away the questions like he always did, leaving only the sweetness of their bodies together.

That afternoon she washed Rose's clothes, hanging them out to dry in the sunshine on the line outside the kitchen door, so that Clare might know that she cared; if Clare knew anything about her, that is; if Clare even knew that she existed – which she probably did not.

'You don't have to do that,' said Adam, as she ironed Rose's summer dress, pressing the cotton creases away.

'It's OK,' she said. 'I hardly ever iron anything – never in London – but I quite like doing it here. It's just a little dress, anyway.' Suddenly, shamefully, she felt as if she wanted to cry – remembering herself at Rose's age, no, younger, that summer alone in Elverson. Everything had been ironed for her then – the sheets of the truckle bed, and her dresses, her shorts, her t-shirts, even. One night, soon after she had arrived in that long-ago August, Kate had dreamt she was trying to smooth out a large white sheet – maybe bedlinen, or perhaps it was paper – but it kept getting creased and dirty and it was too big for her to manage; she could not keep the mess away. Never, never, would she ever, could she ever, sort anything out. Sometimes her heart felt creased, like her face these days.

'What's the matter?' said Adam, touching her cheek.

'Everything's a mess,' she said, staring down at the ironing board.

'It only seems that way,' he said. 'But it's going to be OK. I promise.' His reassurance made her want to cry even more, but she did not let herself, holding her breath as she kept on ironing.

It was misty when Adam and Rose left early the next morning, as if the sky had settled like a feather eiderdown over the trees. Kate stood by the front door, Sam at her side, waving goodbye. 'Come back soon!' said Sam, breaking away from her, chasing the car down the drive, but he could not keep up. 'What are we going to do by ourselves,' he said to her, 'all alone and lonely?'

'Bake a cake?' she said.

'No, that's boring.'

'Go for a walk?'

'Boring, too.' Reading a book would also be boring, he said, kicking at the gravel, and as for building sandcastles on the beach, 'It's no fun when it's just the two of us.' The dog looked equally disconsolate; quietly pining for Bella, and probably missing Adam now as well. In the end she took them both to the nearest beach, the pebbly one, where Sam could throw stones into the waves, and the dog sniffed the air, scanning the blurred horizon where the grey sea merged into the pearl-coloured sky. After Sam had vented sufficient frustration on the rocks, they bought crab sandwiches and chips to eat, perched on the dry top of a shingle bank, guarding their lunch against the seagulls and feeding the crusts to the dog. 'It's not fair,' said Sam, as the dog regarded them with her melting brown eyes, 'Poppy should have a sandwich of her own.' So Kate relented and fetched her a ham roll; and soon all of their moods were improved a little, though the dog still sighed from time to time, as if possessed by a passing melancholy.

The phone was ringing when they got back home, but stopped, infuriatingly, just as Kate reached out to answer it. 'Who was that?' said Sam.

'I haven't got a clue,' she said, 'but I'm sure they'll ring back if it's important.'

'Maybe they can't,' he said. 'Maybe they're lying in a

ditch, close to death, and that was their final call, and now their mobile has run out, and you didn't answer the phone. How would you feel about that?' She did not answer him, feeling distracted, but trying to retain her good spirits from the beach.

'Well?' said Sam.

'Well, what?'

'You never *listen* to me,' he said, slamming the front door behind him and going to skateboard on the terrace, which he knew annoyed her, because of the noise, like grindstones. She sighed, like the dog, and then resolved to occupy herself with an improving activity – yoga, perhaps (except she couldn't remember how to do yoga, from her limited experience at an ante-natal class when she was pregnant with Sam). The problem of her fading memory, she decided, related not only to yoga but the task of how to be alone. She had been perfectly competent at the art of self-sufficiency until spending too much time with Adam these last few days; and now she was crumbling, letting self-containment spill out into neediness. That was the mess that was bothering her . . . that was what she needed to put right again.

And she would have been fine, except bloody Adam didn't bloody ring. Why didn't he ring her? What was he doing? Working everything out again with his bloody wife? Kate wanted to stamp around the house and slam doors, like Sam did when he was angry, and then be comforted, as she comforted Sam. But she couldn't, could she? She was in charge, in control – facing up to facts. Except what *were* the facts? They seemed to have escaped her, again.

When the phone rang that evening she skidded across

the wooden floor to answer it in Charles's study, so that Sam would not overhear her conversation, just in case it was Adam. 'Hello?' she said, trying to sound cool and restrained.

'It's me,' said Harriet.

'Oh, hi,' said Kate, now trying to be enthusiastic, instead.

'You sound a bit disappointed,' said Harriet. 'Were you expecting someone more exciting than me? Your tall, dark, handsome friend?'

'And who might that be?'

'You know – what's his name? . . . Adam. Lovely smile, bad history, but you can't resist him, because there's that tiny muscle that quivers in his cheek when he's angry or on the verge of kissing you. I just spoke to Julian, who said he'd been there yesterday. Adam, I mean, as well as Julian . . .'

'Well, he's gone now.'

'But not for good?'

'Who knows . . . I'm sick of thinking about it, anyway. Can you come and see us soon? I'm pining for adult company.'

'Can't till next week, my darling. But I'll see you then.'

Kate put the phone down and started absent-mindedly flicking through Charles's diary on the desk, before remembering where she was. She shut the diary, feeling guilty, but did not leave her uncle's study; she'd never been alone in here before, and there were so many photographs to look at on the walls: his parents, never more than the most shadowy figures in her memory, both dead now, yet framed forever here in their wedding portrait, bride turned lovingly to groom, her handsome man, facing the camera with steady confidence, like Charles, like Julian (and Kate remembered his wedding day, watching him say his vows with Jessica in the Elverson church, and she'd felt so bereft, though Pete was beside her, whispering that he loved her, but her head had been full of Julian). And then there was Charles's younger brother, Luke: long gone also, dead of a heart attack – it must have been twenty years ago or more; not that Kate had ever really known him, for he had emigrated to Australia just a few months after her parents had divorced. There were two photos of Luke on the wall – one of him alone, a student, maybe (he had gone to Cambridge, too, hadn't he?), looking very like Charles – how strong those Reid genes must be – yet smiling in a way that Charles would never smile: jaunty, teasing – like Julian, really. In the other picture, Bella and Judith stood arm in arm, laughing, with Charles and Luke on either side of them, framed by the greenery of what Kate guessed to be a Cambridge college garden. How strange she had never seen that photograph before – they looked like newly-weds, the four of them, celebrating their good fortune at finding one another.

There was part of her that wanted to piece together another plot – of two brothers in love with twin sisters, boundaries blurred, emotions confused – but surely someone would have told her that story by now? Her father would have mentioned it before; or Isabel – shrewd judge that she was – would have guessed something. Luke was a red herring, she decided – and turned her attention instead to the framed photographs on her uncle's desk: Bella, of course, alone and with the children; Julian and Paul, in shorts and ties and blazers, at the beginning of a new school term; Harriet, on the cusp of adulthood, a beauty emerging from beneath her dark fringe; Isabel, on her graduation day, unwavering blue eyes meeting the camera's gaze. Kate felt slightly disappointed that there was no picture of her on the desk; but then noticed one on a bookshelf on the other side of the room in which Judith cradled her – a baby, still – on her lap. 'Mum,' she whispered in the empty room, 'make everything turn out right, please?' She imagined her mother, occupied elsewhere – in that unseen, unheard place beyond the stars – catching her words, the whisper that blew across the sky . . . and then what? What could her mother do with her daughter's hopes? Weave everything together with stardust? It seemed almost blasphemous to think such thoughts – magical, childish, impossible – in her uncle's study. This was a place for figures and equations; for rigour, not nursery rhymes. She closed her eyes – for if she could not see her uncle's room, then it would not judge her – and said the magic words, anyway. 'Wish I may, wish I might, wish upon a star tonight . . .' And then she stopped herself, because she had to see the star first – and how could she see it, eyes shut, in the study?

She called Sam – who appeared to have forgiven her when he emerged from the kitchen, with the dog, trailing biscuit crumbs behind them – and they all went outside to the terrace, where the high summer sky was turning to darkness. 'First one to see a star gets a wish,' said Kate, looking at her son's lovely face as he searched the sky. 'There it is!' said Sam. 'Over there, above the oak tree! I wish . . . I wish it would be this summer forever, and all my friends came here to stay, and we were all happy, amen. Do you believe in God, Mum?'

She was tempted to ask, 'Does God believe in me?' but

decided instead to err on the side of safety. 'I believe in love,' she said, believing this as she spoke, but thankful that Sam was her only witness (her only child, her everything).

'We had a teacher who said God is love,' said Sam, 'but she just came for one day, when Mr Evans was off sick. She was funny, that teacher – she hummed all the time, and her bracelets jangled.'

'Funny ha ha, or funny peculiar?'

'Peculiar,' said Sam, 'but me and Robbie went ha ha when we were in the playground. Robbie says his mum says she doesn't believe in God, and he says he doesn't believe in Father Christmas. But I do, even though I know you bring me some of my presents, because I saw you creep into my bedroom last Christmas Eve when I was asleep, before Father Christmas came.'

'Maybe you were dreaming,' said Kate.

'Maybe,' said Sam. 'Mum, can I have a drum kit for Christmas?'

'Maybe,' said Kate.

'That's what mums always say,' he said, but seemed happy enough, and ran back into the house, arms stretched wide like wings, pretending to be an aeroplane, she guessed (though it would be nice to think of him, just for a few seconds, as an earthly angel). And before she turned and followed him, she tilted her head up to the sky and smiled at the evening star. 'Thank you,' she said. 'Thank you for everything . . .'

Thirty-One

In the days that followed, Kate realized – and clung on to that realization in moments of doubt – that even when her life seemed not to be progressing, it was, because life moved on, as time did (whatever her uncle said). These phrases were clichés, she knew, but the truth contained within them seemed real to her, for now. Adam had rung the morning after he'd driven Rose back to London to say that he'd tried, twice, to ring the day before, but first there had been no answer and then the phone was engaged; and anyway, could he come back to Elverson tomorrow for another day or two?

Sam seemed happy to see Adam – and even expressed regret that Rose was not here, too – and Adam seemed happy to be back. 'How was Clare?' said Kate, tentatively, when they sat down together in the kitchen just after Adam had arrived.

'Oh, she graced me with her presence for a few minutes,' said Adam.

'What presents?' said Sam. 'Did she bring presents for you and Rose? I want a drum kit, but Mum says I've got to wait till Christmas, but that's ages and ages away.' He rattled on, leaving no room for any more questions, or answers, but maybe that didn't matter. At sunset they all walked to the woods together, so that Sam could inspect the tree house and bang a few more nails into it; and as they crossed the wide lawn he took each of their hands. 'Swing me up into the air!' said Sam, beginning to run, pulling them along with him.

'You're getting a bit big for this,' said Kate, but tried anyway, and with Adam's help, up went Sam, up and laughing at the sky, as the three of them ran towards the woods. There the sun slanted between the leaves, a soft, golden light that she wished she would remember forever (the gorgeous, ordinary light of just another day, another precious day). When Sam rushed on ahead of them, the dog at his heels, Adam took her hand for a moment and examined it, as if he might find what he was looking for inscribed there. 'Palm reading?' she said.

'No, not really – I was just wondering if Julian was going to return, to claim you.'

Kate tried not to stiffen, to keep her hand relaxed in his. 'What makes you say that?' she said.

'The look in his eyes when he looks at you. Don't worry – you don't have to tell me about it. Some things are best left unsaid – or have I said that before? I have, haven't I?'

'Sometimes words don't say the right thing, or they get in the way of what you really mean. And if you don't quite know what the truth is, then words confuse things even more.' She paused, thinking of the tangle of words that rustled through these woods for her, haunting her family; but if she said this to Adam, it would sound melodramatic – and meaningless, for the truth was more delicate than that. 'It's hard to explain about Julian,' she said. 'But there's no future in it. I mean, I love him, because he's my cousin – and because of the past – but I'm not going to let myself fall in love with him all over again. And he'll never leave Jessica – he's very loyal, like his father was . . .' As she spoke, she wondered why she had used the past tense about Charles – for he was still alive, still loyal, presumably. But it was as if she had been resolving something; deciding for herself that Charles had been true to Bella, had not had an affair with Judith – at least not after he'd married his wife; had behaved honourably, as Kate felt she had done when it came to Julian.

'That's one way of looking at things,' said Adam.

'I know you could interpret it in any number of ways,' said Kate, 'but that's the way I see it.' She knew that this was not entirely truthful, for had she not spent her time – years and years of it – trying to understand her family from different points of view? But what she said would have to do for now; would do for Adam, it seemed, for he was smiling at her, not angry, not accusatory (not her father, who had been driven half mad, perhaps, in his efforts to pin her mother down). Oh, she didn't want to *think* about it any longer – she wanted just to kiss Adam, to lose herself in kissing him, pushing words away, embracing speechlessness. But Sam would see, and she had not yet explained to Sam about her relationship with Adam – hoping that it would happen naturally, that everything would fall into place.

'Don't look so worried,' said Adam. 'I love you.'

'I love you too,' she said.

And they were the right words, after all.

Thirty-Two

September came, like a new beginning, like it always did. Sam went into his second year at junior school (impossible, surely? It had been such a short time since he'd started at the infant school, solemn-faced, determined not to cry when she'd said goodbye on the first morning). Adam and Clare seemed more separated than before – she was temporarily in Manchester again, apparently living with her boyfriend, Rob, for the duration of a new series. Kate had not yet met Clare, nor Rob, and therefore still pictured them only in Rose's words (the nose-rubbing, tongue-tangling scene), having decided to avoid watching Clare on the television. Sam had no such compunctions, however, and became strangely involved in the soap opera of Clare's screen life. ('She's very pretty,' he'd told Kate, 'with these big eyes that look like she's going to cry, and I thought she was nice, but now she's run off with her cousin's husband – he's the goalie for the football team. I suppose he's her new boyfriend. Poor Adam.' 'It's just a story,' Kate had replied. 'I do *know* that, Mum, I'm not stupid,' said Sam, 'but that guy, the actor, is her boyfriend in real life; that's what Rose told me.)

By the end of September the children seemed to have accepted that Adam and Kate were – ghastly word – 'involved'. 'Are you my mum's boyfriend?' Sam had asked Adam on a Sunday-afternoon outing to the park, in the lovely, dwindling warmth of an Indian summer. 'Because if you are, I don't mind. And I was wondering if you could build me a mini skateboard ramp for our back garden, if that's OK?'

Adam had said yes, on both counts, and fortunately Rose appeared to object neither to the ramp-building nor to the presence of Kate. It was hard to tell exactly what Rose was really feeling, deep down, but the tic in her eye had lessened and she negotiated a tolerable relationship with Sam. 'I'm not going to stand around watching him skateboard,' she'd said, arms folded across her chest, 'but I don't mind going swimming with him.' Despite her best intentions, Kate had never quite got to grips with the local swimming pool – that murky bottom and those grubby changing rooms, last resting place of soggy Elastoplasts – but Adam was happy to take the children every Monday evening, leaving Kate at home on the sofa, pretending that she was about to start practising her yoga.

The four of them were not living in perfect harmony – they weren't even living together, for a start. And the symmetry that Kate had imagined at the beginning of the year – two single parents, brought together in a neat solution – seemed ridiculously optimistic now, because there were other people to complicate the equation: Clare and Pete, and all their histories. To be honest, Pete seemed even more of a blank to her these days – what had she ever seen in him? (But was it her fault – her lack of focus – that made him fuzzy around the edges?) Occasionally Kate wondered if she'd somehow mistaken him for someone else, convincing herself that his bland neutrality had been calmness, when it was nothing of the sort, just nothingness. (That's what comes of having a father who said too much: a husband who said too little.) But Pete was amiable, all the same; and when she worried that his apparent blankness might rub off onto Sam – not that blankness could rub out anything, actually – she reminded herself that she had not turned out like her own parents, not really. Anyway, it was possible that Pete had hidden depths as a father; and that maybe what she now saw was merely a front, to keep her from coming too close.

What did it all add up to, she wondered? Contentment, mostly, with the occasional burst of anxiety in the early hours of the morning when Adam was not in her bed, mixed up with flashes of pure joy when the four of them were at peace with each other, and he looked at her, this man she loved, over the heads of their children. Could she love Rose? It was too soon to tell – but she felt for her; felt her prickles of uncertainty, and wished to protect her from that.

Did they constitute a family? They were not like any other Kate had known – they did not live together, did not discuss that possibility – but something bound them together, threads that looked fragile, when regarded separately, yet were winding into a rough-edged whole. They were . . . viable – that seemed the right word; not solving the problems of her past, nor holding the key to the future, necessarily, but getting by, getting together, happily enough. Absorbed as she was by this, Kate did not much notice her father's silence, nor her mother's. Julian rang only occasionally – Jessica was on Prozac now, just a low dose, nothing to worry about, but life was far easier, he said. Harriet had dumped the Seattle boyfriend, and taken up with a likeable paediatrician instead. 'Not as handsome as George Clooney in ER,' she'd said, 'but lovely, all the same.' 'And his job will come in handy when you're married with kids,' Isabel had said; and though Harriet scoffed, there was something in the way she laughed that made Kate agree with Isabel's predictions of their future happiness. And Isabel? Isabel went on in her own quietly mysterious way.

The weeks passed, and the leaves began to fall, and they did not return to Elverson, living only in the present, day by day. Sometimes life felt chaotic – Sam never wanted to stay the night at Adam's flat if there was school the next morning and Rose was equally reluctant to sleep at Kate's house during the week, which meant that their evenings were fragmented, and often frustrated. Sometimes Adam annoyed her – he left shaved stubble and soap scum in her basin and tramped his muddy boots (hellish Mephisto) through the hall. But that smile of his, and the dip in his chin, where her little finger fitted . . . and he never behaved like a little boy in bed (unlike other needier men she had encountered – too irritating for words).

In October Bella asked them to come for Halloween, which fell on a Saturday night that year. 'But we won't be able to go trick or treating,' said Rose, disconsolate. 'I don't like it there, in the middle of nowhere.'

'You could go around the village,' said Kate. 'There are quite a few houses – how about giving it a try?' Rose shrugged and the corners of her mouth drooped, and Kate suppressed a sigh.

'I'd like to go,' said Sam, seizing the opportunity to prove himself more lovable than Rose.

'I think,' said Adam, 'that Rose will be in Manchester that weekend, and maybe I should stay in London to work – I've got to get that conservatory finished for Helena's horrid neighbours.'

'Horrid Helena, horrid Helena,' chanted Sam and Rose in unison, while Kate put her hands over her ears.

So Kate ended up going only with Sam to Elverson, which piqued her slightly, though the irritation was tinged with a kind of relief (at least there would be nothing to negotiate with Rose, or Adam for that matter). It was cold by now, an east wind blowing, and the remaining leaves were shivering on the trees. She did not much like autumn in London – too much dirt hidden beneath the sodden leaves on the pavement – but in Elverson it was more exciting, more reckless, when gales tore branches from the trees and clouds ran ragged across the wild sky. Bella had collected ruby-red hips and haws, as always, filling the vases in the house; and there were the voices of other children in the garden and upstairs – Julian's children, and Paul's twins, more unexpectedly; a source of excitement for Sam, for the boys were eleven years old. They were a little less identical than Kate remembered them – Jack was slightly broader and Danny's hair was darker than his twin's – but she could see Sam studying them, to make sure he remembered which was which.

'I didn't realize Paul and Becky were here,' she said to Bella, heart sinking at the thought of the scratchy conversations to come.

'Just Paul,' said Bella. 'Becky's doing some writing at

home – she's working on a novel, I think. And Jessica is in London, catching up with some friends – a hen night, apparently, for someone she used to work with.' She paused for a moment, still scooping out flesh from a giant pumpkin, to join the other lanterns on the kitchen table. 'Am I an impossible mother-in-law?' she asked. 'Maybe I'm doing something wrong.'

'You're lovely,' said Kate.

'Yes, but you're not my daughter-in-law,' said Bella, 'though I sometimes wonder if Julian didn't wish you were.' Kate felt herself flush, hot embarrassment rising from her neck to her face, which she tried to cover by bending over the smaller pumpkins that the children had carved. It was so unlike Bella to say such a thing, and Kate could think of no response; wondering, in fact, if she had misunderstood her aunt's odd choice of words – so she did what Bella might more usually do, and simply changed the subject.

'What were Charles's parents like?' she said. 'I hardly remember them.'

'Slightly intimidating at first,' said Bella. 'They were very self-contained, so I was never quite sure what they thought of me.'

'Sounds like your parents,' said Kate.

'No, they were more silent than mine. This house always seemed so quiet to me when they were living here, as though everything anyone had said, or even just wanted to say, was somehow absorbed into the walls.'

'And Luke? I can't remember much about him, either – just that he drove me to Elverson that summer when Mum and Dad split up.'

'Did he? I'd forgotten that. I always think of him as a

boy, even though he was only a year younger than Judith and me. We were friends, of course, at university – but he seemed such a puppy, and Judith always wrapped him round her little finger.' Bella smiled to herself, looking not at Kate but into the middle distance of memory. 'Charles's mother rather disapproved of us in those days – "You girls," she used to say, "leading my boys a merry dance." She never realized they gave as good as they got . . .'

'So why did Luke go to Australia?'

'I'm not quite sure. It was a shame – I'd always hoped that he and Judith might get back together again after she and your father split up. But maybe that was just me wanting a happy ending . . .'

'So they'd gone out with each other already?'

'Well, sort of, at Cambridge, before Sebastian came along.' Bella smiled again, a secretive smile, which reminded Kate of Isabel, and she wondered – though did not say so – if perhaps her father might have had some reason to feel suspicious, after all. Judith had always accused him of being paranoid; but it must have been unsettling, thought Kate, for him to see, or sense, the shifting allegiances between those twin sisters and that pair of brothers – even more unsettling, perhaps, because Sebastian as an only child could not have known the loyalties and rivalries with which siblings were entwined. Poor Sebastian, who had suspected plots in everything – capitalist plots he'd railed against, when she was still a small child and didn't understand his words; and anti-Semitic conspiracies that he suspected amidst his colleagues at work; and family stratagems, directed against him by his parents at first ('monstrous people, dead to me') and then his wife ('What were you doing in the water?' But, no, don't start up on that again, not now . . .). He'd spent so many years searching for answers and solutions – *schemes*, whereby everything would at last come clear: Marxism, post-modernism, structuralism, all those edifices and diagrams he'd been at pains to explain to her over the years; none of them sufficient in the end, all crumbling beneath him, eluding him, as disappointing as a faked map of buried treasure; sad Sebastian, like dusty Mr Casaubon in *Middlemarch*, lost in his useless search for 'The Key to All Mythologies'.

She'd wanted to ask more about Luke (What did he do in Australia? Was he married there?), but then Julian and Paul came into the kitchen together, Paul slightly awkward, Julian with that familiar provocative look of challenge. 'You're so appallingly bumptious,' Paul was saying to his brother.

'Better bumptious than squashed,' said Julian, thumping Paul on the back a little too hard.

'The unquashable hero, as ever,' said Paul, looking as if he might like to hit Julian even harder. 'How do you put up with him?' Paul went on, looking at Kate in a slightly accusatory manner, which made her want to blush again. (What was it with this family today? They all seemed to have leapt to absurd conclusions.)

'Come on,' said Julian, putting his arm around her shoulders, 'let's go and find our delightful children.' She let him steer her outside before shaking herself free of him.

'What was all that about with Paul?' she said.

'Oh nothing, really – history, I suppose, but dressed up as a discussion about modern economics.' His eyes sparkled, and he looked very much more pleased with himself than the last time she had seen him, in the summer. She told him so and he told her that it was simply the pleasure of seeing her again; but she guessed that something else – or someone other – was the cause of his good humour. A promotion at work? Or an affair, more likely, a girl at the office, perhaps, in high heels and a tight black pencil skirt – bold, like Julian, but enjoying this secret with him. Whatever the despondencies of his marriage, Julian could always bounce back; it was infuriating, but also part of his charm – for he would never lose himself in melancholy; his attention span was too short for enduring despair. 'So, what have you got planned for me tonight?' he said, smiling his dazzling smile. 'Trick or treat?'

'Oh, treat, of course,' she said, happy to flirt with him, knowing that they were safe with each other; safe from one another, for now. 'Speaking of which, who is going to escort our children around the village this evening?'

'I've already volunteered my father,' said Julian, 'but we can both go, as well, if you like.'

'Charles? Trick or treating? You've got to be joking.' But he was not: and there was Charles, striding across the lawn, five children lined up behind him already dressed in monster masks and fake blood – and Charles, most surprisingly, swathed in a long black cloak. 'What's come over him?' she said.

'Autumn – season of mellow fruitfulness,' said Julian. 'Maybe he's finally mellowing into old age.'

'But he's not old,' said Kate, unable to take her eyes off the procession through the garden. She ran towards them, to catch up, Julian behind her. 'Can we come to the village with you?' she said.

'Only if you dress up,' said Jack. When Kate explained she had nothing to wear, Julian told her to wait for a moment and disappeared into the house, returning a few minutes later with two more dusty black cloaks. 'Where did you get those?' she said. 'Have you lot been running a secret coven at Elverson without my realizing?'

'I don't know where they first came from,' said Charles, 'but they've been knocking around for years, for as long as I can remember.' She slipped into her cloak, which was velvet and hooded – like a widow's, she thought – and saw Julian, similarly hooded in his. Sam regarded her, with approval, she hoped, but he looked a bit frightened so she reached out for his hand. 'Do I look too scary?' she said.

'Mum, I'm not a little kid,' he said, moving away, clearly wanting to impress his older cousins. But when they were further from the house, on the path through the woods to the village, he did take her hand, in the darkness; and she was glad of it, because there was something quite spooky about being there, following Charles with his candle-lit pumpkin. Julian was carrying his daughter on his shoulders, fairy wings attached to her crimson jumper and a wand clutched in her fist; Rafael was walking hand in hand with Charles, who seemed to be explaining the history of Halloween. 'It used to be called All Hallows Eve,' he said, 'the night when people thought that the veil between the living and the dead was flimsiest.'

'Do you believe in ghosts?' said Danny. 'My parents say it's a load of rubbish.'

'What do you believe?' said Charles. Danny shrugged his shoulders, while his brother smirked. They'd reached the lychgate into the churchyard, but kept on the path towards the village, just a hundred yards or so away.

'Where are the witches and ghoulies?' said Madeleine, lurching on Julian's shoulders as she twisted around to look.

'In the cupboard back at the house, I suppose,' said Rafael.

'Why are they in the cupboard?' said Sam.

'My mum says there're lots of skeletons in the cupboards at Elverson,' said Rafael.

Julian was talking, loudly as usual, to Charles and the twins, so Kate guessed that none of them had heard Rafael's remark, but for once she felt Julian's wife had rather endeared herself to her, and wished – for the first time – that Jessica were here. And just as she had glimpsed her father's point of view earlier this evening, now she could see why Jessica and Becky might feel an unwillingness to be drawn into Elverson: not because Bella was a nightmare, but because the family – like most families, doubtless – had its unsettling, even sinister, side (and as she was thinking that, she remembered herself as a child, and her father explaining to her the other meaning of sinister – 'on the left side', he had said, 'in heraldry, the left side from the point of view of the bearer of the shield.'). Tonight Charles carried the pumpkin like a shield, with Rafael on his left side; the child Julian believed to be an angel; the boy who saw the skeletons in Charles's cupboard. Kate was being absurdly whimsical, she knew – but if there were ever a time for magical thinking, then surely it was Halloween.

By now they'd reached the village – just a couple of lanes, meeting at the crossroads by the church. She didn't know how many children lived in the village these days – there'd never been many, not enough for a school – but there seemed to be half a dozen or so out tonight, carrying lanterns, and mostly accompanied by parents. Charles seemed to recognize them all, even the family that was here just for the weekend, in their second home. (Another side to him, as well – this unexpected sociability.) 'I'm not sure if some of the more God-fearing old ladies in the village will approve of trick or treating,' he was saying to the twins, who had just donned their rubber monster masks, 'so do be polite monsters, if you can.' But, as it turned out, the old ladies were charmed by Madeleine (and by Charles's impeccable manners, of course) – none more so than Mrs Cox, Bella's retired housekeeper, who asked them in for toffee apples and mulled wine after they'd finished their brief tour of the village.

'Look at you, Kate, in that cloak,' said Mrs Cox, 'the image of your mother.'

'Do I look like her?' said Kate. 'I suppose you never know what you really look like – because mirrors show you the wrong way round, don't they?'

'Reversed symmetry,' said Julian, 'or is that not right? I can never remember that stuff.'

'And aren't you two a proper pair,' said Mrs Cox, 'just like each other in those old cloaks – now where did you find them? I haven't seen them for years – they was the ones you used to dress up in when you were little. Opera cloaks, I think they were – they'd been in a trunk in the attic, used to belong to your father's grandmother.' She was making hot chocolate for the children – 'They need something warm inside them, so they don't catch cold' – and kept sliding glances at Sam. 'Don't take after no one in the Reid family, do he?' she said.

'Well, he wouldn't,' said Julian.

'Though I seem to recall your grandmother might have had red hair when she was a little girl.'

'That was my father's mother,' said Julian, 'no relation of Sam's – unless you count her as an in-law, I suppose.' Mrs Cox appeared to take no notice of him, simply humming to herself and handing out the toffee apples. 'Well, nearly eight o'clock, better be off,' said Julian, picking up Madeleine again, now chocolate-smeared and drooping. 'Thanks ever so much, Mrs Cox . . .' Outside her house, as they set off back home, he whispered to Kate, 'Does she think Sam's my son? She must be going batty.'

'I don't think so,' said Kate. But she had started wondering: did Mrs Cox think that Sam was Charles's grandson? What if the old lady suspected that Kate were Charles' daughter – or Luke's, perhaps? She was seized by an impulse to run back to Mrs Cox's cottage, and ask her outright. Would it be waking the dead to do so, or laying ghosts to rest at last? Kate kept walking, swept along by the others, unwilling to turn around, yet hesitant, too. 'Oh, for goodness sake,' said her mother's voice in her head, out of nowhere, as their little procession turned the corner around the graveyard, 'do stop fretting. You're just like your father – your *father*, Sebastian – with all these thoughts of plots and mysteries. There *is* no mystery – you are his daughter, though I do appreciate why you'd rather not be; why, in fact, you feel it to be such a mystery that he is your father. And I do see your point – he's a hopeless father, but he's yours, and no one else's.'

'But what about Luke and Charles?' Kate asked her mother, not out loud.

'What about them?'

'Well, Mrs Cox said—'

'Mrs Cox said nothing. Oh, Mrs Cox had a sense of something, yes, I grant you that – but it was gossip, making two and two add up to five.' Her mother's ghost seemed to giggle, laughter rippling through the dead leaves. 'Bella and I made two, and so did Luke and Charles – but you were not the mystery fifth to the equation. I flirted with Luke, even after I'd fallen for Sebastian – just like you still flirt with Julian, you know you do, you know I see you. And Charles – well, I'd loved him once, in a way. But Sebastian – he was the one for me, my own disaster, my chosen one. That's the mystery here.'

'You sound remarkably cheerful, for a dead person.'

'Speak for yourself.'

'But I'm not dead.'

'No, but you're cheerful, aren't you? And so you should be – if you can just remember to look to the future, rather than the past.'

This seemed such an unlikely thing for a ghost to say that Kate was almost convinced that she'd invented the entire conversation herself – another piece of conjured whimsy, spun out for Halloween. (But why did her dead mother seem more alive now than she had ever been?) And if Kate hadn't made it up . . . well, she'd never know, not in this life, and maybe this life was all there is. Wasn't that what her mother was telling her? But how could a ghost tell you that there was only the here-and-now, not the here-after? The voice that had seemed so clear a few seconds ago was already fading, vague and hazy like a will o' wisp, lost in the night again, trickling into the stream. Kate began to feel confused – though not unhappily so – and there seemed to be nothing for it but to keep on walking through the darkness, following the light of Charles's lantern, back to Elverson.

Thirty-Three

The clocks went back that night – the end of summertime, as if they'd needed reminding, when an icy wind whipped around the terraces of Elverson and the oak tree sighed. Just after midnight, on her way to bed, Kate found Charles in the hall, adjusting the grandfather clock, turning it back to eleven. 'I'm on my circuit of the clocks,' he said, 'though I've never been able to get them to chime precisely in time with each other. Maddening – it must be something I'm doing to the clockwork . . .'

'The Uncertainty Principle,' said Kate, thinking of her drunken night with Harriet (their last lost hour, for the time being).

'So you've taken up with Werner Heisenberg at last?' said her uncle, locking the mahogany clock cabinet with a tiny silver key.

'No, not really – Harriet tried to explain it to me, but she said she'd never really understood it herself.'

'Of course, she does,' said Charles. 'She's a very clever girl, just as you are.' He was walking into his study by then, and gestured, almost imperceptibly, for Kate to follow him.

'Two more clocks in here,' he said. 'Absurd, really, how many there are in this house. That was my father for you – a great believer in Newtonian mechanics.'

'I thought he was a Classicist?' said Kate, who remembered, vaguely, a dusty set of the first Professor Reid's Greek translations, a life's work, lodged somewhere in the house.

'Exactly,' said Charles, 'I rest my case.' Kate didn't really know what he was talking about, but, emboldened by the simple fact that he was talking, decided to tackle again the question that her mother had advised her to forget. ('I'm sorry,' she imagined calling after her mother, chasing the winds across the angry sky, 'but it's now or never – and after now, never, I promise; I won't ask again.') If it was all down to your point of view – to where you were standing – as to whether or not something had a sinister aspect, then surely it was right she asked Charles about that scene in the water, in the woods, wherever it was, whatever it might mean . . . Now, she told herself, was the best time to ask him: in this limbo, this extra hour that existed only tonight, when the clock moved backwards and the dead walked the earth. 'The thing I'm most uncertain of,' she said, as Charles opened the second clock face, humming to himself under his breath, 'is how things stood between my mother and you. My father, you see, seemed to think you were having an affair. And when I was little, I heard him saying, "What were you doing in the water?" I know he sometimes imagined things, when he was at his craziest, but I do seem to remember being there – watching, though maybe I'm inventing it – seeing you with my mother, in the water, and you were kissing her . . .'

'Which is why you think she killed herself?' said

Charles, not looking at Kate, examining the workings of the clock as if the answer lay within it. 'All those years later, for lost love?'

'I don't know,' said Kate. 'That's the point – that's what haunts me, not knowing.'

'And that's what haunts me, too,' he said, 'and what haunts everyone as we grow older – not knowing what might have been. But it was no more than that, Kate – if you're remembering the same scene as I do – just a moment in time, the swiftest of innocent kisses, a gentle reminder of what was long gone. I love Bella, and your mother loved your father – those were our choices. But there are rare instances – you must have had one yourself – when you glimpse how the past might have taken a different course, and the past intersects with the present, in a flash, and then it disappears. And maybe you witnessed that instance between myself and your mother – a vanished moment, except in your head.'

'And in yours? You didn't forget it?'

'No, I didn't. But I don't regret the trajectory of my life – though I do regret the ending of your mother's. And I know you want to understand – want me to explain her death to you, perhaps, to tell you whether or not it was an accident. But I can't do that for you – though God knows, it's tormented me – because I wasn't there when she crashed, no one was, apart from your mother, and it has to remain inexplicable – impossible to unravel into a neat set of facts.' He spoke more rapidly than usual, his sentences less measured, his hands still fluttering inside the clock.

'But what about that stuff you said to me at the beginning of the year, about Aquinas and whatever it was he said? You know, accidents waiting to happen . . .'

'As I said at the time, that's just *an* answer – not *the* answer. And not a very good answer, either.' He turned to Kate, at last, looking at her directly, instead of at the clock. 'I'm sorry, I haven't been very helpful, have I? I wasn't very helpful to your mother, either. She wanted my advice about your father's mental collapse – and I was hopeless, I'm afraid, absolutely useless. As a matter of fact, it frightened me – the chaos in his head, that seemed to seep outside, towards the rest of us. I didn't do enough to protect you from that, either of you.' His dignified face looked crumpled, suddenly, its familiar smooth lines sagging, and she feared that he might cry – but no, that would be impossible, her uncle would never cry (though what was it Harriet had said about seeing Charles sobbing, after Judith's death?).

'It's OK,' she said, 'you gave me Elverson as a refuge – my safe house. And it never seemed chaotic here, I always imagined it as a place of perfect symmetry.' But as she said it, Kate felt just for a moment that his study – this building they stood in – was suddenly not solid, as if previously invisible cracks in the walls might open up, might swallow them. And it struck her how imaginary Elverson had been to her: more ordered in her mind than it ever really was; for people had cried here, and quarrelled, and despaired of the random messiness of their lives. She should have listened to the uneven chiming of clocks, the clue that in Elverson's apparent order there was irregularity, when time did not run smoothly, ran its own course and was lost . . . 'Come on,' she said, touching her uncle's sleeve, feeling unexpectedly amused by her earnest efforts to understand everything ('the effing ineffable,' Harriet had once said). 'Let's go and change that clock in the kitchen, if you haven't already done it, and find something to drink.'

Julian and Paul were sitting at the table drinking whisky by the flickering light of the candles inside the pumpkin lanterns. 'It's rather dark in here, isn't it?' said Charles, his voice controlled again.

'We're conjuring up the dead,' said Paul, slurring his words just enough for Kate to guess he was drunk. 'Hell of a lot of ghosts in this house, aren't there? Hell of a house.' Charles merely raised his eyebrows, poured himself a glass of water, and made for the door, murmuring a quiet 'goodnight' on his way out. 'What's up with him?' said Paul. 'Did I say something wrong?'

'Perish the thought,' said Julian. 'You are, as ever, the essence of charm.' Paul stood up, swaying slightly, and announced that he was going to bed, punching Julian, hard, on the shoulder, as if in farewell.

'That looked like it hurt,' said Kate, when Paul had gone.

'It did,' said Julian, 'but it's too late to get into an argument with Paul, and he's had too much to drink.'

'Did you fight when you were kids?' she said, wondering why she had never noticed the tension between the brothers, or if it was something new.

'We were always incredibly competitive,' he said, 'and I suppose it's still there. I don't know – I don't see him that often. We're forever promising to have lunch with each other in the City, but then something always comes up. Not very fraternal, is it? Or maybe that's what most brothers are like . . .'

'I wouldn't know,' she said, remembering only that she had envied them as children, believing them to have been united in comradeship. What a curiously unobservant child she must have been – or maybe she noticed only what she wanted to; fixating on the tiny details, unaware of the bigger picture. She looked across at his face, shadowy in the candlelight, studying it, and tried to fix it in her mind – grown-up Julian, not the boy he once was.

'You look exactly the same to me as you always did,' said Julian, as if guessing her thoughts. 'Same green eyes that turn yellow when you're angry.'

'And when am I ever angry with you?'

'Not as often as you used to be. Not nearly as often as Jessica.'

'But things are better between the two of you, I thought.'

'We're OK,' he said. 'And I could never leave her, never – I couldn't bear what it would do to the kids, the havoc it would wreak.' She flinched, slightly, and he looked embarrassed. 'Oh, God, I'm sorry – that was tactless of me. And stupid – I mean, just look at Sam. He's a great kid – a good advertisement for divorce, actually.'

'Don't be absurd,' she said, smiling; relieved not to feel the usual hostility rising between them.

'Katie, Kate,' he said, pushing a lock of hair back from her face, as tenderly as he might to a little girl. 'Let me walk you up to your bedroom, to keep the ghosts at bay.'

'I quite like ghosts,' she said. 'Sometimes they're easier than the living.' He took her hand and pulled her up from the chair. They climbed the stairs together, still hand in hand, like they did when they were children, and on the first-floor landing he kissed her on the cheek. 'Sweet dreams,' he said. 'See you in the morning.'

Kate looked in on Sam first, sleeping in the little bedroom beside hers, the dog curled up beside him, his Halloween costume discarded on the floor amidst piles of sweet wrappers. She stroked his cheek, soft as a butterfly's wing, and then climbed into her own bed. Downstairs, the clocks struck midnight again; still not in unison, but with an odd harmony all of their own.

Thirty-Four

When Kate came downstairs the following morning, Paul was already up – bleary-eyed, but less pugnacious – doing a Sunday-newspaper crossword with Bella, his dark hair (a little greying now) bent close beside his mother's faded light brown. 'Six letters, diagram of astrological signs,' he said to Kate. 'We're stuck – any ideas?'

'I haven't got a clue,' she said.

'That *is* the clue,' he said, jabbing at the newspaper. 'Fifteen down, diagram of—'

'So you said. I'm sorry – I've always been hopeless at crosswords.'

'But you're an English graduate!' he said. 'You're supposed to be good with words.'

'Not those sort,' she said. 'Scrabble, crosswords, all that stuff – can't get my head around them, unless it's really easy clues.' Paul looked bored and turned back to the newspaper on the kitchen table, staring at it, waiting for the puzzle to become clear. 'The person you need to talk to is Harriet,' said Kate. 'She knows about astrology.'

'Does she really?' he said. 'How extraordinary – I always thought she had a mathematical bent.'

'I have an idea that there was a time when mathematicians used to be interested in astrology,' said Bella. 'The two don't necessarily preclude each other.'

'But one's mumbo-jumbo and the other's scientific!' said Paul, looking rather more invigorated at the prospect of a friendly quarrelling match.

'Well, you say that,' said Bella, 'but there are occasions when mathematics seems like utter mumbo-jumbo to me. Honestly, when your father starts talking about the equations for parallel universes, I haven't got the foggiest what he's going on about.'

'Dad doesn't believe in parallel universes,' said Paul.

'It's not a question of believing or disbelieving,' said Bella. 'The mere possibility is of mathematical interest to him.'

'They had parallel universes on the telly last weekend,' piped up Sam, who had been listening quietly at the other end of the table, eating his way through a large bowl of cornflakes. 'You can get there through a black hole, I think, or something called a worm – not a real worm, but a sort of worm hole, that wiggles through into the other side.' He looked for approval at the twins, who stared blankly back at him; and though Kate wanted to intervene on his behalf, she knew not to, because it would embarrass him, and anyway, Sam seemed undeterred by these signs of incipient adolescence in his cousins (or maybe they were just rude, like their father). 'Do you want to go outside and skateboard?' he said to the twins, putting his empty bowl in the sink.

'Whatever,' they said, shrugging, but getting up, any-way.

It was a mild, muggy morning, All Saints' Day, and Kate imagined the ghosts of last night safely at rest: not buried in their graves, too dreadful a thought, but coasting through the air, in the clouds; free at last from the voices of the living, released from the clasp of those they had loved. The cloud was so heavy, so low in the sky, that the spirits would be hidden from view, but still they were close, ready to revisit the earth again tomorrow for the feast of All Souls'. These occasions were printed on Bella's desk calendar, by the telephone in the hall: without the neatly typeset reminders, Kate might have forgotten that such religious observances existed (and surely the dead did not obey the rules of a church calendar; nor the bereaved, come to that, but wandered together, in limbo, out of time).

She'd never gone to church with her mother – nor had Sebastian taken her to synagogue when she was a child, for he was in his aggressively atheist period then, and anyway, he told Kate on her sixth birthday, she couldn't be Jewish with a Christian mother. This had confused her, because Judith didn't seem very Christian to Kate, though she did say 'Oh, Jesus' a lot when she was cross. But at Elverson, church had been part of the fabric of their lives: not that they were particularly holy, but it felt intrinsic to the house, as much as the family – the path at the side of the front lawn leading directly through the woods to the church, like a fairy tale, it had appeared to Kate as a little girl.

She did not intend to go to church today – what did All Saints' Day mean, anyway? It occurred to Kate this morn-ing that her erratic attachment to the Elverson church had been another element in her search for pattern and structure – and now she liked the idea of being in a kind of free fall, floating like an autumn leaf from a skeleton tree. While Sam and the twins skateboarded on the asphalt stretch of the drive, she wandered through the garden in the twilight of the November morning, cloud blurring into mist rising from the ground, everything colourless. You could hear more than you could see; though the children's voices were also muffled in the haze. There was a bonfire, somewhere, she guessed, sniffing for the wood-smoke, but it must have been smouldering in the damp air.

As Kate walked, she tried to work out the answer to the crossword clue; it seemed somehow important to get it. A chart – wasn't that the name for the diagram that astrologers drew up, based on a client's birth time? But 'chart' was only five letters long, so it couldn't be right. One of Pete's flakier fashion friends had presented them with Sam's astrological chart a few days after his birth; she'd read it once or twice, but it didn't seem to make very many specific predictions, nothing that might come in useful, like, 'Your parents will split up when you are still a toddler, but never fear, you will overcome such difficult beginnings.' She'd kept the chart somewhere – buried in her desk, probably – and never consulted it again, like an inaccurate or obsolete map.

So, no charts then; but what was the right word? Six letters . . . her brain was foggy, like the day, like her dreams. She ran through the alphabet, A to Z . . . zodiac: could that be the answer? Zodiac – six letters; imagine how many it would score on a scrabble board if you got it in the right place. Zodiac – that had to be right; the astrological diagram of the twelve star signs. She started walking back to the house, to tell Paul, feeling pleased with herself – and then suddenly couldn't be bothered. What did it matter, anyway? She imagined the mist enveloping Paul's crossword puzzle, the black grid disappearing before his eyes, his hands clutching at the piece of paper, but it vanishing, the printed lines and the words and the numbers, all dissolving into thin air . . .

Thirty-Five

Back in London, the mists continued through the early days of November. Kate woke every morning in a light that was more like dusk than dawn, and walked Sam to school along the dampened streets. Maybe it was the dim imprecision of the weather that made him ask, over and over again, what time it was, what day of the week, and who would be picking him up from school. She tried to answer him without irritation, keeping her voice light under the heavy sky. 'I'll be there at quarter past three,' she said, waving him goodbye as he trudged across the playground, tugging at his backpack, tugging at her heart.

Guy Fawkes Night was on a Thursday, but the fireworks went off every evening, as they had been doing for at least a week; the constant explosions unnerving their cat, who retreated to Sam's bed as soon as it got dark every afternoon, emerging only in the early morning to eat and sniff the air outside. 'Poor puss,' she said, stroking the cat, which purred for a little while and then batted Kate with semi-retracted claws.

Sam was not wildly enthusiastic about fireworks;

certainly not at close quarters, though he seemed to have recovered from his overwhelming fear of them as a toddler (his only apparent phobia, apart from a horror of clowns, which seemed entirely justified to Kate, though that too had passed). Adam was taking Rose to the big display at her school, but Sam said he'd rather stay at home to look after the cat and watch the fireworks from the attic windows. Kate didn't mind – she liked the view from up there, away from the crowds, but close enough to see the lights in the sky. It had rained and rained that afternoon, a downpour that had died down to drizzle by 7.30, as if dwindling into the ghost of water, when the display began. The biggest fireworks, the ones that soared highest, were almost obscured by the mist and the smoke from the bonfire, but they were still beautiful, like the briefest of rainbows in the clouds, or falling stars, visible only for a few seconds, silvery and perfect and then lost. 'Would a firework be big enough to blow up a house?' asked Sam, standing on a chair beside her, craning his head to see the flares to the north, and another display over to the west of them.

'No,' said Kate, 'though you must never let off fireworks inside the house.'

'I *do* know that,' he said. 'But how come Guy Fawkes thought he could blow up the Houses of Parliament?'

'He was using gunpowder,' she said, 'not fireworks. The fireworks are just to remember him by – little explosions, to remember the past.'

'They don't sound very little to me,' said Sam, as a volley of crackers went off in the street outside. 'It sounds like a war. What is it that makes the fireworks explode, then?'

'Gunpowder, I think,' said Kate, aware that she was stepping into a different minefield.

'But you said that's what Guy Fawkes used, not fireworks?'

'Well, he did use gunpowder, but there's also a little bit of it in fireworks.'

'So what makes them go up in the air then, before they explode? Because they've got to go up first, haven't they? They can't just explode on the ground.'

'I don't know, Sam,' she said, giving up the struggle to explain. 'I'm sorry, but you'll have to ask someone else.'

Later, when he was asleep, the cat curled up beside his feet underneath the duvet, Kate rang Adam. 'When am I ever going to see you again?' she said.

'Tomorrow and the next day and the next day,' he said.

'And after that?'

'After that it's Monday.'

'And then?'

'And then we could start looking for a place to live together,' he said.

Kate was so surprised that she didn't answer him at first. 'Hello?' he said. 'Are you still there? Have I said something terrible?'

'No, not at all,' she said. 'Just unexpected. What about Clare?'

'What about her?' he said. 'We're getting a divorce.'

'Are you? You didn't say . . .'

'It's not about her, anyway. It's about you. I want to live with you. I love you.'

'OK,' she said, which was an inadequate response, she knew, but words failed her – were entirely absent, in fact.

Adam seemed not to mind; he was not the sort of man who liked talking on the phone, anyway. He said goodnight to her and that he'd call her in the morning. 'OK,' she replied, for the second time, and that was the end of it.

But it wasn't the end, was it? It was the beginning, again. That was what was so frightening. She wished she had an astrological diagram that could show her the future: just a rough guide, a map with warnings of dragons and precipices and chasms; or a compass, at least, that would point her in the right direction. But there was nothing to guide her, no stars visible in the cloudy sky; and she could not afford to take a wrong turn again, not with Sam by her side. She had to get it right this time, and the thought froze her. No wonder her mother had sunk into inertia, into petrified melancholy, after Sebastian had gone. Not that Kate would allow that to happen to herself; she would not, could not, be like her mother; inertia turning into something out of control, though what was the point of fighting the uncontrollable? 'Stop it,' Kate said to herself, as her mind whirred and wavered. 'Don't panic, OK?' OK – she muttered, again; shorthand for the unsayable, the unspeakable, the unknowable. OK didn't sound very much – but it would simply have to do.

The winds blew that night, sweeping some of the clouds away, so that Friday was a little brighter, a wraith-like sun in the washed-out sky. Kate was up in the attic again, supposed to be writing, but staring out of the window. A helicopter hovered in the distance, too far to hear through the closed window, and then moved on, out of sight, but she could make out its sound when she couldn't see it. She turned back to her computer screen. No new emails; just

yesterday's reminder from the features editor of the magazine that they needed her article on the cultural significance
of the January sales: 2,000 words, please, by Monday
morning. Kate started writing. It wasn't so hard to come up
with those words; sentence followed sentence, turned into
defined paragraphs, formed a beginning, a middle and an
end, and the end referred back to the beginning in a neatly
constructed circle, just as it should. She was breathing more
easily now; there was nothing to worry about, up here, in
the silence.

Kate worked solidly for several hours, stopping only to
make cups of tea, and by 2.30 she had finished a first draft.
Her head was aching by then, so she switched off the
computer and went downstairs, lying on her bed for ten
minutes, eyes closed. Into her mind drifted the memory
of her mother writing, the tip-tap of an old typewriter,
unintelligible to Kate at the time, but comforting, nonethe-
less. What had her mother been writing? A fairy tale for
grown-ups, she'd said, but Kate had no sign that her mother
had ever finished the story; nothing but that sole-surviving
handwritten page. She imagined her mother writing now in
the sky: cartwheeling, skywriting, a bold hand drawing the
ribbons of clouds and jet streams into a message for her
daughter. Kate opened her eyes and looked out of the open
window, out above the roof of the house across the street,
above the television aerial and the chimney where the crows
perched, up into the empty sky. It was a beautiful nothingness, peaceful; no answers there.

She looked around the room: walls the colour of
lavender, white ceiling, bookshelves on either side of the
bed, a framed photograph of her mother on the marble

mantelpiece and snapshots of Sam propped against an old watercolour that had belonged to her grandmother – a girl in a pink dress, hiding behind a gauzy veil. It seemed inconceivable that she might leave this room, this house: pack it up into boxes, and move somewhere new. It was not perfect, not like Harriet's flat: Sam's fingerprints were on the wall beside the stairs, a little higher every year, as he grew taller, but still trailed across the white paint, even though he no longer needed to steady himself. Piles of papers gathered on spare surfaces, and Sam's toys colonized every room, despite her efforts to tidy up. The skirting boards in the hall were scuffed by his shoes and skateboard, and by the long-gone buggy that had been parked there when he was too young to walk; but it was their house, and she loved it. She remembered the night she'd moved there with Pete – hating it all, hating the bathroom that still smelt of strangers, and the dark kitchen cupboards and lino floor. She'd been pregnant, and everything smelt odd then, heightened, nauseating, repellently meaty. But now the house had cleanly stripped wooden floors, and a white bathroom that had belonged to no one before her; and the kitchen was full of light, with units painted the colour of the pale Norfolk sea in summer – a shade she'd spent hours choosing, mixing it herself, and then brushing it onto the raw wood late at night when Sam was a baby, with careful strokes. Pete had paid for the new kitchen, and its limestone floor, not long before he'd left her; she'd believed it to be a sign of his commitment to their shared domestic future, but when it turned out to be something other than that – a guilty feathering of the nest he was about to abandon, perhaps – she did not resent the house he had forsaken. She'd painted it often since then: smooth white layers, except for the coloured walls of her bedroom, brushing away the dust and the dirt brought in from the outside, making her house into a creamy cocoon.

But while she could not imagine leaving her home, nor could she envisage Adam moving into it with Rose. The attic room was tiny – and anyway, it was where she worked, piled high with books and reporters' notepads; and the spare back bedroom on the first floor was almost as small, with space for nothing much but a single bed, a bookshelf and a chest of drawers. That left only Sam's room, and Rose couldn't be expected to share it with him. And her bedroom – where would Adam fit into it? Night after night, his Mephisto boots beside her bed; Adam inside her.

She sat up hurriedly and ran down the stairs. Time to get to school; time to fetch Sam. 'Friday afternoons are my favourite day of the week,' he said, cheeks glowing, allowing her to take his hand as they crossed the road opposite the school gates. 'Who decided that the weekend would only be two days, and the rest of the week is five?'

'I don't know,' she said.

'What are we doing this weekend?'

'I'm not sure – something nice.'

'Is Adam coming over?'

'I think so.'

'And Rose?'

'Probably.'

'But I want Robbie to stay the night tomorrow.'

'Well, maybe they can both stay.'

'Course they can't!'

'Then Robbie can stay another night.'

'That's not fair!'

'Sam, we didn't see Adam and Rose last weekend, so we're seeing them this weekend, OK?' He didn't answer her, just chewed his lower lip, pulling his hand out of hers. How could they be arguing already? 'Are you hungry?' she said. He shook his head. 'Do you want Robbie to come round now, for tea?' He shrugged. 'Where is Robbie, anyway?' she said.

'Dunno. He played with Tom today. It's not fair – I was all by myself, I didn't have anyone to play with.' He was close to tears by now, and though Kate knew he was not friendless (his teacher had said only last week how sociable he was), she could not stop herself from worrying.

'I tell you what,' she said, 'let's stop off at Robbie's house on the way home, and you can see him and I'll have a cup of tea with Maria – I don't think she's at college this afternoon.'

'I don't want to go to his house,' said Sam.

'Well, I do,' she said, hoping she didn't sound childish; but as it turned out, there was no answer when she rang Maria's doorbell. It was then that Sam started crying out loud.

If it was this hard to spend a weekend with Adam, she thought, how could they ever live together? How was she supposed to cut up her life with Sam, like a photograph, and rearrange it into a different picture, one that incorporated Adam and Rose? It only worked when she didn't think about it, just did it, one day at a time; but the thought of making solid what had been nebulous – well, that seemed impossible. When she was younger she'd longed for confirmation that life was built on immovable bedrock; now, after her marriage to Pete had dissolved, she was happy to drift in the slipstream.

As it turned out, the prospect of seeing Rose was worse than the reality for Sam. Adam had arrived at six with pizza and sparklers; and after they'd eaten, the four of them went out into the garden, looping their sparklers in the dark. 'Can you see what I'm writing in the air?' said Sam. Kate couldn't guess – the glowing lines were gone in a fraction of a second – but Rose got it first time. 'Your name,' she said. 'Sam! Look, I'm doing mine!'

When the sparklers ran out, they went back inside and watched *EastEnders*: all of them bound up together by the familiar plotlines, discussing the likely outcome of the latest cliffhanger on the television screen. Sam and Rose assumed their usual positions on the sofa, side by side between Adam and Kate, separating their parents, united in doing so. But Adam's arm reached behind the children, like the first time they'd watched television together on that long-ago Sunday evening at his flat, his hand taking Kate's, their fingers laced together now.

They went to bed as soon as the children had stopped whispering in Sam's room, the giggles having subsided into the even breathing of sleep. Kate began to talk, hesitantly, about what Adam had said on the phone, but her sentences dissolved in his kisses. 'You were saying?' he said, running his hands down her body. She tried to answer, but found she could not speak, she only sighed, and then was lost, losing herself like always, with him.

In the morning it was raining, raining and raining, solid sheets of water, it seemed from the inside. Kate made pancakes for breakfast, flipping them in the pan, and then Adam played Monopoly with the children, which she hated but they loved. As they inched around the board, buying their properties, staking their claims, she could hear other negotiations taking place between them. 'My dad lives near there,' said Sam, a little too loudly, as Adam landed on Marylebone Station.

'Do you think he'll mind if I buy it?' said Adam.

'S'pose not,' said Sam. 'He's in New York a lot, anyway.'

'And it's OK with you?' said Adam.

'Yeah,' said Sam.

'Marylebone it is, then,' said Adam, handing over his paper money. Watching them, Kate remembered an evening when she was a child and her mother had gone out, leaving her with a babysitter. Sebastian must have left by then, and Kate was tormented by fears that her mother would be kidnapped. Huddled in her bedroom, she could hear her babysitter, a student who lived nearby, saying something, indistinctly. And then she heard a man's voice – a stranger, stranger danger, like they learnt at school – saying, 'Give me £500.' Kate's heart had thumped so loudly she thought it would explode, for she was sure now that this was the kidnapper, come to demand her mother's ransom money. She had stayed in bed, agonized, too scared to cry; and at last, after hours it seemed, though it was probably only a few minutes, inched her way from the bedroom along the hall to the living room, where the voices were. And there, through the slightly open door, she had seen her babysitter, her betrayer, laughing with the kidnapper. Then the kidnapper leant forward to kiss the girl, the babysitter, and Kate knew that she was trapped; it was inescapable. She'd crept back to her bedroom, waiting for the worst, and then suddenly, in bed, it came to her, the detail in the living room that she had missed. The Monopoly board – they were playing Monopoly, the babysitter and the kidnapper – no, he couldn't be a kidnapper, he must be the girl's boyfriend. Still not trusting herself, or what she had seen, Kate lay awake until her mother returned home. 'Had a good evening?' said the kidnapper to her mother outside in the hall.

'Lovely,' she said. 'And you?'

'Oh, we've been playing Monopoly,' said the babysitter. 'He won, of course.'

In her bedroom, Kate had said nothing, and later told no one of her fears that night. She'd kept so much quiet, as if she were living in a cult that could not be spoken of in the outside world. When her father was in mental hospital, she'd kept that a secret, as well. At thirteen, sitting with her friends in a cinema, an advertisement came on, recruiting psychiatric nurses. 'Do you care?' said the voice-over, almost accusatory. Yes, Kate did care, she cared very much; but she did not know what to say, her face hot with embarrassment and shame in the dark cinema, her friends laughing by her side, oblivious.

Poor Sebastian. He'd always said too much, never knew when to stop, even when he was depressed. When that blackness descended upon him, he would sit in silence for an hour or so, but then the words would come pouring out, like bile, acidic, like an assault. The worst times were when Kate had been alone with him. Her mother had decided it was important that Kate spend every other weekend with Sebastian. At first, he'd seemed almost oblivious to her presence; that was when he was depressed, and when he was manic, he was flying, beyond anyone's reach. But then he'd started saying terrible things, making her skin burn, burning her insides. 'If we lived in Africa, you'd be having sex with me,' he'd said, looking at Kate as if he hated her. 'Did you know that?'

She'd shaken her head, mutely. 'You don't know?' said Sebastian, jabbing his finger at Kate, pushing it into her chest. 'Haven't you read any social anthropology? What kind of fucking awful school does your fucking awful mother send you to? She's a fucking witch, she is, just like you – you deserve each other, the pair of you.' He said other things like that as well, too awful to repeat, too awful to remember; Kate had buried them at the back of her mind, where they'd lodged, those ugly words, covered over with the silt mud of memory. No wonder, now, her conversations with her father were so infrequent, and so stilted; that these days so much was left unsaid.

Kate knew that she should ring him today; it was weeks since they'd last spoken, months . . . He didn't ring her, either; but that wasn't the point. Why couldn't she just pick up the phone and talk to him? But she still didn't know what to say; nor did she know how to talk about him, not after all those years of silence. She'd tried to describe what her father had been like, just once, to Pete, but it seemed impossible; or at least, Pete seemed to not want to hear; to not want to know. Who could blame him, really? Other people's unhappy families, like other people's dreams, can be so boring: that's what Pete had said – not then, but another time. He preferred pictures to words, anyway. 'No one reads your magazine for the words in it,' he'd say, nudging Kate, as if she'd enjoy the joke. 'Don't know why you bother writing, darling, not in a glossy. Readers just want something pretty to look at.'

'Then why call them readers?' she'd replied, not smiling.

'Lighten up, babe,' he'd said.

It was hardly surprising, thought Kate, washing up after the pancakes as the Monopoly game progressed, that she was anxious about what would happen next with Adam. Her record with men was not good: fractured relationship with her father; failed marriage. Surely she was right to be cautious? But how wonderful to be free, to throw caution to the winds . . . How did you do that, exactly? She imagined a woman standing on the edge of a cliff, scattering ripped-up bits of paper, grey-black legalese turned into confetti, swirling over the edge.

'All right?' said Adam, looking up from the Monopoly board.

'All right,' she said.

Thirty-Six

So that was that, mind made up; she told him on Saturday evening that yes, they could live together. By Sunday morning Kate had changed her mind, and changed it back again on Sunday afternoon, after she'd read her horoscope in the colour supplement. ('Gemini: You can begin to see yourself living a very different life, in a very different setting.') On Sunday night, after Adam and Rose had left, she lay awake in bed, fretting about what Sam would think, about what was best for him. They hadn't discussed it yet with the children, or Clare, or Pete for that matter. Pete wouldn't care: he'd make some money out of the sale of the house; but Clare . . . Kate wasn't entirely sure where Clare was planning to live, or whether she intended to keep Rose with her. She had a flat in Crouch End, bought after she and Adam had split up and sold their house, but that had been rented out ever since she'd got the part in the Manchester soap opera. Lately, whenever she'd been back in London, she'd been staying with her boyfriend, who also owned a flat nearby. (Why this preponderance of soap stars in Crouch End, wondered Kate? You'd see them, buying their milk in

Budgens and want to say hello, thinking they were friends, and then realize, in the nick of time, that you knew them but they didn't know you. It seemed like a strange place for them to gather, but Adam said it all started when an EastEnder moved in, because when one soap star settled somewhere, the rest usually followed, like a flock of starlings.)

Anyway, the influx of minor household names into the area had pushed up property prices, as Kate discovered the following morning, after she'd dropped Sam at school. True, her house and Adam's flat might therefore be sold for a substantial amount of money – but even so, after Pete had taken his half share, at least, of the house, Kate wasn't certain that they'd have enough to buy a new house, big enough for all of them, not after they'd paid stamp duty and solicitors and everything. And there didn't seem to be much for sale – nothing very nice, as far as she could tell, reading between the lines of the fulsome estate agents' brochures. 'It's a bit of a quiet time of year,' said the friendly girl at the estate agents next to the health club (which reminded Kate, she still hadn't signed up for the sodding yoga class there). 'It's usually busier after Christmas,' said the girl, handing over a meagre assortment of house listings. 'But do you have a property to sell yourself?'

'Yes, I mean, no,' said Kate, feeling flustered. 'Maybe – I'm not quite sure yet . . .'

'Well, if you do have a property to sell,' said the girl, 'it's better to have it under offer before you make an offer on a new property.'

'But I haven't found a property yet,' said Kate. 'And there's nothing I really want to see.' She backed out of the shop, smiling inanely, and scuttled to the cafe next door for a large almond croissant. (The health club would have to wait until tomorrow.)

Her mother had been a great one for browsing through estate agents' windows and scouring the property pages of the Sunday papers. 'Look!' she'd say to Kate, 'if I sold this minuscule flat in Marylebone, we could live in a Gothic mansion in Lincolnshire.' Judith had never done anything more than look – a habit that Kate found herself picking up even though she knew it was an insidious form of displacement activity. Her particular fantasy – like Judith's had been – was to buy a little wooden house by the sea: a perfect cottage, in the sand dunes, with a garden gate that led straight to the beach. Inside there would be sun-bleached linen and walls the colour of seashells; shelves made out of driftwood and a worn teak floor. Outside would be clean air and golden light, the crash of waves beyond empty expanses of unlittered, perfect sand. She'd seen pictures of similar houses in glossy interiors magazines; but none of them was her house, her very own Shangri-la.

At home, after the failed expedition to the estate agents, she switched on her computer, but instead of starting work on her new piece ('The Sole of Perfection: great moments in shoe history') Kate began roaming the Internet, searching through property websites. There was a sweet-looking flint cottage on the north Norfolk coast, in a pretty seaside village not far from Elverson, £200,000, in need of total restoration; but no, that wouldn't do, not really; and a lighthouse-keeper's cottage in Cornwall which sounded interesting, except not very convenient for work; oh, and a Suffolk barn for conversion, that might be nice, plenty of space there, except she didn't really want to move Sam from his school. If only she could find the right house, then everything would fall into place – that was the theory, wasn't it? That families flourished when contained in a happy home; that goodness might be mixed in with bricks and mortar. The right house would be like a perfect sonnet: the elegant yet solid structure that contained an abundance of human emotion (but houses were more expensive than sonnets, these days).

Just as she logged off the Internet and tried to concentrate on the shoe that might best epitomize effortless elegance (difficult, given that she was wearing a pair of slippers so old that they had holes in them), the phone rang. It was Clare.

Kate felt immediately flustered – even more wrong-footed – but that was absurd, she had done nothing wrong. She tried to keep her breathing steady as Clare suggested that they needed to meet, and now, preferably. The way Clare said 'preferably' – with a sort of venomous hiss – suggested that she was not feeling well-disposed; nor did she soften at Kate's conciliatory tones. This morning wasn't very convenient, explained Kate – she had a deadline to meet, before picking up Sam at 3.15. 'So what about lunch?' said Clare. Kate said that was the problem, she'd be working until she fetched Sam, but that tomorrow would be easier.

'Tomorrow's no good for me,' said Clare, 'I've got to get back to Manchester for filming. So it'll just have to be today.' She said it in such an assertive manner – yet with a subtle undercurrent of having been hurt, as if she were the injured party – that Kate found herself agreeing to meet

Clare at two o'clock. She also agreed, against her better judgement, to go to Clare's boyfriend's flat, because Clare said it wouldn't be a good idea to see each other in public. Kate couldn't tell if this was because Clare felt herself to be too famous to be spotted in a Crouch End cafe, or because the encounter would be too acrimonious. Nor, as it turned out, could she discover whether Adam knew, or approved, of this meeting, because his mobile was either switched off, or he was in a basement somewhere, digging doubtless, underground and out of reach.

So appalling was the prospect of the 2 p.m. meeting (a sort of delayed High Noon, Kate felt) that she managed – for possibly the first time that year – to entirely bury herself in her work, as Adam had done. Shoes were never more soothing than now; and in contemplating the vagaries of fashionable footwear, Kate discovered a temporary escape from the hell of imagining her coming ordeal. She kept writing until quarter to two, and then stopped to put on some make-up (warpaint, more like) and a pair of leather boots. Unfortunately, halfway to Clare's boyfriend's flat, which was a ten-minute walk away, it started raining – so hard that Kate's feet were soaking by the time she arrived, and her hair dripping onto her already sodden clothes.

'Goodness, it's wet,' she said, smiling, as Clare opened the door. Clare did not smile back, simply stared at her with some distaste.

'I suppose you'd better come in,' said Clare – as if she'd rather Kate didn't; as if *Clare* was the one who'd been forced into the meeting. She led Kate into the kitchen but did not offer her anything to drink, though Kate was desperate for a cup of tea, with several sugars in it, for comfort and to occupy her hands. Clare lit a cigarette, and blew out the smoke in Kate's direction; it was such a stagy gesture that Kate wanted to laugh, but restrained herself. Her instincts were to talk – to fill the silence, to smooth things over – but she told herself to keep quiet; to let Clare say whatever it was she had to. And though Kate would have preferred to look out of the window or at the floor – anywhere other than Clare's face – she made herself meet her gaze. Clare was pretty, there was no doubt about it: familiar looking, from the snatched seconds Kate had seen her on the TV; expensive blonde highlights in naturally fair, shoulder-length hair; big blue eyes that looked like they might brim with tears for the camera, but right now were still staring at Kate.

'Well?' said Clare, accusingly, eyes flicking down over Kate's clothes, a quick one-two, like a *Vogue* fashion editor.

'Well, what?' said Kate.

'What's going on?' said Clare.

'I'm not quite sure what you mean by that,' said Kate. 'You're living with your boyfriend—'

'And you're living with my husband.'

'I'm not, actually.'

'But you're planning to.'

'That's none of your business,' said Kate, immediately regretting her words, knowing she'd made a tactical mistake.

'Oh, I think it is,' said Clare, tossing back her glossy hair (Kate's was now in limp rat's tails) and rapping her manicured red nails on the table (Kate's were ragged and unvarnished). 'I've got my child to consider . . .'

Kate wanted, very much, to point out that Clare did not

show a great deal of consideration for Rose at other times, gallivanting off to Manchester for weeks at a time, not to mention cavorting with her boyfriend in front of a confused little girl. But she restrained herself, again. If she'd learnt anything from many arguments lost against her father – a man who used an abundance of insults in attack – it was that words often failed her in defending herself; that quiet contempt was a better form of armour.

'Haven't you got anything to say for yourself?' said Clare, who had been rattling through Adam and Kate's iniquities (having Rose to stay the night in Sam's room; not making social arrangements via Clare; giving Rose sweets, which were lacking in any nutritional content and would rot her teeth; feeding Rose ice cream, which would make her fat).

'Not really,' said Kate, 'though I hope we can be civilized with each other.'

'You want a battle, do you?' said Clare. 'If you want a fight, I'm going to win. I'm not giving up custody of Rose.'

'No one's asking you to,' said Kate.

'So you don't want her? She's an inconvenience, is she?'

'No, she's a delightful child. But maybe you and Adam need to resolve some things together.'

'He still loves me, you know. He's only seeing you to try to make me jealous, to win me back.'

'OK,' said Kate, standing up. 'I'd better go now – the school's a bit of a walk from here.'

'Go on then, run away.'

'Whatever,' said Kate, shrugging, finally allowing herself a small smile (just like Paul's twins – and equally infuriating, she guessed). She left the flat feeling as if she'd walked away from a theatrical set (surely real people didn't live in kitchens with no evidence of food, or sit at a polished Conran cherrywood table, completely clear of bills, scribbles, or newspapers?). But she also felt irritated with Adam. How could he have married such an awful, hysterical woman? OK, so Clare had a neat figure – curvy in the right places, flat-stomached, pert bum – but she was dreadful, wasn't she? (She had been wearing *leather trousers*, for God's sake, and a black lace shirt.) And if Kate started living with Adam – well, she'd be landed with Clare as well, phoning her in that imperious manner, sulking and scheming and standing her ground.

Kate marched down the road in the rain, furious, wanting to stamp in puddles, and by the time she'd reached the street that led to Sam's school she realized that she was half an hour early, so brief had been her conversation with Clare. It was too wet to wait outside, not enough time to start working again, so she ended up in the cafe next to the health club for the second time that day, with a cup of tea this time (three sugars for good measure) and an apple Danish pastry (for the nutritious fruit). Then she bought Sam a jam doughnut to eat on his way home from school – an irrational act of defiance against Clare, who was clearly anorexic, with her size eight figure and those bonkers rules about food.

Maria was already waiting outside the school gates, sheltering under an umbrella, when Kate got there. She asked Kate what the matter was – 'You've got storm clouds all over your face,' she said. 'Can't really talk now,' said Kate, as the boys ran towards them, 'except to say I've just met Adam's ex-wife.'

'And was it awful?' said Maria, thrilled.

'Hideous.'

'Best stick to secret affairs,' said Maria, giving her hand an affectionate squeeze. They ended up back at Maria's house, eating oat flapjacks in the kitchen. 'Very good for us,' said Maria, dipping a flapjack in her tea. 'No wheat, you see, so very slimming.'

'Aside from the tub of golden syrup in the recipe.'

'Organic,' said Maria, 'and therefore more easily metabolized.'

'You've been reading Good Housekeeping again.'

'I know – it's my favourite magazine these days. Isn't that sad? That's why I was at home making flapjacks at ten o'clock last night, instead of swinging from a hotel bedroom chandelier.'

'Are you beginning to hanker after your former life as a Scarlet Woman?'

'No, not really . . . too complicated, too boring. What's the point of having a lover who says all the same things as your husband?'

'That his wife doesn't understand him?' They both laughed, and finished the plate of flapjacks with a little help from the children. Maria cheered Kate further by telling her that Clare's soap opera was not nearly as popular as EastEnders ('It's only on once a week, Sunday evenings on Sky'); and also pointed out that Clare, though undeniably pretty, looked like the footballer's wife that she played. 'Well, of *course* she looks like her,' said Kate, who was feeling slightly drunk with friendship and an excess of sugar. 'That's because she's acting the part.' Maria said that wasn't what she meant; that Clare actually looked like a footballer's wife in real life.

'How do you know?'

'Because I saw her with Adam in the corner shop a couple of weekends ago. High-heeled shiny black boots and slightly stripy blonde highlights – a bit girl-band, I thought, except she's too old for it.'

Kate felt suddenly discomfited: what, exactly, was Adam doing in a shop with Clare? Buying Sunday newspapers to read in bed together? Maria told her not to worry; Clare was too ghastly to waste time fretting about. But after they'd said goodbye, Kate found that she couldn't quite get Clare out of her head; she'd lodged somewhere, like an incubus, or a bad cliché – like a punishment. She told herself it wasn't fair that Clare had cast her in the role of husband-stealer turned wicked stepmother. What on earth was Clare thinking of? Did she have no insight into her own actions?

Back in Kate's own house, cooking spaghetti for herself and Sam (with extra nutritious peas and pesto), she wondered what Clare was doing right now. Peeling some raw carrots, perhaps, for Rose's dinner? Worrying about Rose, but trying not to? Kate tried to see it from Clare's point of view – and, for a moment, she felt a surprising pang of sympathy (like the twinges she'd begun to feel for Jessica; a kind of heartburn, she thought). At least, so far, Kate had not had to face the prospect of Sam staying with Pete and a new girlfriend: Pete never seemed to have a girlfriend who hung around for long enough to introduce to Sam (or maybe Pete was more tactful than she gave him credit for). But if she were in Clare's shoes, Kate knew she'd find it hard not to feel anxious – and presumably Clare did feel anxious, otherwise she wouldn't have behaved as she had – which meant, perhaps, that Clare and Kate had something in common, aside from Adam.

She drained the spaghetti and called Sam to come and eat. 'Can we have it in the living room?' he asked. 'It's just I really want to see this new episode of *The Simpsons*, and I want you to sit next to me.' Kate was about to refuse – as if to prove to the absent Clare that she *was* a responsible mother, she really was – when she stopped herself. Spaghetti on the sofa with Sam and *The Simpsons* sounded perfect – just what they needed, someone else's family to laugh about; the two of them together, alone . . .

Thirty-Seven

The next day it had stopped raining and a watery sun shone on the sodden back garden, though the morning weather report on the radio had forecast something called 'organized rain' spreading in from the west. How did rain organize itself? wondered Kate, as she sat at the kitchen table, finishing her second cup of tea, watching a fat grey squirrel dig up her crocus bulbs on the edges of the lawn. She'd given up chasing the squirrel away – given up on the poor crocuses, too, because the squirrel found them so irresistible, and at least when it had crocus bulbs to eat, it left the snowdrops alone. Kate was contemplating the garden – a mess, to be honest, because she hadn't swept up the fallen leaves, and her pots on the patio were ragged with the sad summer annuals that should have been taken out a couple of months ago. But though bedraggled, the garden still had a certain charm – weathered brick walls covered in ivy and jasmine; grey stones from a Norfolk beach disguising the gaps along the borders. When they'd first moved into the house, the garden was completely out of control – uncut lawn, with bald patches, like an aging hippie's hair, and bindweed choking the magnolia and the apple tree. Her father had spent an afternoon helping her cut back the weeds – an unusual show of solidarity on his part, for he tended not to become involved in domestic matters (though maybe the garden was sufficiently undomesticated to be acceptable to him).

A postcard from her father lay on the kitchen table in front of her; his handwriting was the reason that she was looking away at the squirrel, instead of reading his card. His writing always unsettled her: angry black italics, which seemed to carry with them the sound of his grinding teeth. The picture on the front of the card was faded – he'd probably bought it years ago, on a trip to a museum; it was a detail from *The Resurrection*, Stanley Spencer's painting of the dead climbing out of their graves in the Cookham churchyard. Kate examined the woman's figure that seemed to be coming out of the church, like a bride, beneath an arch of white flowers. Was she dead as well, wondered Kate, peering at the woman, who appeared to be carrying something – a baby? And there was someone else standing behind her, a weirdly flattened man, with his hand resting on the woman's head. It made Kate shiver; the man reminded her of her father.

On the back of the card her father had written to say that he wanted to come to see them soon, to light Hanukkah candles with Sam. 'I won't be a nuisance,' he added, as a postscript, underlining the final word. Kate was not sure if she could cope with the idea of her father staying the night, let alone the reality of such a visit. The last time he'd tried to celebrate a religious occasion with them had been disastrous: two years ago, when he'd found them wanting as companions for the Jewish New Year. Kate had told him to shut up when he'd started complaining about the failings of primary education (because Sam didn't know any Hebrew) and then she'd felt guilty for her rudeness, but there was no space to apologize because he was accusing her of anti-Semitism; finally he'd left the house in a rage, saying he'd rather catch the milk-train home to Herefordshire than stay a moment longer with her. 'You're heartless,' he'd said, slamming the front door, 'just like your godforsaken mother.'

Both 'heartless' and 'godforsaken' had seemed to Kate to be interesting choices of words; but she'd been too angry with him – and with herself, for allowing the argument to happen in the first place – to want to think about the encounter ever again. Now, though, as she looked at the postcard of the resurrected dead, his words came floating back into her head. Wasn't it her father who had forsaken God, by not believing in Him, despite his religious observances? And if her father didn't believe in God – and she had no reason to think he had changed his mind – then how could he also believe that God had chosen to forsake her? As for being 'heartless' – well, maybe she had a splinter of ice in her heart, at least when it came to loving her father.

Kate shook her head, amazed to find herself so disturbed by the memory of her father, by his handwriting, when she'd thought that she had moved on: grown-up . . . accepted and forgiven him. 'Unforgivable' she whispered to herself, trying out the word on her tongue – but she knew as she said it that forgiveness was mandatory when it came to her father, because she couldn't face the alternative, of hating him. (An irrational equation seemed to have formed itself in her head, which was that if she hated her father, then Sam would grow up to hate her.) Anyway, when he wrote that he wouldn't be 'a nuisance', perhaps that was his code for saying he wouldn't come looking for a fight. Or was he simply trying to make his peace with her? Kate sighed, and shook her head again. Were all families so impossibly complicated? Which reminded her . . . she must ring Adam, who'd left two messages on her answer phone last night which she'd not yet returned. She'd been too busy checking that she'd locked the back door before she went to bed; in fact, had come down the stairs twice after getting into bed to make sure that she had not unlocked it without realizing.

Kate chewed her nails and looked back into the garden again. The squirrel had been joined by a blackbird – the one that sang in the summer, but now seemed intent only on digging up a worm. This was the downside to not working in an office, these solitary mornings that drifted by with no form to them; just her muddled thinking, floating around the kitchen. She imagined the words in her head, contained in bubbles – real bubbles, like the ones that Sam blew – streams of soapy bubbles, hovering, then popping, and the words falling to the ground; a single word in every bubble: 'hate', 'squirrel', 'heartless', 'crocus', 'godforsaken', 'locked', and then the words lying on the kitchen floor, random, disconnected, soon to be swept away, like house dust and stale crumbs.

She stood up and went to the phone, and rang Adam. His mobile was switched off. Missing each other, again. But did she miss him sufficiently to be certain they should live together? And if she said no, would she be missing the

moment? Oh *God,* she was sick of the scratchings and the
noise in her head; she was driving herself round the bend,
just like her mother did . . .

Just then the phone rang. 'It's me,' said Adam. 'Are you
OK?'

'No,' she said, almost wailing, almost ironically.

'What's wrong?'

'Everything. I met your wife, and my father wants to
come to stay.'

'Poor you,' he said. 'Shall I come round and see you?'

'Now?'

'Yes – just for half an hour.' And so he did, and she
buried her head in his jacket, which was cold, like the
November air outside, but his hands were warm, cupping
her face and kissing her. 'Don't worry,' he said. 'It's all going
to be fine.'

'But Maria said she saw you in the corner shop with
Clare.'

'Did she? Well, there's no sinister subtext to that
encounter. Clare had accused me of not returning a video
that she'd rented for Rose, and I said that I couldn't be
expected to, given that it was in her boyfriend's flat, and
Clare said it wasn't, that Rose had taken it home – anyway,
it's boring, but I was trying to sort it out with the man that
runs the shop.'

'And did you?'

'What?'

'Sort it out?'

'Well, I did with the corner shop, but not with Clare –
but that's not your problem, OK?'

'It is – she is – she's going to torment me, and I'll be

stuck with her, and it wasn't even me that married her, and it's impossible, I can't bear it, I'd rather go back to a simple life with just me and Sam.' Kate meant the things she said, but she was laughing at the same time, and Adam did not take offence – not like her father would have done, not that her father was anything to do with it, not now – and he kissed her again, lifting her off the floor, so her eyes were level with his.

'I love you,' he said. 'That's all that matters in the end. I love you.' And then he put her back down, and brushed his fingers against her cheek, and went back outside into the cold day; but she was warm, and her head was clearer. How could she not love him? No, that wasn't the right way of putting it: she *did* love him . . . For someone who used words for a living, thought Kate, she really should be more precise about what it was she felt. At school, like the other teenage girls, she'd drawn biro hearts in her notebooks with an arrow driven through them, and her name linked with whoever her boyfriend happened to be at the time (the written inky names clearer, usually, than the more tenuous link between her and the boy in real life). She remembered a tree on the school playing fields, carved with hearts and names and dates, disfigured by those protestations of love. But she'd never added her own name to the tree; it seemed to be tempting fate, too permanent, because the tree would still be standing, long after the exercise books were faded and stained and thrown away.

Still, that was twenty years ago, and she should know her own mind by now. 'I love Adam.' She said it out loud, in the silent kitchen. 'Adam loves me.' What could be simpler than that?

Thirty-Eight

Towards the end of the week, Kate was suddenly struck by
an idea, which was that in a spirit of openness and hope
and whatever the opposite of heartlessness was, she would
invite not only her father for the Hanukkah-candle ceremony, but also Adam and Rose and Pete and Clare and
Clare's boyfriend (and if Pete did want to bring a girlfriend,
well, that would be fine as well). She was spurred on, in
part, by the feeling that there would be safety in numbers –
not that company had ever stopped her father behaving
badly in the past. (There had been a memorable Christmas
Eve when she was six months pregnant with Sam, recently
married and misguidedly attempting to engender a sense of
family harmony, when Sebastian had accused Pete's father
of being a fascist and Pete's mother of being an emasculat-
ing bitch.)

She'd never risk a Christmas fiasco again – and anyway,
her father seemed happier at home by himself reading Sartre
at that time of year – but the stakes weren't as high for
Hanukkah, because no one was Jewish aside from him,
which would mean he could be the master of ceremonies

(surely good for him) and everyone else would have the unfamiliar ritual to concentrate on, instead of each other.

Adam had looked doubtful when she told him her plans, but said if that was what she wanted, to go ahead and give it a try. Sam and Rose were more enthusiastic – both of them were still young enough to enjoy any kind of cere-mony, especially if it involved presents (which Kate said it might do, but they shouldn't expect anything big). Pete was as easy-going as ever – 'Sure, babe,' he'd said, 'sounds like it could be a laugh' – which left only Clare to invite. It took Kate all day to steel herself for the encounter, but after a large gin and tonic she managed to make the call – only to discover, much to her relief, that she was talking to Clare's answer machine. She left a message anyway, and an invita-tion for both Clare and her boyfriend to come to the Hanukkah dinner.

And then she realized that she hadn't yet responded to her father's card – nor asked him whether he minded the extra guests. So she drank another gin and tonic, and rang him to explain her plan. 'Marvellous,' he said, in a gloomy voice.

'You don't sound very pleased,' she said.

'That's just the way I talk,' he said. 'I don't do fake jol-lity.'

'But you still want to come?'

'Of course I do,' he said. 'Unless you don't want me to.'

'Dad, that's why I'm ringing you – to make these arrangements.'

'OK, I'll see you then,' he said, and put the phone down, before she had a chance to ask what it was she was expected to provide on the night, given that they'd never celebrated Hanukkah before.

She was beginning to think that the whole idea was a terrible mistake when Clare rang, still wary, but friendlier than the last time they'd talked. She wasn't Jewish, she said, but Kate told her not to worry, that none of them were, except her father, and he didn't believe in God, anyway. 'Actually,' said Clare, 'my boyfriend's got a Jewish mother, so he's quite keen to come.'

'Perfect!' said Kate, in a voice that made her wince (from Marriage-Breaker to Girl Guide, in a single swoop of insincerity). Afterwards she briefly considered ringing Isabel and Harriet to ask them along, as well – at least they'd be on her side – but she decided against it. If things were going to work with Adam – and this new, unruly, jumbled family – then she just had to get on with it, to face it herself.

The trouble was, it was hard to know where to begin. Kate knew it was childish to look for a set of instructions – there were none, anyway – but nevertheless found some brief sense of purpose by consulting Sam's illustrated concise encyclopedia, which said that Hanukkah was a feast of lights to commemorate the re-dedication of the Jerusalem temple in 165 BC and the miracle of a one-day supply of oil lasting for eight days. No mention was made of what food you were supposed to cook, but Kate had a vague idea that cheesecake would be a good thing, and maybe a couple of roast chickens. (Why didn't someone write a cookbook with recipes for happiness, she wondered: a simple guide to pouring oil on troubled waters, and whisking it into a soothing gravy?)

There would be eight of them, because Pete seemed not to want to bring anyone with him, which meant they'd just about fit around her kitchen table, so she embarked upon an extensive cleaning programme (not that any of her guests were likely to care that she'd thoroughly scrubbed the living-room skirting boards). It was while Kate was polishing the kitchen sink that she caught sight of a squirrel perched on top of the trellis opposite the window, apparently staring at her. She couldn't tell whether it was the same squirrel that she'd seen before, eating the crocus bulbs; it seemed identical to her, but didn't all squirrels look alike? Kate remembered a friend saying that after her grandmother died she used to see a squirrel in her garden, and became convinced that it was the grandmother, returning to watch over her. Kate could not imagine the grandmother she had known – her mother's mother – returning from the dead in such a guise (she'd have been horrified by the very idea of reincarnation, though Kate could just about envisage her as a rather haughty pedigree cat); but as the squirrel continued to regard her, unblinking, Kate wondered whether this was a visitation from her father's mother, whom she had seldom met in life. Her name had been May – May Linden, a lovely name, Kate had always thought – and as a child she'd imagined her unknown grandmother in garlands of blossom, even though her father had said she was a monster. She had not seemed like a monster to Kate when they met – a small, round woman, greying hair in a bun, dark beady eyes, not unsquirrel-like, now Kate came to think about it. May Linden and her husband, Gerald, had lived in a house on the very outskirts of London, a faraway place where the city met the fields. Kate could only remember a single visit there, a year or so after her parents had split up, though she'd been told they had seen her occasionally as a baby. Sebastian had driven her to his parents' house on a Friday evening, after school, stalling and jerking through the rain and the traffic jams, cursing the weather and his family, his face pressed close to the car windscreen, hands gripping the steering wheel like it was a weapon. May had cooked chicken soup with dumplings for dinner, for her only son, her only grandchild. Kate had eaten it, quietly, like her grandmother, not saying anything except for please and thank you, as her father had argued with his father, their voices filling the dining room, heavy with anger, dark as the mahogany table. Sebastian had got up to go before Kate had had a chance to finish her second piece of apple strudel, which was a shame, because it was delicious; as they left, her grandmother had taken Kate's hands in hers, and there were tears in her eyes. 'Don't forget us,' she'd said to Kate, 'don't forget where you came from.'

'She didn't come from here,' Sebastian had said. 'She's got nothing to do with you, thank God.' Kate had wondered, then, why he was thanking God, given that he had been arguing with his father about God being dead. But she didn't say anything more, except goodbye to her grandparents, and 'Thank you for having me.' Later, she tried not to forget them, but their faces faded in her head, leaving only the imagined may-blossom, soft as her grandmother's voice. They'd died before she was a teenager – May first, Gerald less than a year later – and her father had wept, sinking into a long depression that had lasted for the winter and beyond, even when the new buds unfurled in the park.

Still, here she was, planning a Hanukkah celebration with her father, remembering her grandparents, despite everything. That had to be good, didn't it? Kate knew that this was as glib – or as childish – as searching for the meaning of Hanukkah in Sam's encyclopedia; but she couldn't let go of the idea of a hopeful resolution, of people coming together, if only for a night, lighting candles in the darkness. Miracles *could* happen: that's what Kate kept telling herself, anyway, right up until the evening itself, when the house was cleaner than it had ever been and a fire was burning in the living room, and the chickens were roasting in the oven. Adam and Rose had arrived first, with flowers and wine (white tulips and red burgundy – he was good at things like that). Sebastian came next, his Menorah candelabra wrapped in a prayer shawl, inside a plastic bag. 'What's that?' asked Sam, as Sebastian put the Menorah in the middle of the table, and Kate held her breath, waiting for her father to express outrage that his grandchild did not know about the sacred symbols of Judaism. But Sebastian simply launched into a long explanation of the Menorah (seven candles for the seven planets, but eight for Hanukkah), and Sam seemed happy to listen, though Rose backed away, taking Adam's hand. Clare and her boyfriend, Rob – Kate muttered his name to herself, so as not to forget – arrived at half past seven, in a taxi from the station, having caught the train down from Manchester that day; and Pete was only a few minutes late, which showed he was making an effort.

The first five minutes were taken up with polite introductions – Adam had met Rob before, but not Pete, and Sebastian didn't know any of them, apart from Pete, whom he hadn't seen for years. Fortunately, Clare seemed to have adopted sparkling form for the evening – at least with the men in the room, though she more or less ignored Kate. And Kate didn't care that Clare wasn't talking to her, because she was charming Sebastian instead, which was a great relief.

'That's fascinating,' Clare kept saying, head cocked to one side, tinted eyelashes sweeping over her baby-blue eyes. She was wearing black velvet trousers – snugly fitting, inviting to be stroked – and a matching blazer, buttoned up, but with nothing underneath, aside from a red lace bra, so that when she reached over the table for a glass of wine, you could see the curve of golden skin. Kate looked at her, and was reminded of the most popular girl in her class at secondary school – also called Clare, as it happened, and more adored by boys than girls; indeed, most adored by Kate's first boyfriend, Max, who dumped her on the bidding of that other, equally flirtatious Clare, who didn't really want him, anyway, not for more than a week. And despite Kate's wish that harmony would descend upon her house tonight, like a ray of golden light, she could not rid herself of the knot of jealousy inside her stomach, acid and twisted and sour. She hated herself for feeling that way, and for caring that Clare's velvet suit was far more desirable than her faded black jeans (the wrong sort to wear with her black polo-necked jumper because the blacks didn't match – and why on earth had she not washed off the red biro shopping list written on her hand – and why wear red biro at all, instead of red lace?).

Fortunately, Pete seemed not overly impressed – Clare was probably a bit too obvious for him, and she had breasts, unlike the stick-thin models he preferred – and Adam appeared not to succumb to Clare's hand brushing his more often than was necessary. Sam was full of admiration, Kate could tell – but that didn't matter; in fact, it was a bonus, because it ensured his good behaviour, which reflected well on both of them. As for Rose – it was clear that she was nervous, the tic in her eye starting up again whenever she looked at her mother, as if what she saw – and both resented and adored – was too much to take in.

Kate looked at them all, but said little, too busy getting the food out of the oven, and making sure the gravy didn't boil over. 'Roast chicken – my favourite,' said Rob, who seemed likeable enough, though Kate had to keep reminding herself that he was not an old friend simply because she recognized him. (Which television series had she seen him in, apart from the current footballers one? He looked like the handsome sidekick from any number of detective stories; or was he the good-hearted young doctor on Channel 4?)

'Is it kosher?' said Clare, pointing at the chicken, like she cared.

'It's free-range and organic,' said Kate, trying to arrange her face into a smile. 'Now, Dad do you need to say your stuff before we eat, or afterwards?'

'Before,' said her father, who was beginning to look anxious. 'Sam and Rosa can light the candles with me.'

'Rose,' said Sam, 'her name is Rose.'

'That's what I said,' replied Sebastian, his hands trembling as he tried to light a match; and, watching him, Kate was engulfed with pity, rather than the unease she more often felt in his presence. She wanted to take his hand, to calm him down – but she could not bring herself to touch him, in case it made him more anxious; in case he flinched. Instead, she switched off the kitchen lights, as Sam and Rose, with infinite care, lit the candles, so that the adult faces around the table disappeared into the darkness, leaving only the children, now shadowy as ghosts. Her father started saying a Hebrew prayer, and Kate stood between Sam and Adam, both of them holding her hands, though no one else would see them; only she could feel their touch. And then the prayer was over, and Rob – alone in understanding that her father had reached a conclusion – turned the lights back on, and they all glanced at one another, and lowered their eyes again, to the food.

'So important to have a spiritual dimension to life, isn't it?' said Clare, who was fingering a necklace that Kate had only just noticed around her neck – a diamond crucifix on a white gold chain. Kate recognized it as an accessory that her magazine would describe as 'an absolute must-have': in fact, she'd spent long enough writing fluffy captions to fashion stories to be able to identify it as the work of a particularly sought-after London jeweller. Crucifixes were in last Christmas; this year it was keys (and next year, for all she knew, it would be Satanic runes). But she could tell from the look on her father's face that he might not have realized that Clare was making a fashion statement rather than a religious one.

'And what might your spiritual choice be?' asked Sebastian, teeth bared and eyes glittering, hovering on the edge of no return.

'Well, I've always felt very drawn to Catholicism,' said Clare, not recognizing the danger signals, as Kate did; not knowing that his anxiety in the company of strangers might tip over into violent rage. 'I wasn't raised a Catholic, of course, but it seems such a beautiful, *beautiful* religion.'

'Tell that to the Jews,' said Sebastian, 'betrayed by the Catholic Nazis.'

'Dad,' said Kate, 'would you like chicken breast or leg?'

'Don't try and change the subject,' he said. 'Though obviously, you've never shown the slightest interest in the Holocaust.' He was grinding his teeth by now, and glaring at Kate – as if it were her fault that Clare was wearing a crucifix on Hanukkah. 'The trouble with the fucking Catholics,' he said, enunciating his words very clearly, 'is that they blame the Jews for betraying Jesus – so they've spent the last two thousand years punishing us. What they've forgotten is that Jesus was Jewish. Jesus was fucking Jewish!' He stabbed his fork at the chicken, as if it were the Pope, apparently unabashed by the silence that had fallen at the table.

'So, Sebastian,' said Pete, 'still as committed as ever to the cause . . .'

'Committed!' said Sebastian. 'What would you know about commitment?'

Pete shrugged, and helped himself to roast potatoes; Adam caught Kate's eye, and gave her a small, encouraging smile. She wasn't sure whether to smile back, or start crying, or pretend that nothing had gone wrong – when suddenly, Rose started giggling, quietly at first, but then with such abandon that she was almost weeping, holding herself as if it hurt.

'Rose,' hissed Clare from across the table, 'pull yourself together. Now.' But Rose was beyond togetherness, tears running down her cheeks, gasping for air between sobs and shrieks of laughter. 'Oh, for goodness sake,' said Clare. 'I knew this was a bad idea . . .'

'Can't take the truth?' said Sebastian.

'Stop it,' said Kate, to her father, rather than Rose. 'Just stop it right now.'

'Stop what?' said Sebastian, who was getting into his stride, looking almost as if he were enjoying himself, but agonized as well, as Rose was. 'Stop telling the truth?'

'Stop making a scene,' said Kate. But she knew as she spoke that it was too late, that the scene had been made and could not now be undone. 'Broccoli, anyone?' she said, trying to keep her voice level over Rose's snorting and sniggering. 'Rose?' she said. 'Do you want a drink of water?'

'I want to go home,' said Rose. Both of her parents stood up simultaneously, both offering themselves, both wanting to escape, presumed Kate, and who could blame them? But it was Sam who got to Rose first; Sam who hugged her, for she was crying properly now; Sam who persuaded her to stay, and took her up to his room, with the promise of as many games of snap as she wanted to play. 'Don't take any notice of my grandad,' Kate heard Sam whisper, as he led Rose up the stairs. 'He doesn't mean to say rude things, it just comes out that way, even when he wants to make friends.'

Sebastian, meanwhile, had blown out the candles, and was wrapping up his Menorah. 'Thank you for the lovely meal,' he said, with no apparent irony. 'But I must be on my way or I'll miss my train home.'

'You don't have to go yet,' said Kate. 'You haven't finished your chicken.'

'I know, dear child,' said Sebastian, his face frozen into a rictus smile, 'but I've got things to do tomorrow morning – my perennials need pruning. Goodbye, Kate. Goodbye, everyone. See you all soon, I hope – Passover, perhaps?' Clare stared at him, open-mouthed, upstaged for once; but Rob and Pete and Adam recovered sufficiently to shake

Sebastian's hand, and then Kate walked with him to the front door, where she kissed him on the cheek.

'Take care of yourself,' she said, fearing for him, wanting him to know she loved him, yet not knowing how. Suddenly he flung his arms around her, squeezing her tight, so hard she couldn't breathe, and then he left, rubbing his eyes as if he was close to tears.

Back in the kitchen, the tension had dissolved, and Pete was laughing. 'I'm so, so sorry,' said Kate.

'Don't worry, babe,' said Pete, giving her a friendly hug. 'It's not your fault your old man's mad as a balloon.' Kate wanted to disagree: it was not for Pete to pass judgement on her father; but she let it pass, not wanting another argument (she felt too tired for that).

'It's fine,' said Clare, with a sugary smile. 'I think you're very brave.' She'd clearly collected herself sufficiently to play the magnanimous part from now on – well, for tonight, at least; while Rob seemed quite invigorated by the encounter with her father, and regaled them with stories of his paternal grandfather, an Irish protestant who referred to his daughter-in-law, Rob's middle-class mother, born and raised in Surrey, as 'the dusky Jewess'. While the others were laughing – all at once the same generation, united by the awfulness of their elders – Kate crept upstairs to check on Sam and Rose, and to give them some orange juice. They were sitting on the floor together, with their cards, apparently content. 'Are you OK, my darlings?' said Kate, kissing each of them on top of the head.

'We're fine,' said Rose, lifting her face to Kate's. 'Can we stay up late and have a midnight feast?'

'If that's all right with your mum and dad, that's all right with me,' said Kate.

'Well, it's our decision,' said Sam, emphasizing the unfamiliar words. 'And we say it's OK.' Kate wanted to agree with him – surely the best Hanukkah present was to give them some sense of autonomy, one night of freedom from the choices that adults made for them? But she knew she had to tread carefully with Clare; was not free herself to grant them freedom.

'Maybe we should get into bed and pretend to be asleep?' said Rose. Kate sank down on her knees beside the little girl and wanted to enfold her, to protect her (remembering her own nights of pretending to be asleep as a child, pretending not to hear her parents' voices, hoping that if she could see nothing then she would not be seen; but of course she could see, behind her closed eyelids, all the imagined horrors of what might be happening elsewhere). She gave Rose a quick hug – any more might be too much – and made up the truckle bed that pulled out from beneath Sam's. 'I like staying here,' said Rose. 'You always give me lovely clean sheets, and it's cosy sleeping next to Sam.'

'I love it when you stay here,' said Kate. 'You know you're always welcome.' She reached into her pocket and pulled out two packets of chocolates that she'd bought earlier – 'Magic Stars', they were called – and put one on each child's pillow. 'Just remember to brush your teeth afterwards,' she said, and kissed them both on the cheek.

As she went back downstairs, she wondered why it was that in attempting to move forward in her life – to look to the future – the past seemed to be catching up with her. But she did not appear to be standing still, at least; and maybe the past was pushing her onwards, nudging her forwards. It was not a bad feeling – which was why when she walked into the kitchen again, the smile on her face was real.

By then, Clare seemed to have drunk a considerable quantity – and, fortunately, she was suffused with an alcohol-induced sense of goodwill. 'S'lovely,' she said, patting Kate on the arm. 'Glad we could sort things out, like grown-ups.'

'And I'm so glad you came tonight,' said Kate, meaning it, even though she knew the moment wouldn't last. 'Now, would anyone like some cheesecake?'

'Not me,' said Clare, patting her flat stomach. 'No wheat, no dairy – they just don't suit me. But go on, you go ahead, sweetie – you're a civilian, unlike us hardy soldiers in the glamour wars . . .' Kate began hating her again, but the hate was mixed up with a certain grim affection – because they were in this together, and there was no escaping that. And at least Clare didn't make a fuss later about Rose staying the night – both the children were fast asleep by then, Sam on his back, arms flung out; Rose curled into a ball, like a dormouse.

'I'll come back tomorrow morning to pick her up,' said Clare, half threateningly, but kissing Kate on the cheek as she spoke. And then they were gone, the three of them, Pete and Clare and Rob, those awkward, erratic, yet integral figures in Kate's equation: 'Odd numbers,' she whispered to herself as she closed the front door.

'What was that?' said Adam, coming up behind her.

'Oh, nothing really,' she said.

'Well, it was OK, in the end, wasn't it?' he said, hugging her in the dark hall. 'All's well that ends well . . .'

'It's not over yet,' she said.

Thirty-Nine

In the first week of December, Kate and Adam went to see eleven houses: eight of them horrible (dark and north-facing, or on busy roads, or both); the remaining three far more than she and Adam could afford. 'There'll be more coming on the market just after Christmas,' said the girl at the estate agents. 'That's when couples decide to split up.' Kate did not like the idea of preying, like a vulture, on other people's marital misfortunes; she'd rather stay in her own house, she told Adam. 'Why can't we just leave things as they are?' she said, after returning from a particularly dismal viewing of a four-bedroomed house with rising damp, that cost half a million pounds.

'We could try,' said Adam, 'but things don't stay the same, even if you want them to. Things happen . . .'

And he was right, of course. A thing happened in the last week of term, when Pete came to see Sam's school Christmas show (not a nativity play, because baby Jesus did not come to north London boroughs, but what was billed as a 'multi-cultural celebration of song and dance'). Just after

Sam had done an Irish jig dressed as a crocodile, Pete said, 'We should talk about the house.'

'What house?' said Kate, startled, still waving at Sam, as he filed off the stage, snapping his cardboard jaws by way of a goodbye. 'Go on, give Sam a wave – he's looking for you.'

Pete waved, and took some more pictures – he had his digital camera with him, as usual – and then said, 'Our house. We should come to some sort of arrangement, now you're with Adam.'

'Do we have to?' said Kate. 'Now?'

'Not this instant,' said Pete. 'Let's talk about it after-wards.' So they did, over weak tea and biscuits in the junior school hall, in a huddle, which meant that none of the other parents came to talk to them, and Kate felt that they might as well have had signs stuck to their foreheads saying, 'Danger, divorced parents'. But it only took a few minutes because she didn't have much to say, and all Pete said, quite reasonably, was that he'd like half of the value of the house, so that he could buy a flat, because the lease on his rented one was coming to an end. 'There's no rush, babe,' he said. 'It's just that you seem happy with Adam – like you're going to stick together.'

'But I don't know if it's going to work out with him,' she said. 'I mean, you never know, do you? Look what hap-pened to us.'

He put his hand on her arm, and said, 'That wasn't your fault.' She said she knew, she understood that it wasn't any-body's fault, not really – but it had gone wrong, hadn't it? And she couldn't bear to end up with everything falling apart again. 'But that's not a reason to not live with Adam,' said Pete. 'It's not a reason to stop trying. Anyway, you two are far better suited than we ever were.'

'How do you know that? You don't even know him properly – you've only seen us together once.'

'But he loves you – it's obvious.'

'I thought you loved me?'

'I did,' he said. 'I really did. But I wasn't good enough at it.'

'And you're telling me that Adam is? That doesn't seem like a cast-iron recommendation, coming from you.'

'I'm not telling you anything, Kate. You need to find that out for yourself.'

They walked back to her house together, in silence, though Kate felt there was plenty she might have said. (When, for example, did Pete decide he was not in love with her? Before she got pregnant or after? Or was it simply living together that had been the kiss of death?) 'Don't fret about it,' he said, patting her on the cheek, as if he half heard her unspoken words. 'What will be will be, yeah?' She waved goodbye, feeling mildly irritated (he was obviously spending too much time with a neo-Buddhist crowd: Zen and the art of fashion – he'd be preaching the Tao of Pooh next). But it was unsettling, as well. Adam and Pete seemed to be trying to tie up her loose ends, but she still didn't know whether she would end up in knots. She looked up into the pale winter sky, almost from force of habit, but there was no news there; and inside the house the answer machine, like everything else, was silent. Only the cat stalked across the kitchen – just the cat, wanting to be fed, as usual, not her maternal grandmother come back to haunt her – and there was no sign of the squirrel outside.

(Didn't they start hibernating in December, or was that hedgehogs?)

What would her mother say to her now? Kate waited for a voice, something to fill in the gaps. 'Nothing', looped the handwriting inside her head; nothing but the refrigerator murmured. She went over to the desk and dug out her mother's story from beneath the passports and Sam's birth certificate. No changes there: still the same words, still the same woman, alone in her tower, bathed in starlight, no ending in sight. Did the dead change, as we do? wondered Kate. Could they move on, just as the bereaved are instructed to? She could not imagine her mother forever motionless – in fact, she seemed to be soaring further, further and further away, out of Kate's reach, up into the sky and over the horizon, to the edge of the world and beyond . . . But there was still a thread between them, silvery like the starlight, unbreakable, too. Maybe that was the only thing that didn't change. Maybe that was it.

Kate put back the story in the desk and looked at her watch. Time to pick up Sam from school; time to get going, again.

The next morning, amidst the post from various estate agents containing the improbable details of two more houses Kate wouldn't buy – a bedsitter hostel in Finsbury Park with 'fantastic refurbishment potential' (absolutely not); a six-bedroomed 'impeccable property' on the borders of Highgate for well over a million (only in her dreams) – there were three party invitations. One was from Helena Vickers-Green, for 'pre-Christmas drinks' (stiff white card, expensively embossed gold italics – the unmistakable scent of affluence); another from Julian and Jessica, announcing they would be 'At Home on Christmas Eve' (a picture of Rafael and Madeleine riding their white ponies, Jessica's confident handwriting on the back). The third invitation was from Bella, written in her inky fountain pen on a simple piece of creamy notepaper, asking Kate and Adam and Sam and Rose to spend New Year's Eve at Elverson.

Three invitations seemed like a sufficient number to justify a shopping expedition; she could wear last Christmas's black dress for New Year's Eve, and to Helena's, if necessary, but though Kate had absolutely no intention of driving to Suffolk and back for Christmas Eve, she felt the need of something new to be At Home in herself. Jessica would be wearing an expensive outfit by Ralph Lauren – a cropped black cashmere sweater, guessed Kate, over some immaculately well-cut, low-slung flannel trousers, and a pair of very high-heeled Manolos. Kate's daywear wardrobe consisted mainly of frayed jeans from the Gap and ancient, bobbled jumpers: she was like a child, still, when it came to buying clothes, caring only about party dresses, rather than what Jessica would doubtless call 'investment pieces'. She decided, therefore, to combine a trip to the magazine – Annunciata had been making threatening noises again about forward planning – with a quick trawl around the West End.

Nothing much seemed to have changed at the magazine, except for the departure of Annunciata's elegant assistant, who had gone to work for *Vogue*. 'Ungrateful trollop,' said Annunciata, looking peevish. 'You just can't get the staff these days.' Her eyes hovered, alarmingly, on Kate's hair, as if a cockroach were lurking there, but Kate tried to stay calm (Annunciata was probably just lamenting her lack of highlights). 'So, Kate,' she said, 'still doing grunge, I see. But what about next year – when's your new-season look going to kick in?' Kate confessed that she couldn't really think that far ahead: she was still struggling with the notion of how to plan for Christmas and what to wear on Boxing Day. 'We did that three months ago,' said Annunciata. 'It's called, "How To Dress Up While Still Dressing Down."'

'And how do you do that?' said Kate.

'Cashmere,' said Annunciata, 'and heels, except if you're channelling rich Bohemian, in which case clogs are OK.'

'But not trainers?' said Kate, tucking her feet out of Annunciata's sight (pointlessly, given that Annunciata had radar vision for every item of another's outfit; indeed, could probably already tell that Kate was wearing a frayed greying bra from Marks & Spencer).

'Absolutely not,' said Annunciata, with a shudder. 'Sportswear is so last season, we are so not loving it now. But we digress . . . I'm thinking magic, I'm thinking, how to make magic in your wardrobe. You like?' Against her better judgement, Kate agreed to Annunciata's demands for in-depth research (though how on earth was she supposed to find out whether Karl Lagerfeld consulted feng shui experts, or if Calvin Klein was an astrology fan?) and then slunk out of the office in the direction of Oxford Street. She felt too diminished to face Bond Street – couldn't afford it, anyway – but in immediate need of retail therapy, nevertheless. Top Shop seemed the best place to look – cheap, but cheering – so she scuttled past the scouts for Models One at the entrance, on the lookout for thirteen-year-old proto-starlets (as opposed to, say, thirty-six-year-old mothers) and down the escalators to the lowest floor. (Might this be a suitable fashion reference for Annunciata, she wondered: Top Shop as the modern equivalent to Alice's entrance into Wonderland? No, probably not . . .)

Taking care not to look at herself in any of the Top Shop mirrors (not doorways to a magical world, but the fastest route to giving up and getting out, as she'd learnt from past mistakes), Kate trawled the rails in search of 'classic-with-a-twist daywear', as recommended on a regular basis by the magazine's senior fashion editor. But nothing seemed quite right: neither the semi-sheer chiffon blouses with harem pants (hideous, actually, unless you were a lissom sixteen-year-old, in which case you would look lovely in anything), nor the abundance of pink leopard prints (ditto). In the end, Kate settled for a new cord jacket, despite the fact she already had two at home, because this was a toffee-caramel colour, irresistible, delicious (even though Kate knew she was inviting future problems with Matching Accessories).

Back up the escalators she went, clutching her new purchase, out onto Oxford Street for a few yards in the open air (not that the air round here smelt remotely fresh), before returning to the tube station. It was after she'd gone through the ticket barriers that she saw her – a little girl, three years old maybe, dark curls and a pink dress, skipping onto the downwards escalator, out of her mother's reach. Kate ran after her, seeing as if in slow motion the child running on the spot, trying to get back to the first step, but failing, the stairs giving way beneath her feet. Kate reached her a few seconds before her mother did, steadying the little girl with an outstretched hand; the mother apparently unconcerned, blithe, like the child. The three of them descended the escalator together, Kate more shocked than she knew why; the mother still not holding the little girl's hand. And then they were all on the platform for the northbound Victoria line, and the child was running again, too close to the edge, and Kate wanted to cry out to her to take care, but the train had pulled in, and the woman and her daughter had climbed onto another carriage, laughing, ahead of Kate. When she got to her stop there was no sign of them, but she could not erase them from her mind. Why they troubled her so much, she could not explain – the child looked happy, radiant, even, and no accident had befallen her.

But still the memory gnawed at her, making a mockery of her brief belief that new clothes might be transformational in any way – because even when you were in disguise, it was always there, the danger, the uneasy foreboding that a quick slip might spell disaster. Slip – the word stuck in her head (slipping away or slipping up, slipping through time or over the edge; a slip of the tongue or a slip knot . . . and how did you sew a slip stitch?). Slippery words, untrustworthy – jumble them up and throw them all away; let them go, like she'd tried to let her mother go. But she couldn't do it, couldn't forget the child on the escalator, on the edge. Had she misconstrued the scene? Might the problem be with her rather than those she watched?

'Eeyore,' Kate said to herself, walking down the hill towards home. 'Always seeing the worst in everything. Look on the bright side for once.' And then, as if in answer, came another cliché: 'One step forward, two steps back' – that was what her mother used to say. No wonder her mother had made so little progress in life; no wonder she'd driven herself mad, crashing off the road, a full stop at last . . . except for everyone she'd left behind, driving them crazy, too, when they found out that her dead end didn't seem to be an ending at all. (You were told to expect closure with the dead, but they seemed to leave doors open, behind them, just the same.)

Forty

A week before Christmas another postcard arrived from her father. The picture on the front was a Marc Chagall print called *Time Has No Limits*: it looked to Kate like a flying fish on top of a clock, floating above a river; beneath, on the river bank, a man and a woman embraced one another. Kate turned the card over to read her father's message. He had written: 'Basically if it hadn't been for Hare/her madness we all would have lived forever. Moon is more or less eternal and we would have been like him. Her/hare madness means we run away from eternity. Please tell me I am not a Hare but a good tortoise/man/moon-person. Is that clear? Say yes or I will get Moon to split your lip! Kate, really. Dad. Am going to a Torah class – will finish this later. Dad. Remember, time is a river with no banks. Only Hare/her leads us astray.'

Kate's stomach lurched as she read it. He really was quite mad again – either that, or he had sent a fragment of what he was thinking; a fragment that might make more sense as part of a whole; a message that she longed to understand. She showed the card to Adam when he came round that evening (they were supposed to be going to Helena's party together, though Kate felt too anxious to get ready to leave the house; for what if her father was to turn up while they were out, throwing stones at the windows as he once did when she was a child, finally smashing the glass?). Adam read it, frowning, and then said, 'Does your father just do this for effect, or is he really crazy?'

'I don't know,' she said. 'I don't know if he knows, even. But it makes me feel terribly unsettled.' He put his hands on her shoulders, as if to steady her, as if she might otherwise float away, like the flying fish. She waited for him to say, 'Don't worry', like everyone always said. But he didn't. He just looked down at her, with his calm, level gaze. 'My dad's not like this all of the time,' said Kate. 'He seemed absolutely normal earlier this year. It must be something to do with the imminence of Christmas. I think he finds it very stressful – it's hard for him.'

'You don't have to apologize for him, or make excuses,' said Adam. 'He is what he is . . .'

'But I don't know what he is,' said Kate.

'Does that matter?' said Adam. 'He doesn't have to be your problem any more. You've got your own life now – you don't have to live with him.'

'But I didn't have to live with him,' she said, 'not after my parents split up.'

'You know what I mean,' he said. 'Anyway, don't we all grow up believing we have to live with our parents, that we're stuck with them and the consequences of their actions? But it's not forever – at some point we have to let go of them, even if they seem never to let go of us.'

She looked at him, and felt that he could be trusted; that

what he said made sense. And seeing Adam standing in her kitchen – very solid, both feet on the ground – gave her more confidence that she could go out tonight; for Sam was sleeping at Robbie's house, and perhaps her father was only monstrous in her imagination, no more a real monster than his parents had been, no worse than her. Doubtless, all of them – grandparents, son, father, daughter – had felt guilty about each other (and maybe their guilt still tainted the air, when one dwelt upon it for too long), but now Kate ran away from that sour stagnation; ran upstairs to get changed – slipping into last year's Christmas party dress, never worn since, and the same red satin shoes she had been wearing when she met Adam for the first time. This year, though, she was far quicker with her make-up, feeling that she had less to hide – and when that was finished, she put on her birthday earrings from Bella and Charles, and her mother's charm bracelet, which had perhaps brought her some luck: for here she was, nearly a year later, returning to Helena's house with Adam beside her.

'You look lovely,' he said when she came back down to the kitchen just a few minutes later. 'Am I too much of a mess to go out with you?'

'Of course not,' she said; and, in fact, he looked as if he had made more of an effort than usual, his Mephisto boots unmuddied, possibly even polished, an uncrumpled midnight-blue linen shirt over a pair of newish jeans. He drove them to the party, past the Friday-night crowds of office workers weaving their way to Christmas drinks in Camden Town; down to the outer circle of Regent's Park, where the big houses were lit up, in golden pools of light amidst the shadows of the trees and the darkness on the other side of the road. They parked outside Helena's house and walked up the steps together, brushing past the clipped bay trees and the silvery lavender, barely scented in the midwinter night. 'I'm so glad I found you here,' he said, as they waited for the door to be answered.

'Yes, but you didn't want me then,' she said.

'I wanted you from the very start,' he said, 'I just wasn't sure if I could have you.'

The door opened – and inside there was the light and the sound of voices, as if the curtain had risen in the darkness of a theatre, and the scene set as a party, all loudness and laughter and people knowing they were being watched. Adam and Kate took off their coats, and then reached out for each other's fingertips, just for a few seconds, as they walked into the front room. Before long, though, she had lost him – he was talking about subsidence and London clay to a man in pinstripes – and all at once, as if this were last year's party, and the scene was being replayed, like a film, Julian had found her; coming up behind her again, so that she could not see his approach. He'd kissed her on the back of her neck, very quickly, and then taken one of her hands, holding her wrist as he examined the charm bracelet. 'Still wearing the key to my heart?' he said, when he found the two golden charms he had given her for her birthday.

'Of course,' she said, smiling, her voice light, like he liked. He poured her another glass of champagne, and his eyes met hers, looking slightly quizzical. 'So?' he said.

'So here we are again,' she said.

'Plus ça change,' he said.

'Not quite,' she said. 'Adam wants us to move in together.'

'And you? What do you want?'

'To be certain of a happy outcome.'

'But you can never be certain of that,' he said, still circling her wrist with his hand. She nodded in response, and sipped a little more champagne, but inside she felt she was drinking to Adam: to Adam and her, to the unknown future. Julian was saying something about dark horses – something she hadn't been following (and anyway, didn't he have two white ponies?). 'Well?' he said.

'Well what?'

'Have you been listening to me? Honestly, you're just like my wife.'

'Am I really?' she said. 'How terribly unsuitable.' And then she drifted away from him, carried by the current of the party, now in full flow. Jessica was there, listening to Helena's husband with an apparently intent look on her face (maybe it was marriage that made people deaf to each other?), sleeker than ever in another narrow silken sheath dress (the Prozac diet, guessed Kate, because wasn't it supposed to take your appetite for everything away?). And there was Helena, holding court by the mantelpiece, magnificently voluptuous in expensive black satin this year, and diamonds bigger than ever – Henry still making a killing in the City, of course – and Kate imagined her every year after, grander as she got older, turning into the dowager duchess of Regent's Park.

Her eyes circled the room, searching for Adam, and at last she found him, leaning against a wall, talking to several more pinstriped gentlemen. Kate weaved her way through the knots of guests, catching fleeting bits of other people's conversation ('and I said, "sell, it's a bear market", but that idiot wouldn't listen'), and then reaching Adam's side. He turned to her, looking relieved, made his excuses to the pinstripes, and ushered her out into the hall. 'Is it me, or are they getting more boring?' he whispered. 'But the really sinister lot are wearing mauve floral party shirts beneath their suits. They're the ones to watch – not the men in black – because it's the posh blokes in flowery tops who'll be smashing a broken bottle of champagne in your face after too many drinks, pretending it's a joke. Can we go now?' He looked at her hopefully and she smothered a rising giggle, as Helena sailed in from the other room.

'Darlings, darlings,' said Helena, 'you're not to run away, not after I introduced you two in the first place – I won't hear of it, not until I've had a chance to catch up with all your news.' Adam started muttering something about babysitters, but Helena was unstoppable – as ever – and fired questions at them, in the manner of a proprietorial parent. Were Adam's intentions honourable? ('Yes, of course,' he said, smiling politely.) When were they getting married? ('Not yet,' said Kate, fiddling with her bracelet.) What about the children? ('They're fine,' said Adam, evenly.) Where would they live? ('Who knows?' said Kate, beginning to feel irritated by now.)

'Really, I should set up my own matchmaking agency,' said Helena, with a look of such self-satisfaction that Kate wanted to stamp on her elegantly beaded suede shoes. Instead, she thanked Helena profusely, kissed her on both cheeks and went in search of her coat, leaving Adam to cope with Helena's observation that perhaps he might do a reduced rate for her new ensuite bathroom, by way of recompense.

By the time they finally got outside, they were both laughing, running down the steps like children escaping from school. 'Thank God you're not a banker,' she said, skipping towards the car.

'Thank God you're not a banker's wife,' he said, lifting her up in his arms and turning in dizzying circles, whistling a waltz all the while. When he stopped, the world was still spinning, and she looked up into the night sky, towards the stars, and they were dancing, too, leaping free at last . . .

Forty-One

In the final days before Christmas, the postcards from her father continued to arrive, sometimes two or three at a time. He appeared to be making his way through the works of Chagall – more pictures of birds and brides and violins; of people flying through air, and flowers in the sky. On the back of some of them he'd drawn diagrams and maps; in all of them his tone was a mixture of hectoring and wheedling; mostly the messages ended, 'Do you understand?' Kate did not know what it was she was supposed to understand, what it was that her father already understood: something about time and eternity, apparently, but still it did not make sense. And though she knew that what he said was perhaps senseless, she felt somehow guilty, as if she had let him down, even though, as Adam had pointed out, her father was the one who had let her down – if, that is, one wanted to apportion blame, given that his history of mental illness was no one's fault.

Kate feared, occasionally, that Adam might become exasperated with her (after all, he seemed able to deal with his own parents, with occasional, apparently untroubled phone calls) – and though he showed no outward sign of annoyance, it was an exasperating situation, especially now that her father had taken to ringing her in the middle of the night, redialling repeatedly if she did not pick up the phone, to explain some fine point of his theories. Eventually she had unplugged the phone at night: hence the flood of post-cards, and emails as well, accusing her of not understanding him, of not loving him enough. After forty-eight hours of this barrage Kate began to feel some sympathy for her mother's often stated view, in life, that she could never escape Sebastian. It had seemed melodramatic at the time – a sign of her mother's weakness, rather than her father's per-sistence – but now Kate wondered if her mother's death had been a kind of escape; a running away at the wheel, break-ing free from him at last (and maybe she was the lucky one, the one that got away). Kate had once read that one in five manic depressives killed themselves (such a neat figure, con-taining so much human chaos), but for some reason she felt sure that her father would go on living – that it was her mother that had done the dying in the family; that her untimely death was the one Kate had always feared as a child and afterwards.

She knew, too, that this phase in her father's life would pass, as it had always done in the past. Isabel said so, when Kate had rung her for advice, as she had done before (and would do again). 'Manic depression is cyclical,' Isabel had said, and suddenly Kate was beset with the image of her father, whirling around in circles, blown by an unseen wind, like someone in a Chagall painting, except he was spinning beyond the frame.

The thing was, Kate wanted to stop thinking about her

father – to get on with her own life, which seemed slow in comparison to his spiralling volition; the speedy exhilaration of her departure from Helena's party having disappeared, like the stars, behind cloud. She and Adam had still not resolved where they might live together – and therefore the question of whether they should live together remained unclear. Kate did not feel able to make the necessary leap of imagination to pack up and leave her house; could not summon the energy and enthusiasm that would make such a move take place. Meanwhile, Adam was preoccupied with finishing a pop star's new kitchen before Christmas (not a very famous pop star, actually, more of a starlet, who seemed justifiably anxious that the kitchen should be finished before her fame evaporated, so that something concrete – black granite, in fact – would remain as evidence of her brief glory).

In lieu of solving these more complex problems, Kate occupied herself with the question of who would go where on Christmas Day. The logistics were turning into a jigsaw puzzle – setting a precedent for the future, she assumed – because Clare wanted to see Rose, and so did Adam, and Rose wanted to see both of them, but Adam wanted also to see Kate and Sam. Whether Rose wanted also to see Kate and Sam was uncertain: sometimes she did, and sometimes she didn't – an erratic oscillation with no end in sight. The only person who didn't seem to care much about the details was Pete, who said simply that he would prefer not to have to get up too early on Christmas morning, but would drop in at some point in the afternoon, before his evening flight to Reykjavik (ice apparently having replaced sun as the currently fashionable photographic

backdrop; though Kate guessed his trip was as much holiday as work).

She was about to suggest, through gritted teeth, that
Clare and Rob come with Rose to Christmas lunch, when
Adam intervened. 'You don't have to come up with a neat
solution,' he said, 'and anyway, it'll probably work itself
out.' Kate could not understand why he was so relaxed
about the arrangements for the day – not that it mattered to
them as adults, not really, but Christmas could be so loaded
(in all senses of the word) for their children. Still, something
of his sanguinity must have transferred itself to her, for she
did not feel herself descending into gloom, as she had done
in previous winters, brought down by sadness, like a dismal
December virus. She savoured the unfamiliar taste of happiness – precious, like the occasional hour of sunshine in the
rain; but, unlike the sun, the gentle contentment stayed with
her, even when dusk fell in the afternoon. Kate knew that
the happiness was in part Adam's doing: but there was
something inside her, as well, something different. 'Older
and wiser,' she said to herself, walking home through the
park one day, in the pale, translucent light as the sun sank
lower in the sky. But that wasn't quite it – for the getting of
wisdom was not necessarily part of growing older; and anyway, was happiness the same as wisdom? She remembered
a story from her childhood, from one of the Mary Poppins
books that she had read over and over again. The story told
by Mary to her charges (and Kate had counted herself as
one of those children, caught up in Mary's magic, yet also
regarding her with due respect, for she was an unpredictable, sharp-tongued mother substitute, not the sugary
confection she was later made out to be) concerned a fool-

ish king: the King of the Castle, instructed to no avail by professors throughout his land. Only when he met a fool – known to all as the Dirty Rascal – did the king find a kind of wisdom in happiness, and disappeared from his castle, following the rascal over a rainbow and up into the sky. Kate ran through the story again in her head, as she circled the scrubby rose garden around the rusting sundial in the middle of the park. She could find no moral in the tale to apply to herself – no parallels, either, except perhaps the knowledge that happiness, like rainbows and clouds and rain and sadness, is liable to vanish, and also to reappear (as did Mary Poppins); but even so, the rhyme lodged itself in her head – 'I'm the king of the castle, you're the dirty rascal' – repeated in Julian's little-boy chant from all those years ago.

That evening, the Saturday before Christmas, she and Sam decorated their Christmas tree: one of two they'd bought together with Rose and Adam, who would be now similarly engaged at their flat. (Rose was also due to decorate another one at Clare and Rob's place – as if sufficient Christmas trees would provide the material to patch together a broken family.) Kate had briefly entertained the thought, as she did every December, that this year their tree should be tastefully colour co-ordinated, like Jessica's, in elegantly arranged silver and red; but Sam dismissed the idea, as he always did, so they had unwoven the multi-coloured tangle of tinsel, and disinterred the ancient cardboard box of baubles from the cupboard beneath the stairs. Some of the decorations dated from Sam's first Christmas; others had been added over subsequent years to replace those baubles broken by the cat, who was prone to launching frenzied attacks on the tree when no one was looking. 'Shall me and Rose put our stockings by the fireplace, or on our beds?' said Sam, who had just discovered his old red felt Christmas stocking, which looked more like a cartoon boot.

'Whatever you like,' said Kate, 'but I'm not sure if Rose has decided yet where she wants to stay on Christmas Eve.'

'We decided today, me and her, at the garden centre,' said Sam, 'when you and Adam were in the queue to pay for the Christmas trees. She's going to stay here on Christmas Eve, so we can wake up in the morning together and open our presents, and then we can have lunch, and then she's going to her mum's house, but she won't be allowed any sweets there. OK?'

'That's fine,' said Kate, wondering whether Sam had in fact correctly interpreted Rose's wishes; but deciding to trust that he had. And then, without thinking, she went on, 'Would you like it, darling, if we lived with Adam and Rose?'

'All the time?' he said, balancing a glass snowflake near the top of the tree, which may have been why he seemed to be holding his breath.

'Well, Adam would be with us all the time, but Rose would spend some of the time with her mum, as well.'

'But I wouldn't have to go and live with Dad when Rose was with her mum? I don't think I'd like that, because it's too far to school, and he'd be no good at getting up in the morning.'

'No, you'd live with me and Adam, and just go and see Dad at weekends sometimes, like you do now.'

Sam still seemed intent on the snowflake, but she could tell that he was considering what she'd said. 'There's not much space for them here,' he said, after a long pause. 'And I'm not sharing my room with Rose – not every night.'

'Well, obviously she'd have her own room.'

'The little bedroom? It wouldn't be very fair on her.'

'Maybe we could move to a bigger house.'

'Move?' he said, turning to face her for the first time, and looking horrified. 'I'm not leaving my house just so Rose can have a bigger bedroom. I don't want to move from this street – it's brilliant for skateboarding, and Robbie lives here, and it's not fair to force me to go.'

'Sweetheart,' she said, regretting her blundering, 'no one will force you to do anything. We don't have to move – we can keep things as they are.' In the silence between them, she thought only of the past, and it seemed to come rushing forward, like the blood pounding through her head, like a rising tide.

But Sam was moving on, too, swifter than she was. 'Maybe Adam could make our house bigger?' he said. 'He's quite good at that stuff, isn't he? He could make the attic bigger, and then there'd be more room.'

'You know what, Sam,' she said, her panic subsiding again, though she still felt ashamed of herself, 'that's a very good idea.'

'I know,' he said, looking pleased, 'I've got lots of good ideas.'

Later, when the tree was finished and they'd strung more fairy lights around the kitchen, Kate went upstairs to look at the smallest, third, bedroom, and at the attic where she worked. Both had potential for expansion, she could see –

Adam could take down the unnecessarily low ceiling in the back bedroom, and maybe build a platform bed, like Robbie had; and beyond her tiny attic room was unused space in the eaves, currently filled with unpacked boxes from when she had first moved in. Clearly, if there was anything she'd actually needed in those boxes, she'd have dug it out by now – but as it was, she might as well chuck them all away. She wasn't quite sure what Adam would think, but the idea seemed more and more exciting to her: a chance to build something new on the foundations of the familiar. And wasn't that the point?

Encouraged by this thought, Kate decided that she might as well do what she had been dreading and ring her father, to see how he was. Sam was asleep, and though she preferred the idea of going to bed herself to re-read her battered copy of *Mary Poppins Comes Back* (the second book in the series, and her favourite), Kate knew that she would feel guilty if she didn't at least try to make contact with him tonight. She dialled his number, promising herself that she would let it ring ten times before putting the phone down, but when she got to ten, and he still hadn't answered, she kept counting. At thirteen, he picked up the phone, his voice sounding suspicious at the intrusion when she asked him if everything was OK.

'Marvellous,' he said. 'I'm full of hope and happiness, and I'm writing a paper on the structure of medieval cartography, with particular reference to time and motion – I'll read it to you now.'

'I don't want you to read it to me,' she said, trying to keep her voice gentle.

'As ever,' he said. 'Why do you have to be so rejecting?'

'I'm not,' she said. 'That's why I was ringing, to find out how you are.'

'You think I'm a lunatic, I suppose. You're trying to label me.'

'Dad, I'm not, I'm—' But it was too late, he'd already put the phone down. This was a scene that had been played out between them dozens of times before, and what usually followed was that she would start crying, or raging to any-one who would listen. As it was, she felt sad, but briefly immune. It was as if her father, like her dead mother, was receding to the edges of her vision, swept away by the wind or the tide – or maybe it was Kate that was being carried forward while her parents remained in the same place. Whatever happened, she did not expect this to last forever – no doubt her parents would return, back into view some time in the future, borne to her by returning currents; but for now Kate felt able to let them go, knowing they were just out of sight.

She brushed her teeth and retrieved her book from underneath a pile of Christmas wrapping paper, imagining what Adam would say tomorrow when she told him she'd gone to bed with Mary Poppins (remembering all the nights when she did go to bed with Mary Poppins as a child, read-ing herself to sleep). And when she slept, she dreamt that she was standing in the park, watching her father and her mother and Mary Poppins, and some others, people she didn't quite recognize, rising into the sky, carried up by bal-loons, up to the stars, which seemed quite close, and steady now, almost like stepping stones. 'I wish I could come with you,' she cried after them, waving her hand, 'but I have to stay here, I've got to keep my feet on the ground . . .'

Forty-Two

On Christmas morning, Rose and Sam woke up at quarter
past six and rushed into Kate's bedroom to wake her and
Adam. 'Have you opened the presents in your stockings?'
she asked them, struggling to form the words in a fog of
sleep. Yes, they had, they said, and they wanted to show
what Father Christmas had brought them; for though separately they were beginning to show scepticism about his
existence, together they seemed willing to suspend disbelief.
She and Adam had stayed up late last night, wrapping the
children's presents, making sure that neither received more
than the other, so that Christmas (if not life) would seem
fair. After inspecting their booty, and expressing the
expected surprise (both at Santa's generosity in bringing
plastic reindeer that made farting noises and at the disap-
pearance of the large glass of whisky left out for him on the
mantelpiece), Kate begged the children to let Adam and her
sleep a little longer. And Sam and Rose consented, which
seemed like a gift in itself, she thought, hoping to sink back
into dreams; but to her surprise, she could not, lying there
in the dark, listening to the farting reindeer in the next

room, feeling nervous about the day to come; wanting it to be perfect for the children, knowing that it could not be, not entirely, but wishing for magic, all the same.

So Kate got up – no point staying in bed, wide awake and anxious – and cooked pancakes, while the children ran between the tree and the kitchen, both of them begging to be allowed to unwrap more presents; and though she entertained the idea of making them wait until after lunch (like Jessica did, improbably), Sam's enthusiasm triumphed, and the four of them were gathered beside the tree. 'We can't wait any longer,' Sam had said, 'it's Christmas, and anyway, Rose has got to go to her mum's after lunch, so we've got to get on with things now.'

The etiquette of present giving had been new territory for them, to be negotiated carefully. Kate had given Sam several presents, as ever, from her alone, rather than including Adam as the benefactor (and who else but a loving mother would have bought her son the longed-for drum kit?); and Adam had done the same for Rose (not more drums, mercifully, but a guitar). Adam had also bought separate presents for Sam, as she had done for Rose, after careful consultation with one another, so as not to duplicate. Similarly, Sam and Rose had chosen presents for each other, and for Kate and Adam – which combined to create a more abundant Christmas than usual; embarrassing, really – as all of them sought to delineate the boundaries between the two sets of parent and child, yet also express something that blurred the differences, as well.

Oddly, Kate had found it easier to shop for Rose than for Adam, for Sam had been a confident conduit of Rose's likes and dislikes (yes to glitter nail varnish and temporary tattoos, braided bracelets and a tie-dyed T-shirt, but on no account anything yellow, 'because she hates bananas'). For Adam, however, she'd agonized, choosing a soft blue cotton shirt in the end, because it reminded her of him, and a cashmere scarf and hat, to keep him warm on building sites (though what would the builders think of him, clad in periwinkle designer stuff?). He'd seemed similarly uncertain, too – not about the clothes, she hoped, which he'd immediately put on (even, sweetly, the hat) – but about his choice of present for her. 'I hope you like it,' he said, 'and you can change it if it's not right.' Beneath the silver tissue was a small wooden box painted in the shape of a house, two windows either side of a door, and two above, very neat, but with a few wobbly lines, as if drawn by a child. 'Dad made that,' said Rose, 'and I helped do the roses round the front and some other things.'

'It's beautiful,' said Kate, lifting the delicately hinged roof; gasping as she saw what was inside – a diamond ring: and not just one diamond, but lots of little ones, like tiny stars, set all the way around the circle. 'It's called an eternity ring,' said Adam, muffled behind his new scarf.

'To Infinity and Beyond!' said Sam, 'like Buzz Lightyear, who is a bit of a prat.'

'Which finger do I wear it on?' she said, trying to keep her voice steady, though her eyes were stinging with tears.

'Whichever one you want – whichever feels right,' he said, taking it out of the little box, for she had not yet done so, and putting it into the palm of her hand, closing her fingers around it with his.

'Is it OK?' he said.

'I love it,' she said. 'I love you.' It was the first time she had spoken these words in front of the children, but they seemed not to mind – to welcome the statement, perhaps, as the reason for their gathering; though Sam was quick to say, after Adam reached over to kiss Kate, 'yuck – no more disgusting lovey-dovey stuff,' which made Rose giggle.

After lunch Adam took Rose to Clare and Rob's flat, and Pete arrived soon after, with two new PlayStation games for Sam (Kate wanted to disapprove of the games – did disapprove, in fact – but they were exactly what Sam wanted, which was what mattered, in the end). She was wearing the ring by then – not on her wedding finger, but the middle finger of her right hand – and Pete noticed it, even though he did not usually comment on the details of her jewellery. 'So, it's happy ever after, then?' he said, gesturing towards the ring.

'It's my Christmas present,' she replied.

'I've got something for you, as well,' he said, and gave her an envelope. Inside, there was a silver framed photograph, of her and Pete, and Sam, snuggled between them. 'I took it a couple of years ago, remember? The Christmas before last – I set the timer on the camera and then ran over to sit on the sofa with you two. I just thought you'd like it . . .' Kate did like it – it was a nice picture, all of them smiling, arms linked. But she wondered whether there was a subtext to the photograph – a detail previously missed, that Pete had now seen with hindsight (the minutiae contained within photographs were his business, after all).

'It's lovely,' she said, running her fingertips over the glass that preserved their faces, fixed in that moment of togetherness. 'We look so happy.' And though she did not say this to Pete, she was perplexed by the apparent

317

cheerfulness of their faces, her own untroubled smile, because she remembered that Christmas as a difficult one – coloured by her resentment that Pete was able to swoop in like the magical godfather, and then disappear out of their lives again for weeks at a time.

'I remember when you took that picture, Dad,' said Sam, who had come over to look at the photograph. 'That was a brilliant year, when I got my new bicycle, my first one without stabilizers, and we went to the park, and there was snow – real snow, not just frost.' And, suddenly, Kate remembered that, as well – how could she have forgotten? – Sam cycling free across the glittering white park, whooping, and Pete taking her hands in his, to warm them, because she had no gloves. 'Cold hands, warm heart,' he'd said, and she'd known he loved her, if only for that instant, in the unblemished snow, when the sky was high and clear, and it seemed like you could see forever.

'It was good, that day, wasn't it?' said Pete, now; and when Sam had disappeared upstairs with Robbie, who'd come round to play on the PlayStation, Pete took her hand again and looked at her new diamond ring. 'I just wanted you not to forget the good things between us,' he said, and as he spoke, she looked at the picture again, at Sam.

'I thought perhaps there was some trick to it,' she said, 'like a hidden clue in the photograph, that I had to discover.'

'No, it's very simple,' he said. 'Just a nice picture, whichever way you look at it.'

'And that's all?'

'That's all – and isn't that enough?'

'So you don't mind about Adam?' As she said it, she guessed that maybe – against all the odds – Pete did mind, a little bit; that the version of him she carried around with her (careless, carefree – whatever you wanted to call it) was not as accurate as she liked to think; that what she chose to see as blankness was in part her application, like a coat of paint, obliterating what lay beneath, what had gone before, between them.

'Of course I care,' he said, looking down at the picture, not her, 'even though it's my fault. But I know I can't wind back the clock, and anyway, you'll be happy with Adam.'

'Since when have you had a crystal ball?' He didn't reply, just looked up and smiled at her, and his face was as she remembered it, like that moment in the park, and long before, when she'd first fallen in love with him, a fleeting thing, melting like the snow, but she would not wish it away; and it seemed like a blessing – both the memory and today . . .

Forty-Three

It was Sam who told Adam about the idea of the four of them living in Kate's house – Kate had been waiting for what felt to be the right moment, which had not yet arrived, but then Sam said he was sick of waiting and came right out with it, and Adam looked so happy that Kate felt foolish for her delay – and it was Sam, now, on Boxing Day who was helping Adam take down the false ceiling in the back bedroom, ready to turn it into Rose's room before she came back from a visit with Clare to her grandparents. Kate had caught snatches of their conversation between hammering and ominous crashes – Adam's voice too low to make out properly, and Sam saying, 'I thought Dad could move into your flat, so it'd be easier for me to see him, because he might be sad if you're living here, and that way I can go and cheer him up. It would be like a swap – except I'm not swapping dads, OK?' Kate doubted if that particular piece of the jigsaw puzzle would be quite so easy to make fit – Pete had never really wanted to live in Crouch End in the first place ('too full of smug marrieds,' he'd said when they'd moved here, ignoring the fact that they too were a

couple – or meant to be, anyway); and there was no reason
to think he had changed his mind since then. Besides, while
she could see the merits of Sam's plan – no loose ends,
everything slotted into place – Sam himself was just as
inclined to sabotage it: the morning after Boxing Day, having lost interest in sweeping up plaster dust, he told Adam
that he'd preferred the house before 'you messed things up'.
Fortunately it wasn't raining, so she'd taken Sam and
Robbie to the park for a while (trying, and failing, to walk
off the mince pies and brandy butter she'd eaten for breakfast), leaving Adam at work, and when Sam went back to
Robbie's house for a couple of hours, she'd retreated to the
attic, to sort out the boxes in the eaves.

Some of it she threw away – dozens of old reporters'
notebooks, containing her illegible shorthand of interviews
for long-ago magazine stories; and yellowing cuttings from
her first job at a newspaper. Looking at them, she suddenly
remembered how much she'd cared – as if seeing her name
in print had made her alive, when after her mother's death
(and even before, perhaps) she had felt almost transparent,
a kind of ghost, herself. But now it was the old newsprint
that was of no consequence; fading, brittle, like the few
remaining leaves that clung to the plum tree on the far side
of the garden wall.

It was easy to get rid of it all, in three heavy-duty bin
bags; and though she knew she was unlikely to stop writing,
she resolved to hoard none of it any more (newspapers, like
leaves, not being suitable for storage – better mulched into
compost, really). But Kate found it harder to discard Sam's
old drawings and paintings – dozens of them, from first
handprints to playgroup scribbles; nursery class collages

and infant school watercolours. Her favourite she'd already framed and hung in the entrance hall downstairs (one wall remained empty, fortunately, with room for Rose's handiwork); and there were others on the walls of the attic, including his square rainbow. She decided to send half a dozen pictures to her father – he liked having Sam's paintings (better, perhaps, than spending time with a real grandchild, though they'd spoken to each other on the phone this morning, after Kate had rung Sebastian to patch things up, and he had said that he wanted to teach Sam the Hebrew alphabet, and Sam had said that was fine, but not until he was nine and had learned his spellings for school). Kate set aside another three recent drawings for Bella, Harriet and Isabel, which could be sent with a thank-you note for Christmas presents. Then she threw away the most raggedly dog-eared of the remainder; and the rest she put to one side, while she decided what to do with them. (What, she wondered, idly, had become of her childhood paintings? Like her stories and her schoolbooks, they seemed to have disappeared, which was not necessarily a bad thing – even liberating, perhaps.)

The last and biggest box revealed more random hoardings: a pile of bank statements, dating back to when they'd moved into this house – all of which could be dumped in the bin, because the relevant, recent statements were downstairs, the usual jumble waiting to be assembled for her inevitably delayed tax return. Her father, she knew, shredded all such documents before getting rid of them ('You never know who might be looking through your rubbish,' he'd said, darkly); and she started tearing the bank sheets in half, as if ridding herself of those reminders of an uncertain past – but in the end she gave up, just throwing them away, thousands of rows of tightly calculated numbers. (There would, after all, be more such sums to contend with – the hateful, treacherous tax forms, for a start – but why weigh herself down with these?)

Beneath the bank statements was another box – a box within a box – and this, she realized, had not been unpacked since she had graduated from university, even though she thought she'd already rid herself of everything from that time. Inside was a sheaf of dusty party invitations from the weeks after her finals (strange word, finals, when life hadn't stopped; racing to all those parties – more in a fortnight, by the looks of things, than in a year nowadays). Kate had no qualms about binning the lot; but the cards from her mother she kept, three of them sent in her first term at university, in that familiar spidery handwriting. She remembered it then, her mother driving her to Cambridge at the beginning of term, both of them nervous, but Kate exhilarated, too, and her mother nostalgic for her own student past, as they drove into the town along the dappled, sunlit roads. 'What a golden place this is,' her mother had said, as they drew close to Kate's college. 'In autumn Cambridge is full of new beginnings – and it looks like the most beautiful, civilized city in the world.' There had been so little to unpack then – just a suitcase of clothes and books, a cheap kettle, some crockery, two saucepans and a set of cutlery her mother had bought for her at Woolworths. (Only one plastic-handled serrated knife remained – but Kate still used it for chopping vegetables.)

The messages from her mother had been brief, restrained, but there was love between the lines. She hoped

Kate was having fun, Judith wrote in the first one, and making new friends. In the second she reminded Kate to dress warmly, because the wind off the Fens was notoriously icy in winter; and in the third she said she was looking forward to seeing her in London for Christmas. As Kate read that message – written, like all of them, on a plain white postcard – she remembered a phone call that she'd made to her mother soon after, saying that she would be going to a New Year's Eve party with some friends. 'That's fine,' said Judith, her voice cracking a little at the end of the line, while Kate shivered in a college payphone, 'I'll probably drive up to Elverson.' As it turned out, her mother had not gone to Norfolk until the following week, spending New Year's Eve alone in the flat, and the next day, at least until Kate had come home later that afternoon, hungover and monosyllabic, further depressed by her mother's melancholy. 'Grim, isn't it?' her mother had said, as much about the world as the weather. 'Only if you choose to see it that way,' Kate had said, feeling irritable as well as guilty, wanting something more hopeful on this brave first day of the year, before disappearing early to bed.

But that had not been their last day together; those had not been their last words. The morning after New Year's Day, they'd gone for a walk in Regent's Park, past the boating lake, empty then, and crossing the Inner Circle to the rose garden, where the bushes were all pruned close to the ground. Kate had linked arms with her mother for a while, and then they'd separated, but not far, still walking side by side. What had they talked about? Kate couldn't really remember, though afterwards, when her mother was dead, it seemed so important to pin down their conversation – as if it might have saved them both – but it had been blurred, shadowy, like the misty January day; something about the squirrels, perhaps. 'Come along,' her mother had called to the squirrels, 'come along, come along . . .'

The next morning Kate had left for Cambridge, before term started, to catch up with some work, and because she craved the solitude of her college room: its quiet, instead of her mother's unspoken love. She'd caught the train that day from Liverpool Street, saying goodbye to her mother at the platform. That was the last time, then, the very last time: kissing her mother, saying goodbye, though surely neither of them knew it was the end. Her mother had been there as the train pulled out, waving, and Kate was by the window, and it was closed, but even so, she said it out loud, believing her mother would hear: 'I love you.' And on the other side of the glass her mother had blown her a kiss, and Kate imagined it, like a butterfly, light enough to slip through a crack in the glass. ('Give me a butterfly kiss,' she'd said to her mother when she was little, loving the feel of the lashes on her cheek, like Sam did now.) It was cold that day, but her mother's face had been warm; and as Kate waved, their eyes had met, just for a few seconds, before the train got faster, before her mother was gone.

Now Kate put the old postcards together, slipping them into an envelope for safekeeping, though she knew it would be another year or more until she looked at them again. Downstairs, the doorbell rang, and she heard Sam's voice, returning from Robbie's house, sounding cheerful, and his footsteps up the stairs, followed by Adam's. They did not come all the way up, and the hammering started again in Rose's room, in between which Sam was asking Adam for a puppy. 'Maybe,' said Adam, his voice clearer now. 'I'd like one, too – maybe in the spring, when we've settled in.' And Sam was saying everything would be settled before then, and Adam laughed, and then Sam said he wanted to stay up all night on New Year's Eve.

They were going to Elverson for New Year's Eve – that was the plan, anyway, though Kate quite liked the idea of staying at home, just the four of them, because Rose would be back by then, and lighting a fire, waiting for the clock to strike twelve, watching as the old year turned into the new, their hands joined in a circle, while the clock's hands ticked on alone. This morning Adam had said he didn't mind where they were, as long as they were together, and now she heard his voice again, downstairs, mingling with Sam's, and they were singing something, but she couldn't hear the words, just the tune. And in counterpoint, she remembered her mother saying – and Kate heard her voice, from all those years ago, clear again, clear like the winter air coming in through the open attic window – 'On New Year's Eve, think of me when the clock begins to strike twelve, because time stands still between the first stroke of midnight, and the last, and that's when wishes come true.'

'I'll remember,' Kate had said, 'I promise I'll remember.' And she did not forget.